O9-ABI-550

# Sansei and Sensibility

**Also by Karen Tei Yamashita**

*Anime Wong*
*Brazil-Maru*
*Circle K Cycles*
*I Hotel*
*Letters to Memory*
*Through the Arc of the Rain Forest*
*Tropic of Orange*

# Sansei and Sensibility

**KAREN TEI YAMASHITA**

**COFFEE HOUSE PRESS**

Minneapolis

2020

Copyright © 2020 by Karen Tei Yamashita
Book design by Sarah Miner
Author photograph © Howard Boltz

Coffee House Press books are available to the trade through our primary distributor, Consortium Book Sales & Distribution, cbsd.com or (800) 283-3572. For personal orders, catalogs, or other information, write to info@coffeehousepress.org.

Coffee House Press is a nonprofit literary publishing house. Support from private foundations, corporate giving programs, government programs, and generous individuals helps make the publication of our books possible. We gratefully acknowledge their support in detail in the back of this book.

LIBRARY OF CONGRESS CATALOGING-IN-PUBLICATION DATA
Names: Yamashita, Karen Tei, 1951– author.
Title: Sansei and sensibility / Karen Tei Yamashita.
Description: Minneapolis : Coffee House Press, 2020.
Identifiers: LCCN 2019028589 (print) | LCCN 2019028590 (ebook) | ISBN
    9781566895781 (trade paperback) | ISBN 9781566895866 (ebook)
Classification: LCC PS3575.A44 A6 2020 (print) | LCC PS3575.A44 (ebook) |
    DDC 813/.54—dc23
LC record available at https://lccn.loc.gov/2019028589
LC ebook record available at https://lccn.loc.gov/2019028590

Images in "A Gentlemen's Agreement" are from the Yamashita Family Archives,
courtesy of the author.

PRINTED IN THE UNITED STATES OF AMERICA
27  26  25  24  23  22  21  20        1  2  3  4  5  6  7  8

*For Jane Tomi*

# Contents

# Sansei and Sensibility

# I. Sansei

# The Bath

I

In their house, they often say that Mother has a special fascination for the bath. Father pointed this out many years ago. Perhaps it was only in answer to Mother's suggestion that Father might bathe more frequently than once a week on Saturday nights. Father bragged of his weekly bath but only in relation to Mother's nightly affair. Over the years, it seems Mother has taken to early morning baths as well, so Father's comments on Mother and the bath continue with an added flourish. He seems to believe certain habits of Mother's have come together to conspire against him by beginning all at once in the morning.

Mother isn't one to deny such things. She laughs at herself in an embarrassed manner, pressing her lips together and looking at the floor. Father's banter is an old and recurring one, and Mother is not without her usual reply. She defends herself on two accounts, saying that a hot bath is the most relaxing thing. Her other retort is a more defensive stance on the necessity of cleanliness. "You perspire, and isn't it nice to have a clean body? You feel so much better." "After all," she'll finally say, "the bath is my only luxury."

These are statements typical of Mother. They suggest perhaps a certain simplicity. This isn't to say Mother is simpleminded. Not at all. Rather, it is to suggest a sensibility that respects necessities for what they are, a practical sense that finds contentment, sometimes even luxury, in the simple duties of necessity. Mother is simple in that she doesn't carry around anything in excess, be it pretension, desire, or fashionable decoration. As Father says, "She is what she is." Mother's simplicity is, finally, honest. It is clean and naked in a hot bathtub.

It has been suggested that the bath is a return to the womb, to a fetal state. Mother freely admits this must be a part of its pleasure. Nakedness is not something Mother is shy about. Birth and bodies, it's all very natural and beautiful. However, they've had some difficulty extracting from Mother explanations as to processes, actions, and causes in the matter of birth and naked bodies. It's all very much a mystery. Mother's standard answer in these cases is, "What do you have that others haven't got?" That has somehow had to suffice for everything, that which is natural and that, mysterious.

*         *         *

Speaking of the bath, one has in mind the bathroom in the old house where they first lived as a family. It seemed this bathroom was painted all over in pink enamel. The built-in wood drawers and the large wood medicine cabinet behind the mirror: these too were painted in pink enamel. But the amazing thing was the tub itself, an old curving tub standing on four legs like a huge white iron pig in the middle of the peeling linoleum.

In those days, the three of them, Mother and the twins, took baths in this tub together. Mother would squat at the front of the tub, adjusting cold and hot water while her two naked daughters stood leaning into her shoulders, splashing and floating rubber toys and bars of Ivory soap. Mother would take a washcloth and soap and scrub herself and the two children, rinse, and send them out before the aka or tub scum could gather much. Mother did this generally and quickly, in a way they called īkagen. Īkagen is "just so" or "to suit your taste" or "just enough." *Īkagen* is a word Mother used to describe what her mother had said about how much salt or shōyu to use in this or that recipe. If it was īkagen, it was an amount of common sense or taste. Īkagen is descriptive of a general approach Mother maintains toward household duties, secretarial filing, letter writing, reading, and washing children.

But if Mother washed īkagen, shampooing was sometimes a different matter. Not that the general style—a quick scrubbing on four sides of the scalp—wasn't īkagen. It was that every once in a while, she would bring three eggs to the bath. The eggs were cold out of the refrigerator. The twins leaned against the white curve of the old tub as she cracked the cold shells gently on the tops of wet heads. She let the yellow lump fall and the cool slime ooze, dribbling down the backs of ears and over the forehead and around eyebrows, tongue reaching for a taste. Then, īkagen, Mother massaged the scalp, scrambling yellow eggs and black hair. She said, "When I was little, my mother always washed my hair with an egg. It gets it clean and shiny."

After a time, the twins took baths together without Mother. And without Mother's īkagen technique, they were free to develop an entire and gradually complicated ritual surrounding bath time. It probably began with two tiny bodies at opposite ends of that steaming pink enamel bathroom scudding about with protruding stomachs and ramming into each other, laughing.

"My pompom's bigger!"

"Lookit your belly button. It's all itchy."

"Don' touchit!"

Later, Mother would find them performing the entire sequence of "The Hokey-Pokey" from "you put your left foot in" to the final "whole self." In those days, baths were apt to be rather lukewarm. But after Mother had them draw their own bathwater, their ritual accommodated by the creation of a system of fore and aft, as in "two men in a tub." That is, one sat up front weathering the hot water and adding the cold and yelling at appropriate intervals, "Row! Row left!" while the other twin in the aft paddled, stirring up the incoming hot or cold. Sometimes they were able to coordinate several rounds of "Row, Row, Row Your Boat," changing directions at new verses. By the end of these songs, they were in a virtual whirlpool, water spilling over the sides of the tub, warping the linoleum.

The bubble bath was a new challenge to bath time, calling for an exceptionally delicate rowing technique to get the water stirred with the greatest and deepest amount of bubbles. They sat fore and aft in a tub of white bubbles, hardly daring to move or breathe. These were almost silent baths. They moved slowly, whispering like cloud people, listening to the soft snapping fizzle of dying bubbles. These were often lengthy bath times spent waiting silently for the bubbles to pass before getting to the business of washing the body, which was by now quite a minor portion of bath-time fantasy.

Emerging finally, skinny bodies flushed and wrinkled, the twins watched the gray aka accumulate in a wide scummy ring, and the water finally disappear in a tiny rushing whirl, the old tub sending up a long sucking noise beyond the dark rusting drain, its navel.

Now they came often to watch Mother at her bath alone. They would usually find her lying deep in the tub, her head and shoulders propped up in a curve against the slope of the tub, a square washcloth floating over her soft mound of stomach and hair. She would say, "Come in and close the door. It's cold air."

They leaned over the edge of the tub, talking. "Mommy, you have a scar on your tummy? Isn't that where I came out of you when I was a baby?"

"No, that's when I had my appendix taken out."

"See, I told you."

Watching Mother was never much entertainment. She never used much soap but scrubbed her skin generally. It was in the usual manner of īkagen, the horizontal soaking being the thing.

It was quite a different thing to watch Father's weekly productions, which were extravagant in soap and water and flourish. He sat at the edge of the tub with a bar of soap, rubbing it into a thick white lather all over his body. He seemed to be very hairy. And there was his bad leg and the wound in his right hip; a scarred hole, it seemed as big as one's small hand.

"Daddy, you hurt your leg in the war?"

"No, I was a bad boy and fell off a fence."

"Oh."

The best part of his bath was to watch him, a hairy lathered man, plunge into deep white water, all the gray foam rising in waves, splashing water up to his chin. And when he rose, the water surged beneath him, and the tub echoed the din and squeak of his body and flat feet beating and rubbing against iron, and there was that wonderful and unbeatable amount of gray aka. It never occurred to them then, but the reason Father washed with the soap bar, always melting it to half its size, was probably that the washcloth somehow remained draped between his legs throughout the bath.

It was perhaps Grandmother who had the ultimate flair for bath-time ritual, and when she came to visit, they followed her around the house, watching to see what she would do next. It wasn't simply the bath, it was everything that led up to and continued after. Grandmother was a proud and somewhat stern woman, but they were able to talk with her through her broken English. She said so herself, "I bery broken Engurish."

She was a plump woman, fat at the middle, and she had long gray hair braided up in a longish bun at the back. They came to her like two young pages, volunteering for buttons and zippers, but mostly they were fascinated with her heavy under-armor: a stiff, thick, pink corset with metal catches and a crisscross of lacing up the middle. The twins, each taking an end of lace, tugged and unhooked step by step, attached to Grandmother by corset strings that slowly stretched across the room.

Grandmother always went to bathe with a long strip of cotton cloth, a tenugui for washing decorated with Japanese writing and designs. In the tub, the thin cloth adhered to the fat folds of her old body, Japanese characters and woven ends trailing off in the clear hot water. Around her stomach, they saw the tight crisscross and wrinkles embedded by the confining corset swell and disappear.

She would begin by washing her face, working over the entire surface of her body to her toes and using the cloth tenugui in a variety of ways, expressing a versatility remarkable in a thing so simple. The tenugui, grasped at both ends across her back, scoured every inch of skin in a see-saw fashion. The tenugui could bunch up in a soft round sponge with a smooth woven surface. She rubbed in circular motions over and under the loose layers of freckled flesh and sagging breasts. Finally, the tenugui, squeezed within a breath of being dry, served to soak up and even dry her entire body. Now she stood outside the tub, steamy and damp, mopping the perspiration on her forehead. Grandmother and her tenugui in the tub seemed simply self-sufficient.

After came creaming the face and brushing and braiding her long gray hair. Then they would join her in pajamas on the large double bed for a group exercise session. These motions ranged from rolling the head in circles and hunching the shoulders to bicycling upside down while lying in bed. These things the three did simultaneously while Grandmother expounded on their obvious virtues. "This berry good for regs. Now you do. Old be much bettah."

It wasn't until many years later, in Japan, that they saw another tenugui like Grandmother's. In fact, it would be many years before they saw another aging body naked at bath. It wasn't that one missed seeing Grandmother in her bathing, but that in rediscovering the bath in Japan, there was a vibrant sense of an old intimacy that seemed to radiate through the steam and crouching jostle at the public bath. It was Great Aunt Yae on Mother's side who first introduced one of the twins to the public bath, the sentō.

II

She came in February to Kyoto, cold with a barren sense of an old winter. She had just turned twenty-one and had been studying Japanese in Tokyo since the fall. She had never been so far from home.

Great Aunt Yae and her husband, Chihiro, lived retired in an old, small house of polished wood and deteriorating paper and mats, a house perhaps over one or two hundred years old, with the wear and darkness of time passing—passing through the war, when Chihiro had been an officer in the Imperial Army; passing with the birth of children, now married and gone; passing through the bitterness of war and the poverty after.

But of this past, the twin knew little, and it seemed she had passed into an old folktale beginning, "Mukashi, mukashi": "Long, long ago there lived an old man and old woman in a little house at the bottom of a hill. They were poor. They lived alone. They had no children. Every day the old man went out to chop wood to sell, carrying his heavy bundle on his back, trudging through the snow." This is the simple beginning of a recurring story; it seemed to convey the sad, gracious charm of an old couple whose lives are simple and resigned.

Her old uncle was hard of hearing, and Yae was continually yelling into his ear, repeating words her niece had said or reminding him of various details he had forgotten. Yae, on the other hand, was rather blind; squinting behind thick wire spectacles, she read newspapers and letters two or three inches from her nose. Sometimes her niece found her washing dishes, inspecting bowls and cups a few inches from her face, shifting her spectacles and poking at cracks and spots.

Yae said she and ojisan couldn't live without each other. She said, laughing, that they were sometimes like cartoon characters. One day she had heard rain on the roof above and announced to her husband that it was raining. Chihiro looked up from his newspapers and said, "That can't be. I don't hear anything . . . Look, no rain today. Omae, you're wrong."

Yae went to the door and slid it aside. Looking out, she saw nothing, and she came back to confirm that it wasn't raining after all.

Yae disappeared into the kitchen, but the old man's curiosity drew him to the door. Looking out, he saw the falling rain and called his wife to the door, tugging at her hand and pushing it into the rain. They stood there at the door, looking out to the garden and the pouring rain, laughing.

\*       \*       \*

At the door, Yae puts her niece in a pair of her old wooden geta. They are so worn down at the outer toe that she is forced to walk awkwardly, imitating Yae's pigeon-toed trot. Yae hands her a small plastic basin in which she's placed a folded tenugui along with soap, shampoo, and combs. They step out. A light snow is falling, disappearing into the gravel about their geta. Nodding over her basin to curious neighbors, Yae leads her to the sentō.

There she sees the layers of kimono fall away and Yae's thin, aged body, plump and wrinkled at the stomach. Yae stands naked, slightly stooped in those thick wire spectacles, scrutinizing her belongings and folding everything into a small pile.

They enter the bathroom gripping their plastic basins, swimming through the warm steam that billows as the glass door slides aside. Rows of squatting women and children wash before running faucets. Yae leads her between the rows and echoing commotion of spilling water. Women, flushed and dripping, emerge from the deep pools. Others meditate silently, squatting low in the great tubs, hot water caressing their hunching shoulders; black wisps of fallen hair cling to cheek and neck. Finding two free places, Yae goes off to steep herself in the hot tub.

Women of every age and shape scrub their bodies with the tenugui, busy at wash, vigorous and skillful in their movements. Women kneel and squat, never sitting on the tile, filling their basins and sending cascades of water over an area almost confined to their bodies. All stretching and standing returns to a compact crouch before the faucet or in the tub.

Under the bright shiny lights of the bath, their skin is a beautiful clear white, smooth rich flesh, full at the thighs and hips and small and round at the breasts. She watches a woman with her back turned, following the curving back to the nape of the neck and the fullness of the shoulders sloping forward over breasts and skin, shaking. Turning to draw the tenugui over her back, she blushes to see her own shoulder.

The woman next to her kneels with her baby. She washes the baby gently. Leaning forward, the child rests in the curve of her arms, its head supported in her hands. Her breasts hang swollen with milk. The baby's stubby arms and legs flap and kick.

Yae is now at her place squatting and scrubbing vigorously. She and other elderly women kneel and squat easily, without the brittle quality that would seem to signify age. Old women, small and folded, scrub their skin, rich luster lost to a worn toughness, thin, loose folds once fat and swollen, now useless.

A young woman rises from the water. Her steaming, flushed body waddles forward, full and round with child.

Yae crouches behind her niece and offers to wash her back. She scrubs with a vigor the girl hasn't felt since her mother did so. Finally spreading the damp tenugui over a well-polished back, Yae sends hot water in a smooth stream that, penetrating the cloth, clings. Yae peels the tenugui carefully up from the bottom edge to the shoulders; old skin falls away.

She turns to wash Yae's back. She's embarrassed, not being able to wash Yae in the same way. Yae turns, squinting and laughing, saying it doesn't matter, taking the tenugui from her niece and turning to continue her own washing. Yae is brusque in a way that doesn't indulge in matters that can't change or sentimentality that forfeits honesty or pride. She's frank but with a wry humor that can't make one take offense.

There are children in the bath. There is a beautiful girl child, her feet padding across the wet tile from the tub to her mother, then to another woman who must be her grandmother. She follows the girl's small protruding stomach and thin shoulders and dark eyes.

*          *          *

Before arriving in Kyoto, she had been to Ise, alone, carrying a small blue backpack with all the necessities for a month and a half of travel. The days on the Ise-Shima were cold and crisp and the sky a deep blue. She found herself traveling in silence, listening to the noises and conversations of her surroundings, attempting to remain an unnoticed observer, another Japanese youth fading into the background and comfort of nondescription. In her attempt to melt into scenic obscurity, she found herself a sensitive observer as to whether others were indeed aware of her and what they might have to say about it. She wanted to be alone and an observer and yet constantly felt the paranoia of her situation: acting the part of a traveling Japanese student, yet beset by an anxious desire to know if she had succeeded in her disguise and anger at any evidence of failure. So she came on pilgrimage alone to the great Shinto shrines of Ise, walking in silence through the ancient woods of hinoki cedar, pausing as others did to wash in the clear waters of the Isuzu River.

Leaving the shrines, she found a small Buddhist temple that had recently opened its rooms for traveling youth. She was the only one to stop there that evening.

Two small children, a boy and a girl, beautiful with dark eyes, leaned into her window. They scuttled around in the back and stood shyly leaning against the edge of the door. Slowly their voices eased into her room, filling silent travels with a warmth she had forgotten. They watched her unpack with curiosity, standing or sitting, leaning elbows and faces against the low table.

"Are you really from America? Really?"

"No, you don't look like one."

"No, it's a lie. Really?"

"Teach us English, please. My older sister learns English in school."

"Hurry, teach us English!"

"Say something."

Then as if some other curiosity had aroused their attention, the two children were drawn away. She heard them running with excited voices.

She sat a long time in the doorway, like a cat warming herself under the last rays of evening sun. Below her balcony, a young pregnant woman was hanging clothes to dry, sliding the damp pieces along a bamboo pole, reaching to expose her full, blooming bag. The woman was the proprietress of the hostel. She said the two children were not her own but a neighbor's. She scolded them gently for bothering her guest.

But when the woman left, they came again, this time with a friend and more aggressively, stepping inside the room to examine any recent changes.

"Are you really from America? Really?"

"Speak English! Hurry, hurry. Teach us English. Hurry!"

The young woman's voice called from a distance. Only the girl child lingered at the door. The child had been munching from a small bag of potato chips. "These are potato chips," the child informed her, leaving her with the small bag, calling after the others.

She sat in the doorway awhile longer, eating the remaining chips, and the cold air and shadows came slowly. Distant in America, Grandmother was dying. Mother had written, "Grandma wakes every morning and says, 'Mada ikiteruno ne.'" Still living.

The proprietress slid open the paper door and passed through from the hallway. Her face shone clean like a wet peach. The warmth of the bath seemed to radiate from her body and the wetness of her hair. Her stomach was round like a balloon, the weight of a child beneath her knitted dress. She said, "You may take your bath now."

*           *           *

Naked, Yae trots toward the steaming glass doors and steps out. A billow of steam follows her, and so does she.

III

At a wayside inn, a young man slipped into a small bathroom. Clothed or unclothed, in Japan he was a gaijin, blue-eyed with brown hair and a bristled mustache beneath a longish nose. The sansei woman was already there bathing. She ignored him momentarily, washing in one corner with her back turned to him. She handed him a basin and soap, and he squatted in another corner. Soon he was a mass of lather and hair, spilling water from the basin over his head, sputtering. He removed the wooden boards from the steaming tub and stepped in. Only his head bobbed there above the tub.

Droplets dribbling down his forehead and from his mustache, he squinted. He said, "You know I used to think you were like Audrey Hepburn. You know what I mean? Not the way she looks but, you know what I mean? I mean, Hepburn is simple and what you might call innocent, but she's not stupid. Hell, she's pretty darn intelligent. I don't know if you understand, but, well, I'm not so sure anymore. Now I think you're more of a coquette than she is. In fact, you'd make a pretty fair Japanese hostess."

The woman looked up at him from shampoo suds spilling about. He smiled curiously. He looked blind without his glasses. She rinsed her hair and sent water splashing around the room. He rose from the tub, dried himself with the tenugui, and slouched out.

The woman stayed to continue her bathing. They had been traveling together for the weekend. He had wanted to fish in one of the lakes surrounding Fujisan, but it had rained continuously since their arrival. Instead they had played cards and read inside the six-mat room at the inn. When sun seemed promised, they had stepped out for walks and returned muddy and soaked, or they had sat at one of the two cafés on the lake among the rubber clad fishermen, sipping tea. Most of the people served and ignored them politely, but the innkeeper had seemed rather curt. Sometimes shopkeepers would address her first, expecting her to translate. He had tried not to be annoyed, and she had tried never to answer for him.

The woman stepped in the tub. He had continued throughout to elaborate on his various and evolving impressions of her. He had discovered in her mysteries and attractions he continued to muddle over. Over the weekend he had at various times become moody and confused. Simply, he was in love but didn't want to admit it, knowing she was not. There was something threatening and cynical beneath her affections.

One could not be sure of the reasons people came to foreign countries; perhaps to search out exotic peoples or beautiful visions of the distant past. Maybe he had come to Japan to find Audrey Hepburn—something respectable, innocent, and elegant. It wasn't fair to make fun of him, for the woman too had come for similar reasons, and it was pleasing to think that another might perceive in her these same traits. He had created an illusion she longed to step into, but finding his elaborations ultimately trite, she could trust neither his observations nor his sensitivity. Even the simplicity she felt natural to herself cast doubt at his innocent world.

He had bought her a small white clay cat, a four-inch replica of the larger maneki-neko that beckons customers into shops and restaurants in Japan. The white cat sat on its haunches with wide eyes and one beckoning paw. It had a red string collar with a small bell. He put the cat on the tokonoma. He had bought the white cat because it reminded him of her.

She slipped her damp body into the yukata robe provided by the inn. In the room he seemed asleep. She turned the lights out and slipped beneath the quilts near the floor. There was a stirring. He went out to brush his teeth.

Suddenly she was under a mass of quilts, trapped by the heavy darkness and his body, which hugged and enfolded. Laughing, she squirmed, groping to find the surface, to find air beyond the tossing quilts; they rolled. Her hand reached for the dry scrap of matting, and elbows squeezed and pushed away the billowing robes. Escaped, she knelt on the matting, watching. He threw the pile of quilts, dumping it over her. "I used to do that to my little sister."

He stood, shaking the quilts and fanning them out over the bedding. "You know, when I saw you in the bath, sitting there with your back to me and your hair wrapped up over your head, you know what you looked like? You looked like an ukiyo-e print, like an ukiyo-e woman in the bath—"


## IV


In late September, the twins were together again in Japan. After a year, one was about to leave, and the other had just arrived for a year of study and travel.

She came downstairs to the bath initiating her sister to the various buckets and faucets that had by now become quite commonplace. A long time since childhood baths together, they found themselves in the warmth of the small bath, talking.

Her sister, shaped more as Mother, was full-breasted and thin-legged, reminding her of how beautiful Mother's figure must have been. And too, her sister and mother were alike in their realism or practicality of outlook. They moved forward with an eye on the minimal expectation, her sister with a saucy flamboyance defying, Mother with a stark energy accepting, the time and the people and the circumstances that came to change their lives. They seemed to experience the events surrounding them more immediately, more honestly, because their peripheral vision was wider, more encompassing. Their reactions, whether silent or expressed, were the mire of sensibilities and possibilities thought of in the past tense.

To meet again after a year was to meet themselves at a new juncture. She saw herself in her twin at some former time, although she couldn't fully see what the time or change had come to. Now perhaps she could say she had gone to Japan in search of something uncomplicated even as her own sensitivity and those around her were complicated in a way she hadn't reckoned and couldn't so easily abandon or disregard. Then, too, she had thought of coming to Japan as a ritual to be performed and observed in its symbolic nuances, a return to the past, not simply as a time in life to be lived. In part, she had wanted to recapture a sensibility about life that her grandmothers had known.

She told her sister of a young man she had met while traveling in Nara. His name was Moto, and he had a car and had offered to drive them to Karuizawa for the weekend.


*            *            *

Arriving in Nara by train after solitary wandering on the Ise-Shima, she had stood in front of the station with backpack on her back and pink scarf bag in hand, trying to decipher the map. A swaggering, skinny Kubo Moto threw his pack at her feet and, assuming her to be a lost young sixteen-year-old, proceeded to give directions and to handle telephone reservations with a brusque self-assertion. She was disgusted, yet resigned to his aid. Besides, he didn't guess her identity, and this game pleased her. Likewise, she assumed him to be an eighteen-year-old high school traveler with a small knowledge of English he bandied about when he discovered her seeming inadequacy at Japanese.

A state of confused identities continued for a portion of the day until they finally decided to abandon a game of bantering for confessions that were more startling than the game itself. Moto was a twenty-four-year-old college graduate who had spent the previous year traveling in Europe and had returned ready to enter the business world, the company.

To explain herself was difficult and unconvincing for all the suggestions implied in their game. It wasn't simply that she was American-born. She had yet to concede to herself that her general dress and appearance were indeed quite young. Sacrificing style for practicality and any conspicuous foreign quality for nondescription, she had also succeeded in becoming by some standards rather childish, devoid of any sophisticated flair or manner. Sophistication of a sort in Japan would have called for cutting her long hair and wearing makeup, and that she found repugnant. There was a need to preserve a basic philosophy about being natural. But moreover, there was a curious pressing need to be the same. When that sameness was seemingly recognized, she felt the comfort of acceptance and for the time being escaped the humiliation of being thought of as Chinese or Korean, a child of mixed blood or a copier after American tastes. It shouldn't have been humiliating, except for the crude manner and exploitative attitudes that often accompanied these assumptions.

Interestingly, a disguise had come about by a discarding of Americanisms, styles and manners that meant nothing to the Japanese. Americans and their pretensions to being more experienced looked silly in Japan. A sansei divested of these American manifestations would seem to become simply another Japanese. Yet it was necessary to take on another set of manners, and her manner had become one of a young Japanese girl with sufficient touches of innocence and certainly reticence, mostly due to difficulties with the language. At least it was the surface manner that others found approachable, or negligible. Even if it were an imitation or cover, there was a kind of comfort that exceeded pretensions or dishonesty.

Yae had explained the meaning of *daikon no hana:* the daikon flower is really, she said, a *nani mo nai,* nothing-much flower, a tiny flower seen in a tuft of green leaves. But beneath the earth, hidden from sight, is the great white root, the daikon. She knew the daikon, a giant white radish that, when grated, garnished fish, īkagen, with a clean, pungent quality like lemon but not as sour—something more mellow, Yae said. "Long ago we used to call some girls 'daikon no hana,' but nowadays there are no such girls. No, daikon no hana have disappeared."

She knew Yae was such a flower, but as for herself, she was probably not what Yae had in mind.

At first, she had playfully experimented with various expressions in the language of the Japanese woman. Gradually these expressions and manners became natural to most communications, and the possibility of successfully performing roles in two different cultures became a sign of advanced knowledge of both. There was, too, the secret delight of perceiving more about one's surroundings than one's image might suggest, of knowing one knew what was what; in other words, of being, after all, more experienced.

Therefore, she herself, unconvincing, put aside suspicions about Moto's maturity, confirmed by age, to see again what might come of it. His forward display seemed to allow for this maturity. In any case, they accepted each other's company for a three-day tour of Nara.

During the same week in Nara, a small cottage in the resort area of Karuizawa was under siege by hundreds of armed policemen. Inside the hillside cottage, members of the Red Guard, a small Marxist band, were holding a woman hostage while police sent torrents of water by firehose to batter the cottage. It was a small war waged on a snowy hillside, police crouching behind fire tanks with rifles and the husband of the hostage wailing through microphones echoing down the valley, "Please, my wife is a sick woman. Please, take me and let her go!"

Moto sympathized with the youth in the cottage. He said they had no choice but to wait and to fight. He couldn't explain why these events had happened, but he said the youth had no choice but to die. They would be killed by police or in the courts.

After a long week, the police finally broke in, killing several youths, capturing others, and saving the woman. Later stories revealed a bizarre tale that had begun in the mountain cottages elsewhere, where members of the guard fought among themselves in a game of power that led to private trials and the systemic execution and burial of their own people, one by one. A woman with child had barely escaped death. Her brothers were dead. Their bodies had been dismembered, buried on the mountainside. A young woman had led the group. Her plain, harsh face stared from newspapers everywhere. Some said it was the woman's plain face that had made her bitter and angry.

*       *       *

Karuizawa was after all a resort area, and Moto's family had built a small cottage there. The long five-hour drive over winding highways was tedious, exhausting. Her sister refused to sit in the front seat and finally said, "That guy doesn't know how to drive. Shit I know—he can't even shift gears smoothly. He's going to get us into an accident. Where did you pick this guy up, anyway?"

Her twin had come a long way to disturb her perspective, but something inside her jumped, an old sense of strength, even of hostility, and she realized she had met and accepted Moto because of a game of sorts, a deception, and urge to imitate. Even if she had tried to suspend judgment or allow another set of values or rules to decide, she wasn't now sure. She didn't know who this Moto was.

The cottage was one of many, isolated among the trees far up on a hill. It seemed wedged into the side of the hill, overlooking a dirt road below. What she had imagined would be an extravagant two-story cabin was rather a two-room kitchenette, compact and convenient. They scrounged for supplies, and she was pleased to cook by putting foods together, īkagen, from a wide range of novel possibilities. She was pleased with her own ingenuity and the camplike self-sufficiency of the arrangement.

The twins talked together constantly. They began to leave Moto out. In fact, they began to wish he might disappear. Moto had at first confused one twin for the other. The initial humor of these confusions long past, he had continued, either due to the growing schizophrenia of his perceptions or a need to release nervous energy, to re-create confusions and ensuing jokes. Her sister wasn't one to conceal boredom or disgust, and Moto couldn't conceal his now-obvious immaturity. The swaggering self-confidence had dissipated into an insipid amiability, and jokes, amusing once because the Japanese had been simple enough to understand, now fell flat.

A typhoon was reported. There was a possibility it would head their way. The resort season had virtually ended. They seemed to be the only people in the area, and the rain threatened to trap them inside the cottage. They prepared for the long, stormy night, setting boards up over the windows.

She cooked, and her twin slept. Moto prepared a bath. Turning from the sink, she heard a huge BOOM! And Moto's body flew backward out of the bathroom. He was stunned and wide-eyed, babbling about fire, about gas. He had lit leaking gas. The burnt ends of his eyebrows crinkled over his forehead. Fortunately his arms had been covered. He wasn't hurt, but she was becoming nervous about this enterprise. And the rain fell steadily.

The twins stepped into that same bath together. Her sister talked constantly and animatedly about all subjects, seemingly unaware of the steady and increasingly loud sound of the rain. The wind blew fiercely outside the boarded windows of the bathroom. Rain pounded intermittently against the thin walls, clanging madly at the tin shielding. Inside that closet of steam and hot water, they splashed soap and bubbles around. Her twin bent over her squatting back and scrubbed, entertaining her with stories and events from the past year, and she could hear the rising scream of the storm against their steaming closet, and the violent chaos was becoming her own fears. She thought of the precarious wedging of the cottage against the hill and the slippage of land and mud and trees; she thought of the deluge and the mass of land that might bury two naked, soapy bodies.

Her sister said of Moto, "You're always getting screwed. He's just like all those other immature Japanese dudes who think they're such hot shit. What a baby. And since I got in that car accident, I'm paranoid about cars, and he can't drive a stick shift. It's murder to try to drive with someone like that."

She turned her twin around, crouching behind, and poured water down her back, peeling the tenugui from her shoulders, trying to work as Yae had. She admitted Moto must be a fool, and foolishly wanted to hear her sister's voice echo forcibly against the tile and wood, harsh or tender but louder than the raging storm. Yet she saw in her mind the crushing weight of a mud wall bursting through that closet and the wild treachery and insipid irony of that disgusting death.

As she emerged from the steam closet, Moto looked up and said, "The typhoon will pass very near. Perhaps it will swerve off, but then again, we may be at the center." He drew the standard shape of Japan on a small scratch pad, marking where they were, where the typhoon was, where it would or wouldn't pass and at what time, with all the authority of a radio broadcast. Then he looked at her; his face looked comically severe and then, just comical.

"Maybe this house will fall down the hill . . . no, the house is probably stronger than that. What I'm more worried about is the car at the bottom. If it slipped off, we would never be able to leave." He smiled, wild-eyed. "Perhaps we'll die!"

She looked at him in disgust.

He continued, "But, in any case, I'll be happy. It'll be like dying with you in a double suicide."


V


She received a letter today from her sister, who is still in Japan. Now she too is traveling alone. She writes that she has found a small beach in Kyushu called Ibusuki, and that she has tried the sand baths there. When the tide recedes, old women come to bury her in the sand. Deep, deep from secret sources beneath the sand, the warm springs rise.

And Mother went out early this morning to weed the garden and came in hot and muddy. She retired to the thing that gives her the most pleasure, her bath. Now she stands in her towel with wet hair, adjusting her glasses.

"Oh," she says, "a letter from your sister. Now what does she say?"

# The Dentist and the Dental Hygienist

Dr. Hashikin's dental office was situated at the very mouth of Gardena. For a town with no obvious boundaries (at least to the unaccustomed eye), over a rambling suburban landscape of fast food stops, asphalt runways leading to shopping centers, and Merit tract homes (vintage sixties), to be at the mouth of Gardena is hardly descriptive enough to locate anything at all. One might point out the dental office's proximity to three major Los Angeles freeways or to the Pacific Square, branch offices of Little Tokyo and therefore a surrogate way to the East. Of course, this attempt to locate the coordinates of Dr. Hashikin's dental office in the disjointed Gardena grid is nothing more than a cheap ploy to throw the Gardena aficionado off track. In the continuing soap opera of tribal life, the ultimate compliment to the author can only be the gossip generated by such stories.

Dr. Hashikin had always lived in Gardena, except for during his adolescence, which had been spent in camp. Some say adolescence is the period in growth when one acquires the cultural attributes that remain for the rest of one's life. It might also be true to say that many people spend their adulthood trying in one way or another to deal with the legacy left by adolescence. Dr. Hashikin had never thought of this seriously, but, going through adolescence in camp, under the close inspection of so many other Japanese Americans at such close quarters, had been memorable. Dr. Hashikin had observed, enviously, that his son could close the bathroom door.

Perhaps it was such an adolescence that prepared Dr. Hashikin better than others to live in Gardena. Dr. Hashikin had never thought of living anywhere else. After finishing his studies, he married one of the Sato daughters and quickly set up his practice in Gardena. In a short time, his business swelled with the mouths of a Japanese American generation brought up on sugar-frosted flakes and Doublemint gum.

Dr. Hashikin and his wife, Betty, began to raise three baby boomers of their own and to weave the spreading floss of their lives through the community. By the time Dr. Hashikin could afford to take every Wednesday off for golf, had joined the Kiwanis, and sent his mother to visit Japan, their first son, Steve, was in the Key Club at Gardena High School. The second son, Craig, hung out at the beach and made part-time money at Shig's service station, and their daughter, Kathy, wore nylons on Fridays in junior high. Dr. Hashikin watched his kids run in a huddle of sansei through life. His house had been toilet-papered six times, twice for each kid. "The only thing left is to flush us away," he remarked with irritation to Betty. The multicolored stuff had been wrapped around his recently trimmed lollipop bushes, which again looked like huge spitballs. But the adolescence of his children seemed to sweep by more quickly than his own, and Dr. Hashikin and Betty were soon left alone to spend most of their time in one corner of a four-bedroom house watching old movies on a video cassette recorder.

It was at this bridge in life that Dr. Hashikin discovered the roots of a canal yet uncharted in all his fifty-seven years. Candy Yuasa was the twenty-four-year-old daughter of his friends and regular patients. Dr. Hashikin had cleaned and treated Candy's teeth ever since she had started kindergarten. Over the years, a relationship of trust develops between a dentist and his patient. Many people continue to see their childhood dentist, often driving great distances over L.A. to keep an appointment with the only person for whom they might condescend to climb into a high chair, wear a bib, and open wide. At twenty-four, this relationship of trust clearly established, Candy kept her appointment with Dr. Hashikin, not for her teeth, but for a job.

Dr. Hashikin was the same kind, congenial man with nice manners and clean breath. Everything in the office, from the white shirt buttoned at his shoulders to the free toothbrush samples, smelled slightly of peppermint.

"Hi, Candy." Dr. Hashikin smiled. "When can you go to work? I've got a full schedule Monday, and I need someone right away. By the way, how are your folks?" There was no interview to speak of, and no question that he might not hire her. If he didn't, it would be extremely embarrassing in light of his personal friendship with the Yuasas. Besides, Dr. Hashikin thought, like most of his Japanese American patients, a Japanese American could always be trusted to do the job. He thought so despite the fact that over the years, he had seen a stream of nisei and sansei dental assistants and hygienists, some of whose temperaments and talents left something to be desired. Despite the stress caused by conflicting personalities and petty office politics, Dr. Hashikin had never had to fire anyone for incompetence. Anyway, he always hired nisei and sansei, and he wouldn't have had the guts in a small community to fire anyone.

Candy Yuasa was right out of the USC dental hygiene program. She had good grades and recommendations. She seemed very quiet and didn't have a great deal to say. Her quietness was slightly discomforting to Dr. Hashikin, but his clientele wouldn't complain. Japanese Americans were used to Japanese Americans.

Dr. Hashikin hadn't always used the talents of a dental hygienist. In the old days, he had done all the teeth cleaning himself. A lot of his old colleagues still preferred to work this way. They liked to keep their operations small and turned away new patients. Most of them, Dr. Hashikin included, weren't much in the way of businessmen or managers and didn't care to take on added responsibilities. Having to deal with a staff of hygienists and assistants, receptionists, bookkeepers, and insurance people, and treat teeth besides, was an uncomfortable ordeal to men who had gone into the profession mostly because they were good with their hands. It was difficult to juggle the artistic talents of capping a tooth with doling out competitive salaries and charging the going rate. Dr. Hashikin had been forced to take one hygienist on staff besides his receptionist, who sided as an assistant, but he was reluctant to let his business grow out of hand. He had realized, however, that he was getting along in years, and a hygienist would lighten his workload considerably.

Candy Yuasa, despite her youth and inexperience, stepped into her position with a certain quiet command. She set up her own tools and cleaned up after herself, and she didn't even mind assisting from time to time. Some hygienists, Dr. Hashikin knew, felt above the tasks of the dental assistant. Candy was agreeable and always quiet.

"Candy is quiet." That's what Dr. Hashikin told Betty in the beginning, but, after a while, he wasn't so sure that was the proper description. It wasn't as if Candy was the sort who required a period of warming up to get to know her. She never really warmed up, and there never seemed to be some hidden someone to get to know. She was always the same person of few words, except when she was cleaning teeth. Dr. Hashikin could hear her talking animatedly above the buzz and squizz of the Cavitron.

But, as soon as the cleaning was finished, the bib removed, and the chair lowered, Candy's chatter stopped. Dr. Hashikin would meet her in the corridor with her sweet, placid smile, ushering a patient out with a wordless nod.

Dr. Hashikin didn't remember exchanging more than two or three sentences with Candy and only on matters of work. That Candy could carry on extended monologues over her captive patients yet have little, if anything, to relate to Dr. Hashikin, even in the normal day-to-day office routine, was curious.

Dr. Hashikin began to slough off the sensation of being slighted and disliked. He chided himself for his childish reaction, as if he had been denied membership into an exclusive club. But, as the days passed, Dr. Hashikin found his thoughts occupied by only one question: Who was Candy Yuasa, and what did she have to say in such abundance to everyone else that she didn't say to him?

Betty laughed at her husband. "She's a young girl, just out of school. You're her boss. She's probably afraid of you."

Dr. Hashikin nodded and returned to the office, trying to assume an unconcerned air with the idea of making Candy relax and feel more at home. "What do you do in your free time?" he tried to ask nonchalantly. "Any hobbies?"

Candy shook her head. "No."

Dr. Hashikin soon ran out of icebreaker questions and began fumbling through the re-runs. "Any hobbies?" he repeated hopelessly. A tiny but perceptible tingle began to nag his lower left molars. Dr. Hashikin crunched down and contracted his jaw, mashing the icebreakers in disgust and near anger. But he was quickly repentant over his hostile attitude. After all, years ago, one former assistant had resigned from his office after complaining, in so many words, that Dr. Hashikin was a poor communicator, that he didn't talk or explain things enough. Dr. Hashikin had always been completely baffled by the complaint. He thought he was certainly better at expressing himself than some of his colleagues were. After that incident, however, Dr. Hashikin had become somewhat self-conscious about projecting himself in the office. He wavered between trying to assume his position as the boss and resorting to democracy. Nothing quite worked. Now, here was Candy Yuasa, haunting him for obscure and even, he imagined, sinister reasons, none of which he could prove, for his own lack of communication.

Linda, Dr. Hashikin's longtime receptionist and dental assistant, didn't confirm Dr. Hashikin's feeling of rejection. "She's shy," was all Linda could suggest. Dr. Hashikin sighed. He himself had chosen Linda for her diplomacy and her inability to entertain catty or inconvenient ideas about anyone. Linda was the most, and probably the only, generous soul in Gardena. Most people considered her naive, but she was, undeniably, the perfect receptionist. In this situation, however, Linda was of no aid to Dr. Hashikin, whose growing sense of insecurity groped about in its solitary and imagined madness.

"I see you've got a new hygienist," said Mrs. Shimizu.

Dr. Hashikin nodded and ran his mirror under her upper molars.

Mrs. Shimizu waited, then offered, "She's an interesting girl."

"Oh?" said Dr. Hashikin, trying not to sound too eager. "What did she say?"

"Well," Mrs. Shimizu hedged, "she mentioned Betty. She knew we went to school together. She even knew Betty and I were in camp together . . ." Mrs. Shimizu's voice trailed off. She decided she wouldn't bother to tell Dr. Hashikin how she had known Betty when Betty was in love with Shig Tanaka, and that Betty had started to date Dr. Hashikin on the rebound from Shig. The strangest thing was that Candy seemed to know all about it too. Mrs. Shimizu waited for Dr. Hashikin to complete the story and explain that he himself had told it to Candy.

But Dr. Hashikin dropped the tiny mirror inside Mrs. Shimizu's mouth, recovering it awkwardly near her chin. "Why would she know about you and Betty?" he asked.

"I thought you'd know," Mrs. Shimizu suggested meekly, her mind immediately punching in all the wild possibilities offered by daytime soaps. "Do I know her folks?" Mrs. Shimizu wondered.

"Yuasa?" said Dr. Hashikin. "Sam and Mary."

"I don't believe so." Mrs. Shimizu shook her head. "That's funny. She was quite accurate about Betty and me," she said more boldly, in part because she was beginning to form a hypothesis in which she might have to defend her old girlfriend Betty, and because Candy's unfortunate opinion of dear Betty was embarrassingly similar to her own. Mrs. Shimizu concluded, by the end of her appointment, that the only person who could have told Candy that Betty hadn't married Dr. Hashikin for love but because of a pessimistic vision of the future must have been Dr. Hashikin himself. "Now," Mrs. Shimizu snapped to her own husband, "you don't go telling a young girl in her twenties personal things like that unless you're trying to make a pass. Imagine, at his age. It's disgusting. Poor Betty. And besides," she pouted, "he let the anesthetic wear off. He hurt me." Mrs. Shimizu discreetly spread the plaque about Dr. Hashikin to a few mutual friends. It got into those hard-to-brush crevices of Gardena, and Mrs. Shimizu and some others took their dirty teeth to other dentists.

Dr. Hashikin rubbed his jaw near that lower left-hand molar. Strange that a dentist had need of a dentist himself. He'd have his colleague Harry check it out for him one of these days. He yawned. He hadn't gotten much sleep, struggling with insomnia and the continuing saga surrounding his hygienist.

Betty quipped, "It's Candy isn't it? I don't understand. Are you hiding something from me?"

Dr. Hashikin shook his head. "I've told you everything. I don't understand it myself. It's uncanny. No, she's downright weird!"

"Maybe you should ask her to leave," Betty suggested.

"I can't do that," Dr. Hashikin wailed. "Sam does my taxes for nothing. We've got season tickets to the Dodgers this year."

So Candy stayed on, scraping the plaque and calcium deposits off row after row of teeth in dozens of mouths every week. There was no doubt that she was an excellent hygienist. Dr. Hashikin recognized the skillful cleaning job, the well-polished tooth, the sparkling new pearly grin. Everything Candy did was technically perfect, except something about the grin. How could he fire Candy for the imperfection of the grin?

One patient after another slumped into Dr. Hashikin's high chair with an expressive grin that seemed to describe every sort of emotion from titillating embarrassment to wretched self-flagellation. Before, they had all had some manner of confronting possible pain—the prick of the needle and the flow of Novocain or the whizzing grind of the drill—but lately, no one seemed especially concerned about whether the dentist would hurt them or not. Instead everyone seemed to be cogitating some private and often shocking discovery. One woman burst into tears, and a young man flew into a rage, screamed incoherently at the dentist, then stomped off, slamming the door and leaving the movement-sensitive bell sweetly ding-donging behind him.

And then there were those who barely got as far as walking across the corridor at the dental assistant's kind invitation. Linda would return after having said, "Dr. Hashikin will be right with you," to find an empty chair and no one to bib down. One anxious girl left in the middle of the x-rays.

"What's this pile of mail?" Dr. Hashikin asked Linda one day. "I thought we were sending our six-month reminders on postcards," he remarked, flipping through the envelopes.

Linda said sheepishly, "These are all x-rays from our files, requested by patients changing to other dentists—" She bit her lip. Lately, every day, she got calls for x-rays and records.

"Bob Kono? Who's he gone over to? Uba? What's happening here? I put in his bridge, and I did all that gold work. Cheryl Miyamura too? I'm the one who got her to stop sucking her thumb! What's got into everyone?"

Linda shrugged. A few months before, she had patients signed up for an appointment at least six months in advance. Now she could squeeze in anyone, if there was anyone, tomorrow or any other day. The calendar looked like a war zone of cancellations. Still, it wasn't as if Dr. Hashikin had been oblivious to the gradual decay of his once-healthy practice. He himself had observed the tiny cavity and the pockets indicating the inception of pyorrhea. He knew the source of the problem, but he wouldn't treat it, as if the excellence of Candy's method would somehow brush everything away.

There was another reason Dr. Hashikin ignored his crumbling business, a reason he couldn't quite admit to himself. He had begun, after the initial trauma of rejection, to listen in on Candy's sessions. In the beginning, he would sneak surreptitiously into the corridor and pretend to look at x-rays outside her door, but, after a while, he merely leaned against the wall outside her room, rubbed his sore jaw, and eavesdropped.

It wasn't as if the patient having his or her teeth cleaned said much of anything. They only had to sit there comfortably, their legs propped up and their minds tilted gently into the headrest. It was Candy who did all the talking. In fact, she talked so much that it had occurred to Dr. Hashikin that she might be too hoarse to say anything to him at the end of the day. The content of her monologues was as varied as the patients who frequented the office, and it was this content that began to attract and preoccupy Dr. Hashikin like a Hershey bar to a sweet tooth.

"I guess you don't like the magazines Dr. Hashikin has in the waiting room," Dr. Hashikin would hear Candy say. "He used to get the big issues of *Vogue,* but Betty must have canceled her subscription. You used to steal those big issues. Now all he has is *Newsweek* and *Time.*"

Dr. Hashikin caught sight of wide-eyed Mrs. Miura, her mouth gaping despite the necessity for it to be open anyway.

Candy scraped away with the scaler and continued, "Did you hear Dr. Hashikin and Betty are getting a divorce?"

This was news to Dr. Hashikin.

"Something about some dental hygienist!" Candy laughed. Mrs. Miura nearly choked.

"But," Candy added, probing a sensitive area beneath the gums, "I suppose you thought about divorcing Joe years ago when he was alive. But it wasn't like now where everyone gets divorced, and Joe didn't do too bad. I mean, he didn't make as much as Dr. Hashikin does, but at least he left you a pension." Candy babbled on to Mrs. Miura, who looked blanched with surprise. "The girls don't understand that. I mean, how you miss their dad even though you bitched and complained all those years. It's hard to make anyone believe you really miss Joe since you never seemed to appreciate him when he was alive . . ."

It was Mrs. Miura who had burst into tears in Dr. Hashikin's office, which came as no surprise, considering the tender subject broached by Candy. Joe Miura had died only last year, and even Dr. Hashikin had thought Mrs. Miura was faking her mourning. No one gave Mrs. Miura much sympathy because they had pitied poor Joe and thought Mrs. Miura had nagged her husband to death. Poor Mrs. Miura. All of a sudden Dr. Hashikin realized what a lonely and frustrated woman she was, and he was sorry he didn't have any more *Vogues* for her to steal.

Then there was Gary Kozawa. He was a young man in his thirties, extremely successful and self-assured. He was an accountant and sped around in a BMW. Dr. Hashikin could hear Candy buzzing in with the prophy angle to polish his nice, straight teeth. He had been coming to Dr. Hashikin ever since he had had braces in high school. Candy pressed the paste to Gary's teeth and said, "You heard from your mom about Dr. Hashikin's dental hygienist too, didn't you? Now you wonder how Dr. Hashikin could be interested in such a woman. You'd never get involved with your secretary, for example. That would be too tacky. You have to keep up appearances. Still, you wonder what would be cool to do when you're in your fifties."

The young man started to pop out of his seat. "What the—"

But Candy pressed him gently back and continued her application of prophy paste. "Of course, your fiancée, Janet—your ex-fiancée, that is—

was only an administrative assistant at TRW. What a low blow. You had the wedding invitations all set up, and Janet pulls a fast one—day before the wedding, she calls it all off. Just like that. You had relatives coming in from all over. Your mom threw a fit."

Gary was actually foaming at the mouth.

Candy went on, sloshing down the paste and generously squirting the teeth with water. "Now you're making payments on that condo she wanted, and she never returned the Porsche. I mean, she returned the ring, but she kept the Porsche. Let her keep the Porsche! I wonder if she returned all those shower gifts. You keep trying to make everyone think it was Janet's fault, like she was an opportunist or something. But you can't buy a woman. No matter how much money you make, accountants are boring."

Gary Kozawa spit out the foaming water and burst into the corridor, running into Dr. Hashikin, whose cheeks were puffed up with suppressed laughter. Even Betty had thought Gary was the most eligible bachelor in Gardena, but Dr. Hashikin hadn't been impressed. Dr. Hashikin thought Gary was egotistical.

Gary screamed a flood of epithets at Candy and Dr. Hashikin. It was the first time he had lost his cool. He hadn't even let himself get mad the weekend of his wedding, self-consciously aware of what others might think. Gary had been so worried about what others thought, he had forgotten what he actually thought himself—that he really wasn't that wonderful and that he lost Janet because he couldn't tell her, in the simplest way, without worrying about the way he said it and who overheard, that he loved her.

Candy made no attempt to defend herself, watching silently as Gary stomped out of the office. Dr. Hashikin looked out the window down onto the parking lot. He could see Gary slamming his BMW over the humps in the lot, the paper bib still fastened under his chin.

Every day, Dr. Hashikin could expect to hear everything, from whose kids were on drugs and cohabiting to the minute details of how the children of one of his dead friends had squabbled over and divided the inheritance. It was as if the entire network of gossip in Gardena reverberated through his office, its singular mouthpiece being his dental hygienist, Candy Yuasa. But Dr. Hashikin discovered that whatever the gossip out there in Gardena might be, Candy usually homed in on the truth, the simple, sometimes painful, sometimes silly, but always simple truth. It was for this reason Dr. Hashikin didn't ask Candy to leave; it would've been against his sense of justice, and besides, he was enjoying himself too much.

Dr. Hashikin was at a loss trying to explain the phenomenon. It was something about the touch of Candy's curette on the nerves of one's mouth. But as informative and entertaining as Dr. Hashikin found the sessions, it couldn't last forever. Obviously, people didn't come to dentists to have their deepest secrets spoken to them as if they had been pre-recorded, and few people, even though they felt relieved by the mental hygiene of Candy's technique, wanted to be subjected to it every six months. Many people felt disturbed and afraid, and others were downright disdainful, assuming Dr. Hashikin's dental hygienist was blabbering these personal things to everyone and anyone who sat under her scaler. Dr. Hashikin ran his tongue over his sore molars. The truth was that no one wanted to hear the truth, and the lips of Dr. Hashikin's practice were now sinking into their toothless gums.

Dr. Hashikin still took his normal golfing days on Wednesdays. His colleagues heckled him at first for putting a strain on their businesses. "We have all we can take. We can't handle your patients too," they complained at first. But after a while, his friends became seriously concerned. "If it's that hygienist, get rid of her," they flatly suggested.

Dr. Hashikin couldn't explain it. It was too preposterous. Even the gossip about his divorce was more probable than this malarkey about tapping the roots of one's conscience.

Harry peered into Dr. Hashikin's mouth. "If it's been bothering you this long, why haven't you had it looked into before?" Harry scraped along the left molars, looking askance through his bifocals.

Dr. Hashikin shrugged. "I asked Linda to take x-rays. They didn't show a thing."

"There's nothing here I can see," Harry agreed. "But you ought to get 'em cleaned."

Dr. Hashikin went back to his empty practice. Linda looked up with a start to see someone come through the door.

He strode into Candy's room and plopped himself on her chair. "I need my teeth cleaned," he announced.

Candy quietly dressed her boss in a bib for the ordeal. She ran through her normal procedure. For the first time, Dr. Hashikin felt the same fear so many of his patients felt facing his drill. But it was painless. The skillful hands worked quickly and delicately.

"You've lived all your life in this community, given your time and talents to these people. In return, you've raised a family and won respect, somewhat tarnished at this point, but . . ." Candy paused and adjusted the overhead light. "It's not that dentistry was a bad choice. There weren't many choices in those days. But you never really enjoyed the profession like some of the fellows. You always spent your evenings watching those animal shows like *Wild, Wild World of Animals* and the *National Geographic* specials on the New Guinea aborigines. The year you went to Japan with Betty was a revelation. You never wanted to come back to Gardena after that, but you did."

Dr. Hashikin stared into Candy's eyes in amazement. It had never been put so simply.

Candy spread the prophy paste and let the little rubber tip spin. "Now that your responsibilities have been fulfilled to your children and to hundreds of mouths all over Gardena, you can do what you've always dreamed of."

Dr. Hashikin smiled. Years of care and irresolution had somehow emptied into the hygienist's mouth. In one simple moment, she had squirted away the uncomfortable ache in his lower left molar. He tore off his bib, sat up suddenly, walked confidently away from his practice, and drove home.

Betty looked up from her weeding. She was pulling the dandelions out of the dichondra on the front lawn.

"Betty," Dr. Hashikin blurted out. "Are we getting a divorce?"

"No." She shook her head and removed her garden gloves. She looked up at her husband sheepishly. "I had my teeth cleaned," she admitted.

"That's good! That's good! That's great!" Dr. Hashikin roared over the quiet and meticulous Japanese American landscape. He shoved Betty, still in her shorts and size-five Nikes, into the car. Betty adjusted her L.A. Olympics sun visor; Dr. Hashikin pulled down the flip-top shades on his glasses and stepped on the gas, whistling past the mouth of Gardena, leaving the movement-sensitive bells sweetly ding-donging behind forever.

# A Gentlemen's Agreement

I am the granddaughter, and Lucio is the grandson. Our photographs are a curious reflection of a time we didn't live in, of a past filtered to us through memories. We suspect and crave a continuum, but we can know neither the things that drew the eyes beyond the photograph's flat surface, nor the inner focus of the mind's eye. We imagine we are seen or dreamed of. We imagine the youth of our grandparents reaches toward us, invokes our respect, guides, condemns, or destines. We imagine.

In 1907, the u.s. and Japanese governments signed a gentlemen's agreement to exclude Japanese immigrant laborers from the United States. In the following year, the first contingent—a boat load of some eight hundred Japanese—arrived at the Port of Santos to begin their contracts on coffee plantations in the state of São Paulo. Moving toward the twenties and subsequent u.s. Exclusion Acts, Japanese immigration to the u.s. dropped off as immigration to Brazil grew. While the u.s. came to house a Meiji-era generation of Japanese immigrants from a Japan somewhat wonderstruck by its opening to the West, Brazil began to house the succeeding generation of the eras of Taisho and Showa*—a time of expanding industries, spheres of political influence, and nationalism. While the dream of the Americas confronting reality would indeed shape emigrant experiences, Japan's national self-perception and its relationship to the West at the time must have molded the way each era of emigrants approached the task of leaving home. While Meiji Japanese coming to the u.s. seemed to set about their purpose with respectful endurance, carefully corralling their children toward good behavior, Taisho and

---

* Japanese historic eras are designated by the lifetime of emperors, i.e., Emperor Meiji, 1868–1911; Emperor Taisho, 1912–1925; Emperor Showa (Hirohito), 1926–1989.

Showa immigrants to Brazil were perhaps more aggressive in their construction of insular colonies that replaced virgin forests, their frank disdain of the Brazilian peasantry, and their Japanese nationalism.

In 1975, I met Lucio Kubo in São Paulo, Brazil. He was a recent philosophy graduate of the University of São Paulo. He had long hair, a scroungy goatee, bell-bottom jeans—the symbols of the time. He surprised me with his knowledge of classical Japanese, French poets, and American jazz, and with his supple and sympathetic mind, his bright wit, and his Brazilian cynicism. Someone told me Lucio was raised and spoiled by his grandmother; it was she who taught him to read Japanese poetry. Other Brazilian nisei couldn't boast of such a formal Japanese education. His friends nicknamed him Shogun.

The four women pictured here were all Meiji-born before the turn of the century and within a decade of each other. Two came from the cultural centers of Tokyo and Kyoto, two from smaller cities in Aichi and Nagano. They were born into a Japan opening to the West, making the transition from a peasant to an industrial society. The transition would be both dramatic and devastating. This opening was also the homeland's implied blessing to leave, to explore the world, to attempt one's fortune in distant places, to alleviate the burden of this transition and the poverty of its people. The four women pictured would all leave their homes and settle in a new world. Two would make their homes in the u.s. just before that gentlemen's agreement, and some two decades later—a time poised between a worldwide depression and a second world war—two would make their homes in Brazil. But none of them planned to leave Japan. These plans were in the stars, in the minds of men, in gentlemen's agreements.

When I left L.A. and that enclave of Japanese Americans in Gardena, California, I didn't know who my counterparts in Brazil might be. I imagined my sansei friends with a Latin feeling. Instead I met a younger Japanese immigration and a generation my age who called themselves nisei, who spoke of integration, of their larger participation in a Brazilian nation, and of the necessity to become respected professionals. I had the strange sensation of meeting my parents' generation in their youth. What was sansei? I was a figment of their imaginations. I had arrived in a time machine; and yet, I hadn't. I had only come from up north. I was American, and every middle-class person on earth seems to know what that means.

## Tomi

Tomi Murakami Yamashita
(Oakland, 1901)

The woman with the bird on her head and the boa around her neck is my paternal grandmother, Tomi Murakami Yamashita. A poster-sized reproduction of this photograph was once displayed in the window of Bushnell's photography shop in Oakland around 1901, shortly after my grandmother arrived in the United States. That a recent Japanese immigrant could attire herself in the Western flamboyance of turn-of-the-century San Francisco says a good deal about my grandmother—that she was beautiful and thought so, and that she was proud, extravagant, and daring—a description of her that remained true until she died in her late eighties. What I loved about my grandmother was that she had guts.

Perhaps a part of her pride came from her upbringing in the urban center of Tokyo. She came from a family of swordsmiths and samurai, and it's said that her mother was a kind of social magnet for artistic and intellectual sorts. Tomi was a convert to Christianity, a Meiji woman with urban tastes and enthusiasm for the West.

When my grandfather, Kishiro Yamashita—a dapper, well-dressed tailor and graduate of the Mitchell Cutting School in New York—appeared with a proposal of marriage and a home in California, she was perhaps only nineteen years old. Tomi and Kishiro came to Oakland and established Yokohama Tailor, catering to the needs of stylish Japanese men in the community.

Tomi was a seamstress in her own right; she patented and reproduced in small quantities a belted contraption called the Abdominal Supporter for pregnant woman. Preserving one's feminine figure must have always been a concern for Tomi, a mother of seven; even at the end of her life, she wore a corset to improve her figure.

Tomi may have had a flair for fashion, but she was never above hard work. When Kishiro died in 1931, the tailor shop closed. Tomi found work in a local sewing shop and later opened Mayfair Cleaners, taking in laundry and cleaning for wholesale businesses and doing custom alterations and pressing. Her work supported the family through the Great Depression and helped pay off debts until 1942, when the family was forced to relocate to a concentration camp in Topaz, Utah.

Perhaps it was because she was long-lived, and the details of Kishiro's life vague and distant, that Tomi became what all of us in her family believed her to be: a matriarch. And yet this photograph, in which she may have only been twenty years of age, defines her in that role in a manner none of us can forget.

When Lucio made his journey around the world, he stopped first in Los Angeles. I remember he joined me to see Wakako Yamauchi's play *And the Soul Shall Dance*. He seemed confused to see this play with English-speaking actors in Japanese roles; it was artificial to his ears. He questioned this Asian American thing. He was Brazilian; in Brazil, it was a question of class, of feeding hungry people, not race.

## Mika

Mika Morishita Akagawa is sitting in the rattan chair. Her story was told to me by her grandson, Lucio Kubo. She was the eldest daughter of a well-to-do family in Toyohashi, Aichi. The family owned an iron works and hardware store. Unusual in those days, Mika received an eight-year education rather than the traditional six for girls. She married her husband, Hidetake, by the strict arrangement of miai, in which Hidetake, under some pretense of visiting the family, observed Mika from a distance. Mika was unaware of these arrangements and only met her husband on the day of her marriage. She was eighteen; he, thirty. Later, she would comment of her relief upon seeing he was, in fact, rather handsome.

Mika followed Hidetake to Manchuria, where he received substantial pay as station chief for the Japan Railroad for a period of eighteen years.

Mika Morishita Akagawa
(São Paulo, 1941)

Upon returning to Japan, however, Hidetake couldn't find work with comparable pay and, with the failure of the stock market in 1931, suffered further financial losses. In a family now grown to nine children, the Akagawas feared their sons would be sent to war with China. Having lived outside of Japan for so many years, perhaps Brazil seemed an easy option in 1933. Still, Hidetake would have been nearing fifty, Mika forty; they would begin again, albeit with a working force of older children.

Unlike most Japanese immigrants who arrived as contractual labor, the Akagawas paid their passage and bought a parcel of land in the Japanese colony of Tietê. Tietê in 1933 was a virgin forest on the far northwestern frontier of the states of São Paulo and Mato Grosso. The Akagawas cleared the land and planted rice, corn, beans, and cotton. Only the sale of cotton would have rendered a return greater than making ends meet, and again, counting their losses, the family moved on to the city of São Paulo. By then, war edicts forbidding the Japanese language and any contact in groups confined them to their house. The children married, went on to other jobs, and left home.

Mika had been a dedicated wife and mother, not engaged in the hard labor of the farm but situated in the home in a traditional manner her daughters somewhat critically said was due to her upbringing as the spoiled daughter of a good family. Yet, she wasn't a social sort, but extremely discreet, reserved in manner. Life in São Paulo became lonely; occasional outings with her daughters to the local cinema may have been a singular source of happiness in those years.

This is perhaps the time in which the photograph was taken. No longer youthful, slightly severe, Mika sits in a rattan chair in the Foto Tucci studio in São Paulo, having traveled great distances, her own story woven silently between the warp and woof of an energetic man, nine children, three countries, war, and the economic and political whims of her time.

Lucio worked as the associate director for Tizuka Yamasaki's film *Gaijin*. I remember my confusion when the film's ending suggested the issei heroine marries a Euro-Brazilian. Even if everything else about the film was realistic (the Japanese characters spoke Japanese!), in my book, that ending never happened; it was a romantic ploy using a famous Brazilian actor.

## Tei

Tei Imai Sakai
(Matsumoto, 1900)

Tei Imai Sakai, my maternal grandmother, was the oldest daughter of a fish merchant in Matsumoto, Nagano. My grandfather Kitaichi came from a small nearby village and married Tei before he left for adventures across the ocean. For seven years, no one heard from him, and Tei's family began to advise her to remarry. But in 1906, an earthquake devastated San Francisco and forced the work of reconstructing the city. It was work that made it financially possible for Kitaichi to write after seven years. "Come," was all the letter said, and Tei went.

Tei made the trip to America at a time when Japanese women were rarely known to travel alone. She joined Kitaichi and they opened the Uoki Fish Market, a Japanese grocery store that remained in business for 103 years on Post Street in Japantown, San Francisco.

Kitaichi, like so many issei men, invested and lost his money in one venture after another, and, unforgivably, an employee and bookkeeper in the store absconded with the rest. It would take Kitaichi's sons a decade of sacrifice to pay off this loss, but Kitaichi had perhaps by then already lost the will that began his adventures so long ago in Japan.

It was Tei who quietly formed the strong backbone of the family, an unwieldy brood of nine all housed in the Victorian rooms above the store. From that time, Tei never lived anywhere else, except for the years during the war at the Topaz concentration camp. Her entire world resided in Japantown, on Post Street, and in the big kitchen where the family and store employees came to eat. Tei rarely spoke a word of English. Her world was insular, enclosed.

And yet, working or at rest, she was the central, solid, most tangible, and eternally patient force behind the family. Perhaps it was the Zen Buddhist in Tei; everything about her radiated simplicity, honesty, humanity, humor, and wisdom. As time went on, she became the elder who spoke few words but always spoke the truth. No one speaks of Tei as having any faults, and it seems strange to report that such a good woman could exist. A peaceful, smiling Buddha—the same woman in the photograph who sits with calm simplicity and a face of young wonder, awaiting a portrait, awaiting a husband gone to America with no word for seven years, waiting at the center of the storm of family and community and life in a new world.

Lucio married Yuri, a more recent Brazilian issei, and I married a Brazilian of European, African, and aboriginal extractions. It's possible to call Lucio's children nisei or sansei, but mine have probably lost these designations to some other identification of their own making.

## Kazue

Kazue Kato Kubo was Lucio's paternal grandmother. She had been married and separated in Japan at the age of twenty-six. A few years later, in Kyoto, she met Tetsu Kubo, a scholar-teacher of Christian theology who had studied at Princeton and spoke English fluently, and who was widowed with four children. Kazue is standing in a kimono, perhaps just moments before she took on the responsibilities of raising a family of six.

Tetsu was a Christian intellectual, and author of several books in Japan. He had Western tastes, drank coffee, and set his sights on a world outside Japan. In 1929, after the Japanese Exclusion Acts, the u.s. was no longer an option. Leaving for Brazil was his decision. Kazue would've preferred to stay in Japan as the prominent wife of a future school director, but she came along.

The Kubos necessarily augmented their family group with two young men and came as contract laborers headed for a coffee plantation northwest of São Paulo. One of the requirements for immigration to Brazil was

Kazue Kato Kubo
(Kyoto, 1926)

that Japanese must arrive in traditional family groups composed of a husband, wife, and at least one child of laboring age, fourteen or older. This was a requirement the government thought would prohibit the excessive entry of young unmarried males, who were considered—in the case of u.s. immigration—to be a source of social problems. Whether it was the fear of young Asian males or the perspicacity of creating conditions for family life, this requirement brought Japanese women to Brazil. And because Japanese woman accompanied men to Brazil, families were born, land was settled, roots taken, homes established.

While the idea to immigrate to Brazil was Tetsu's, the physical reality became Kazue's. Lucio admits his grandfather could never again find his footing in a land that required his physical rather than intellectual labor. From that moment on, Kazue became the major provider and mover of the family's fortune. She tilled the land, planted the garden, established a poultry ranch, sold eggs and produce in the city, and raised four step-children until they left for college and marriages. In later years, being no intellectual slouch herself, she taught the Japanese language. Kazue was a dynamic sort, a woman of energy and charisma. She gave everything she had to the life and sustenance of her family in Brazil. She made Tetsu's dream happen.

We study the formal portraits of our antecedents, recognize statements of fashion and period and familial resemblances. We knew them as older women, as grandmothers with whom the possibilities for communication were more or less difficult. We have remembered or forgotten their stories. What little we know is recounted here. By themselves, the photographs mean nothing—antique curiosities framed for museums and curio shops. But perhaps we remember when our young hands were held by old hands, remember the thin wrinkled skin over tired bones, the deep crevices in the mottled palms.

Lucio is a reader of palms, and therefore, one assumes, the future. I never understood if this was a serious avocation or Lucio's wry method of initiating conversation and meeting women. I don't know if this reading of palms contradicts or complements one of the keenest, most perceptive minds I know. I have never asked Lucio to read my palm.

By 1941, some 190,000 Japanese had immigrated to Brazil. Today, Japanese immigrants and their descendants number over a million and a half—the largest such population outside of Japan. As simple as it may seem, one of the most plausible reasons for this large population must be the presence of women. Women, despite gentlemen's agreements and the myriad plans of men, provided stability, created families, and established homes. While many men may have considered themselves migrant/dekasegi laborers, women were perhaps the true immigrants of the time.

For Japanese women, leaving home meant shedding traditional relationships—an adjustment to the system of joining one's fortune to the husband's family and living under the watchful eye of a mother-in-law. As difficult and physically strenuous as life might've been in the Americas, women achieved a modicum of freedom and equal standing alongside their men. Of course, they were probably too busy to notice. Women's responsibilities were pragmatic and obvious: children, household, meals, garden, work. Perhaps unlike men, women didn't have to succeed; they had to work. Men on the other hand were responsible for an economic and sometimes political, sometimes spiritual vision for their families. So often these visions became muddled; men lost their way. The Americas have a way of swallowing dreams, castigating those who believe, those who yearn. Women made the voyage, crossed the boundaries of time, culture, class, and gender, adjusted to the visions of men in subtle and supple ways, made the thing stick.

I'm the granddaughter, and Lucio is the grandson. I speak an Anglo language; Lucio, a Latin. I live in what is considered the First World in one of the great centers of the Pacific Rim; Lucio lives in the so-called Third World, in São Paulo—the largest metropolitan/cosmopolitan center of South America. As I write, it is winter. Lucio will receive my faxed copy of this document; there, it is summer.

# Bombay Gin

My cousin locked me inside his mother's apartment. This isn't funny, I thought. I jiggled the lock. He had sawed off the stem on the dead bolt so the inside knob wouldn't work. I knew this. He'd already explained this to me. Anyone could knock out the glass on the door, put their hands through, and open the dead bolt. He'd also made sure the windows were secure. I went to try the windows anyway, but he had fixed them so you could open them only about three inches. I'm skinny but not that skinny. I was in a locked box. I guess that was the point.

As locked boxes go, this was a pretty nice one. I mean, it had all the amenities: refrigerator, microwave, TV, telephone, bath, and bed. Well, it had more than amenities; it was a kind of museum and a box of memories. My cousin's mother had died five years before, but he hadn't removed or rearranged a single item in her apartment since. My other cousin said it was like a shrine to his mother, but I didn't think so. It wasn't about any sort of neurosis on my cousin's part; he was just being lazy and comfortable. He really didn't live there anyway. He came in on the holidays, slept in a sleeping bag on the sofa, locked up the place again, and flew back to New York. My other cousin said, "Why does he sleep on the sofa? Why doesn't he sleep in the bed? It must be that he's nostalgic, because sleeping on the sofa is what he did when she was alive." Again, I knew better. He just didn't want to have to change the sheets.

I went to the refrigerator, opened and closed it. It must be a nervous sort of thing, going to the fridge and looking in, as if there's an answer inside that cold space. I've noticed that everyone does it, though. I've seen my kid and even his friends come home, wander into the kitchen, take a peek, make a mental note about week-old leftovers or a dead slab of steak that would take too much time to grill, then shrug away empty handed. I stared at the closed refrigerator for a long time. The doors were a jam-packed collage of two-by-three photos of all the kids in our families, their toothy or toothless grins under a plethora of magnets. My kid was there too, at ages zero to whatever age he was when my aunt died. I stared at everyone, but especially my kid. He was so cute back then. Everyone who visited must have stared at these fridge photos, paying particular attention to their own kids. My cousin never married, never had kids of his own, a fact his mother lamented time and time again. What she would've given for grandkids. Since she had none of her own, she adopted and borrowed everyone else's. I could see and hear my aunt cooing over the photos, naming each one, their ages, announcing the newest baby. This was her future on the door of the fridge. It was her happy moment repeated every time she arrived where I had now also arrived. Or had I?

I opened the fridge again. For some reason, I noticed the salad dressing; it was a Paul Newman vinaigrette. I was sure this was the same vinaigrette my aunt dribbled over salad when she was alive. I checked the date on the mayonnaise; it was even older than five years old. I plunged into that cold box and began ransacking it for old food, checking the dates and tossing anything that looked familiar. Well, five-years-old familiar. Could you have a memory of food from five years ago? I thought I could see my aunt making roast beef sandwiches and spreading the light mayo over sourdough bread. I was convinced it was the same light mayo. Then there was the miso; it could conceivably last forever, or could it? I grabbed bottles of pickled ginger, pasty seaweed concoctions, barbecue sauce, oyster sauce, kimchee, low-sodium shoyu, green pimiento olives, and concentrated lemon juice. I hauled out the tubs of margarine, cans of Sapporo and Diet Coke, even the open box of baking soda. Then, I got into the freezer section and tossed all the cans of frozen concentrate, orange juice, mai tai and margarita mix. I tossed aluminum-foil packages of what looked like wrapped leftovers. Imagine keeping this stuff! I tossed the ice cubes that looked near a state of dehydration, if that were possible. In the far corner of the freezer was a stack of natto. It's the soybean equivalent of the stinkiest aged Camembert you can imagine with the additional quality of being attached bean to bean by slimy strings of its own brown snot. It was already a stinky old slobbering mess when it was fresh, but frozen for five years, it had to be really gross. I threw it out.

From the fridge, I started in on the cupboards. Boxes of instant miso and Jell-O that had hardened into cement. Baggies full of discarded ramen flavor packets, small bottles of salt-free herb concoctions, spray cans of old Pam, boxes of bran cereals. You could tell my aunt was working on the high-blood-pressure/cholesterol angle. These ailments were the nemeses of our family genes, knocking off her sisters and brothers right and left. Still, I knew then that she was always cheating anyway. She said you couldn't live forever, and she wasn't going to sacrifice quality for quantity.

Deeper into the cupboards, there were boxes of California golden raisins in various stages of wrinkled leather and old cans of Campbell's mushroom soup. I checked the dates on the cans. One said 1978. I thought about it; my own son was born in 1978. My cousin never cooked. I thought about him sleeping on the sofa in his sleeping bag with all this rotting food in the kitchen. Pretty soon the trash can was piled high with jars, cans, and boxes. Ha, I thought. That'll show him. On second thought, I replaced the light mayo; he would pay—sometime in the future, he would pay.

My cousin was an only child. His photos were all over the place as well. There were large and small portraits of him, family scenes encased in every sort of framed holder in every room. I went around scowling at all the representations of him, especially the posed one of him at age five. This photo must've been taken just before the war, when the family lived in the Imperial Valley and before they were all shipped off to the Topaz internment camp. Camp and after was part two of my aunt's life, part one being her youth during the Depression. It was all about sacrifice and struggle, and here was her son in a little jacket with a tiny hanky spitting out of his breast pocket, looking like an angel. This was way before I was born, but everyone said he was spoiled rotten. His mother liked to reminisce that he was itazura, as if he were just rascally. When and if he unlocked this box, I was going to break that portrait over his head.

I went out to the back balcony. I supposed I could yell to some elderly resident. Sure enough, I could see someone moving slowly down a sidewalk. Of course she was an old lady; they were all old. This was a retirement community, a leisure world for the elderly. There were seven thousand of them, briskly walking at seven in the morning, tooling around in electric golf carts, shuttling between the pharmacy and their cardiac doctors. I could be counted as the youngest among them. I watched the old lady approach at something like the breakneck speed of a step every sixty seconds. She was dragging two leashes attached to two small dogs that used to be maybe shaggy poodles but were balding in spots and limping behind her at an even slower pace. I realized she was walking as slowly as possible to accommodate her dogs. I imagined I could call to her. "Help! I'm a prisoner!" But it seemed foolish, which of course it was. Any sudden gesture might give those dogs heart attacks. It must've taken her fifteen minutes to cross fifteen feet. Maybe I exaggerate, but it was part of some principle about life at this juncture: having all the time in the world because there was very little time left. Did she know my aunt? I wondered. I decided to say something. At least there would be a witness to my existence in the locked box. "Good afternoon," I ventured sweetly, not wanting to startle her, but the woman and her dogs continued slowly by. "Hello!" I spoke up, but she never looked up. Neither she nor her dogs could hear me. I don't know why, but I stared after the trio until they disappeared in a sort of mirage behind a pine tree.

At that moment, the telephone rang. I ran to answer it. "Hello," I answered angrily. I was sure it was my cousin, calling to apologize. Instead, my hello triggered a recorded message. CONGRATULATIONS! The message blasted into my ear. YOU ARE THE LUCKY WINNER OF A VACATION TRIP, ALL EXPENSES PAID . . . I fumbled with the volume doohickey on the machine. VEGAS! CALL US NOW AT . . . All the phones in the apartment had these gadgets rigged to make the incoming sound louder since his mother and now my cousin were hard of hearing. I got the deafening message lowered and hung up.

I thought about calling 911, telling them I was having a heart attack in a locked apartment. They were welcome to send a fire truck and rescue me via the balcony or, better yet, to break down the door. That's right. Break down the door. Scanning the handy sticker on the phone with its list of emergency numbers, I decided instead to call the condo maintenance department. "I have a problem with the lock on my door," I said. "I wonder if you could send someone to fix it." "We don't do maintenance on locks, ma'am," they said. "It's not in our contract. Here's the number to the local locksmith. They're a twenty-four-hour service, licensed to do these jobs." "But I'm locked in," I decided to tell them. "No problem," they replied. "These things happen all the time. They'll get you fixed up in a jiffy." Who was I to complain? They thought they were humoring an old lady. I even thought they spoke louder, as if they knew I had lowered the volume on the phone. I wrote down the number for the locksmith and attached it to the fridge door under a magnet between all the kiddy faces, then opened the door and closed it again. Right. I had tossed everything. I went to the trash and retrieved an old can of Sapporo. It was still cold enough.

The phone rang again. I popped the tab on the beer, took a swig, and sauntered back to the ringing phone. Now I'd let him have it. But the caller introduced himself as Jeremy Somebody representing a major television station, and wouldn't I answer a few survey questions? Ridiculous, I thought. That's why the polls were so skewed. They were making the rounds through seven thousand old folks with conservative views and no caller ID, who sat around waiting for phone calls and the chance to talk to anyone. No one ever asked me to be a percentage on a national poll. "I'm sorry," I said, venting my anger that Jeremy wasn't my cousin, "I don't watch TV," and I hung up.

I sat down with the Sapporo in an easy chair in front of the television and stared at my reflection in the glass tube. There was a photograph of my aunt and all her sisters on top of the TV. Nowadays, I looked like them, one more sister with matching genes in the lineup. "I don't watch TV," I said to the TV, observing my lips speak inside the box. I pressed the green power button on the remote and watched my lips get exchanged for Martha Stewart's. She and Alice Waters were making salad. What else? They were whipping up the vinaigrette. I walked back to the trash can and fumbled under the pile for the Paul Newman stuff and put it back into the fridge. To hell with it all, I thought, sipping my beer. Martha Stewart doesn't live here. Anyway, that's what the sign above the microwave said.

Next up, *Iron Chef.* "Iron Chef Morimoto-san will take on the challenger! Today's cuisine choice: natto! This is certainly going to be a real test of the skills of these superb chefs, to create an array of dishes using this traditional Japanese delicacy." I watched in disbelief. What did an American audience think this stuff was, anyway? For me, natto was a mark of our family heritage. We were proud eaters of natto from childhood, a tradition passed from our grandmother to her children to us to our children. My cousin loved natto. His mother loved natto. My dad loved natto. I loved natto. My kid loved natto. If I had anything to do about it, my grandchildren would love natto too. It was a badge of something, to love something so disgusting. There were Japanese who wouldn't eat natto. Eating natto made us for real, connected our DNA through our taste buds. I got up and rummaged again through the trash, retrieved the Styrofoam boxes of natto, and tossed them back into the freezer. Thinking again, I separated one box from the pack and left it on the counter. After five years wouldn't hurt to test it with an *Iron Chef* recipe. Didn't paleontologists eat the flesh of frozen woolly mammoths, or archeologists taste the honey from pots in pyramids? O.K., maybe they didn't.

Back in Japan, the Iron Chef was using miso to create his natto extravaganza. "Fukui-san! It looks like the Iron Chef is going to steam that concoction!" I ran back to the trash, retrieved the miso and the light shoyu. Hell, I got the pickled ginger, the barbecue sauce, the olives, and the lemon concentrate too. I sat down on the linoleum, surrounded by bottles and jars. I opened everything, smelled inside, examined the contents. It was all about salt, vinegar, preservatives, and vacuum-packing with a shelf life of forever. Could this kill you? Could it kill you eventually? Could it kill my cousin? Did it kill my aunt? Pretty soon I got most of it back into the fridge and the cupboards.

Lastly I cradled the 1978 Campbell's mushroom soup. It wasn't just the date on the can. I knew why this prefab soup was there. I spied the green index-card box on the counter, filled with all my aunt's recipes, sitting there just as she'd left it, waiting for her next consultation. Now, five years later, I thought, Consult the recipe box. There it was—Campbell's mushroom soup, one of the principal ingredients in the family stroganoff recipe: 1 lb ground beef, 1 medium chopped onion, 1 lb sliced mushrooms, 1 T flour, ½ t salt, ¼ t pepper, ½ pt sour cream, 1 bunch chopped parsley, 1 can of Campbell's mushroom soup! Served over hot rice in Japanese American homes in the sixties. My son, born in 1978, loved this dish. I kissed the can and pushed it to the deep, dark back of the cupboard.

I called my son and got his answering machine. I always got his machines. It didn't matter if I called his cell phone or his land phone, as he liked to call it. He was a busy guy, working full-time, going to school, courting some girlfriend. I was miles away; what could he do anyway, and why would he do it? I hung up.

What else was in the recipe box? I wondered. My aunt made a ginger pork that was to die for. My cousin loved this stuff, and she'd have it ready for him when he came home and ready for him to carry off when he left. My cousin was in the military, would fly in and out with ginger pork. That was how she showed her love for her only kid. Card by card I picked through the box. It wasn't there. Now I remembered. She did that recipe from heart; it wasn't a recipe but her own thing, made the way my cousin liked it. No one had bothered to write down the recipe. Not even him. The expertise had died with her. What about hamyu? I thought. I had watched her make this Chinese sausage patty, package and freeze the stuff. Sad to say, no recipe for that either. Wait! I thought. That's what was in those aluminum packages from the freezer! I flew back into the trash and recovered them for posterity.

Then I found it: the Lois Loehrke Bombay Gin raisin recipe. Nine raisins soaked in gin. It was like my aunt's daily bread. She'd count out the gin raisins and add a few more for good measure. These raisins are small anyway, she'd say. We'd all partake. What the hell. It was medicine. Who was Lois Loehrke? Now I learned it was Lois's *unusual recipe for arthritic relief.* Golden raisins soaked in Bombay Gin with my aunt's note: *must be Blue Sapphire, approx. ½ bottle.* Let stand covered seven days. Step 4 said: *Place raisins in covered container (I use an empty Cool Whip carton) and eat just nine (9) raisins a day.* The disclaimer went on to say that in one month, Lois was able to walk down steps, and that this miracle remedy went back to biblical times when the people of India and Egypt discovered the healing properties of juniper berries. Gin was made from juniper berries. I thought about how the Indians and Egyptians discovered this miracle, but how Lois had somehow encased it in the biblical. Thank the Lord, she said, for her new freedom of movement. I retrieved the boxes of California golden raisins, found the gin and an empty Cool Whip container, and went to work. In seven days, I would find true freedom.

I moved from the kitchen to the bathroom. Her medications were all lined up like yesterday, pillboxes filled with the pharmaceutical promise of an extended lease on life. I scrutinized the dates and shook the plastic containers with their tamper-resistant caps. I thought, Now this could kill you, and closed the cabinet door. Gazing across a fantasyland of delicate cut-glass and crystal bottles spread across the counters, I applied all of my aunt's expensive Shiseido makeup, slathered on the age-inhibitor lotions, spritzed and dabbed myself with a dozen French perfumes, and just like the fridge jars, opened and smelled everything, thinking, A person could be embalmed in this stuff. I gripped the sink, dizzy with sudden nausea, my head in a pungent cloud of her particular smell. I filled the tub with a box of soothing herbal bubble bath and soaked in it until the water was cold and my body prune-like.

My cousin didn't call or come that evening, or the next day or the next. On the second day, I sat on the sofa where he usually slept with stacks of old magazines. His mother had kept copies of *Life* magazine way back from the sixties. There were special editions on JFK, RFK, MLK, LBJ, and Jimmy Carter. My aunt was a card-carrying liberal Democrat. She had joined the Democrat Club in this world of gray panthers. On the other hand, my cousin was a military man, voted Republican, believed the military had the ability to surgically remove evil from the face of the earth and shouldn't be constrained from pursuing its objectives by popular politics. It was difficult to believe a kid raised in an internment camp during the war could think this way, but maybe not. My other cousin said he turned out this way because his mother was domineering, and it was all about rebellion. I didn't buy this, because mothers are blamed for everything, and I was tired of being blamed myself. In any case, they never saw eye to eye, so it surprised me that he hadn't dumped her convictions into the recycle bin. Complimentary to her magazines were videotaped series: PBS biographies of Franklin and Eleanor Roosevelt, *Eyes on the Prize,* and documentaries about the Japanese American incarceration. I plopped in the tapes and let them run continuously, an ear and eye to the TV, my fingers flipping through the now-dull pages of an old magazine world. All day, I wandered through World War II, the Civil Rights movement, the Cuban Missile Crisis, Watergate, the Vietnam War, Reaganomics. That night, I slept on the sofa.

When I awoke the next day, the magazines slipped off me like fish scales, and I thought about my cousin waking up on that sofa as he always did. Above me on the wall was a gold-leaf sumi-e screen, painted no doubt by someone famous, and probably dated in the Tokugawa. I stared at the details, seeing them for the first time. It was a Japanese-countryside scene of folks cultivating tea. I remembered that she had studied this stuff, wanted to retire to an import business in Japanese antiques and arts and crafts. She and my uncle had invested their savings in a small cache of tansu and screens. Along the way, he died, and she gave up this plan and kept the stuff. She also kept my uncle, his ashes in a beautiful bronze box, and talked to the box every day until they could be buried together. This was part three of her life, when the struggle was past and things were collected and comfortable, but there was nobody to share it with. My cousin didn't listen to my other cousin, who told him she was maybe going nuts. I didn't think she was nuts; she talked to everything in the house, especially the live plants, cute dolls, fridge kids, and the bronze replica of the Degas ballerina. She sold some articles, but most of it she kept. She had fallen in love with her collection and couldn't part with any of it. I realized that it was everywhere in the apartment, and this was the museum I was trapped in.

I got up and poked around and finally acknowledged maybe five years of dust over everything. It wasn't just antique chests and gold-leaf screens; it was ceramics, baskets, sculptures, dolls, toys, dishes, lamps, gizmos, fake flowers, and glass fruit. I had never really considered it all. She used to point out a new acquisition from a trip or something she especially liked, but it was all just part of her surroundings. I knew my cousin never paid much attention either. It was her thing, not his. He seemed to move through her house without touching anything. There were small valuables strategically and elegantly placed over every surface, some on special handmade doilies, brocade pillows, or crafted lacquer stands. I had to pick each thing up, carefully wipe or polish it, and try to replace it in the same location. Some things had stickers with dates and names. Sixteenth-century porcelain. Kyushu. Antiques by unknown craftsmen and established artists. Ornate dolls in glass cages. Lacquered candy dishes. Laughing monks. Inside the cabinets and drawers, there was more stuff, wrapped in tissue paper, ensconced in wooden boxes with Japanese lettering. I wondered why she chose to display one thing over another, chose a particular arrangement or location. I tried putting everything back the way it was. I tried changing everything around. I tried to see these artifacts and bibelots as she did, to imagine their significance, to see what she had seen.

When the phone rang, I jumped from the break in the silence. I remembered my aunt's voice on the phone, how she sometimes couldn't talk at first when I called. It took her awhile to oil her throat and get the tongue to wiggle with words. I no longer expected my cousin to call, and I didn't want to croak into the receiver. I almost let it go on ringing and went back to my dusting and polishing. If he thought he was going to bother me now, he was wrong. I was on a roll. Still, the thing was persistent. I cleared my throat and answered, ready to fend off anything. I thought I might even answer a survey or poll. Why not? But it was my son. "Hi, Mom," he said. "How'd you find me?" I asked. "Caller ID," he said. "Oh," I said. "What's happening?" I asked nonchalantly, as if what was happening to me wasn't happening. "Well . . . ," he hedged, "Kirsten is pregnant." Who was Kirsten? I wondered. Had I met her? "Yeah, and so I guess she, well we, well, we'll see." "Are you serious?" I asked. "This has just never happened to me," he whined. "I guess not," I said. "I'm not ready," he said. "Who's ready?" I said. Who was Kirsten? I wondered. Maybe she was ready. He continued like a little boy, "I feel trapped, like I'm in a box. How did this happen to me?" "I don't know," I said. "I feel the same way, although literally." "What?" he said. "Never mind."

The conversation went on like that. I looked toward the fridge door, where the progression of his growth was recorded until five years ago. He might actually have the grandkid my aunt always wanted. I thought, What kind of reward was this? I knew it was just as well my cousin never had kids; he would've made a piss-poor father. At sixty-five, or whatever age he was now, he was still a kid. He and my son had about the same mental maturity. Admittedly I liked that about them—their kidness—but kids are never what you bargain for, even if they grow up to like natto. "Well, keep me posted," I said. "I'll be here for the time being," I added.

I went on with my curating, opening boxes I found in the closets and investigating everything in the apartment. It was truly amazing. There wasn't a corner of storage space that didn't have an archeological find of the highest order. I went into the study and pulled out all the books about Japanese art. I displayed an array of vases on the coffee table and tried to match the designs and glazes to the period pieces in the books. I rummaged through desk drawers and found stickers to make notes of the resembling periods in Japanese art and stuck them to the bottoms of the vases. I began to do this with everything in the apartment. I spent the next three days on this project, but it could take a hundred years. I had only scratched the surface.

While looking for stickers, I found clumps of envelopes bound in rubber bands. I got carried away and started to read all the letters. There were letters from sibling to sibling, mother to child, niece to aunt, distant relative to close relative, husband to wife, friend to friend. It was mostly a boring compendium of things the family did, who was doing what work, whose kid was in which school, who was celebrating this or that, or sick or dying. Who among us cousins would finally succeed, who worthy enough to be called progeny? Of course some of it wasn't so boring, even historic or tender or obnoxious. And there was everything that wasn't in the letters, the stories I'd heard that died with the recipes in the heart: extramarital affairs, love exchanged for familial loyalty, rivalry and hatred, youthful philandering, and alcoholism. Our family through our grandmother back to the Meiji era was Christian, but there were no such artifacts in the apartment to suggest this, only photographs or block prints of the benevolent Buddha and statuary of laughing monks. I pondered my aunt's reason for this, and I thought about our common need for serenity over guilt. In the end, we couldn't count on each other to truly extend ourselves into the future. Our good or bad work and our particular talents were ours alone, and the kids on the fridge wouldn't remember, wouldn't continue, wouldn't respect, wouldn't really care about all our heartfelt or long-gone desires.

In between the hours, I started to use up the old rice, eat up the natto, stir up pots of miso soup. If there were an earthquake, I figured I could survive there for days, even if the provisions might eventually kill me. And by day seven, the Bombay Gin raisins were ready. I filched more than nine, of course, cooing at the kids on the fridge. That's when I noticed my scribbled note with the number for the locksmith tacked between the five-year-old and six-year-old versions of my son. I gave the locksmith a ring, and he was here within the hour. It was that easy. I had him put in a new dead bolt and change the locks. "There it is," he said, handing me a new set of keys. "Shouldn't give you any more trouble." "Not at all," I said, and I closed the door.

# Borges & I

The other one, the one called María Kodama, is the one things happen to. Over the years, I have watched her through our looking glass—her dark straight hair, cut precisely at shoulder length, turn white, her youthful features mature. And yet, I believe her to contain the same dewy innocence and singularity of elegant strangeness in a sea of sameness as she did on the day she first met, in Buenos Aires, Jorge Luis Borges in the musty confines of the university. For María, perhaps that was a moment of complete clarity, the center of the infinite garden, at which she made a choice or the beginning of a choice. I am not sure how one at the young age of sixteen, as sure of ourselves as we felt, can make such choices. For myself, I cannot say it was the attraction of youth to age, but rather youth to knowledge, a hunger planted and fed by the same garden. How I wanted to remain with María in that garden dedicated and extending to our deepest ancestors, but she managed to escape down another path, or at least she thought she had left me behind. Perhaps she had paused to notice my bewilderment; I cannot say. I saw her confident resolve, the flounce of her skirt and hair, toss away from me.

From that moment, I might catch glimpses of María, always with Borges, in newsprint, her image recalled on the stage of some international honorary degree or prestigious award or in a photograph. Though invisible, I was at times not far away. As I have said, the garden was infinite, mapped across the atlas, and so we traveled. In Venice, I saw the swoop of pigeons swirl around her passage across the vast piazza of San Marco. I watched her rise in a hot air balloon over California vineyards. In the Louvre, I too shed tears on the Daru steps at the sight of the Winged Victory of Samothrace. I saw her pet the tremendous bodies of striped tigers. Of course, these events were meant for Borges, and the meaning of being there at his side must have been personal to María. She was to know the shape of constant companionship, the day-to-day routine and needs of a blind man, the acute precision of his oral memory along with the gaffes of eating and hygiene that annoy the sighted and plague the sightless. This was companionship that must fully anticipate the needs of Borges. The work of any companionship cannot be known fully by others. Amanuensis, scribe, secretary, nurse, cook, guide, mother, daughter, caretaker, muse, wife, lover, but principally, gardener. Gardener in the labyrinthine landscape belonging only to Borges. Thus was my invisibility transposed upon a mirror, reluctantly watchful, envious, though safely at the wavering distance of the interpreting eye to its story.

But one day our forking paths would meet at the divine birthplace of Nihon, our feet crunching in unison over the pebbled gravel before the great temples of Izumo. Borges marked this mythic center, calling upon the gods in a swirl of cherry blossoms, their petals falling about him in Bashō's seventeen syllables. What is the garden's atlas to the blind? A geography without vistas, perspective determined by time travel, a folded and reversible map. Yet even the colorblind crave to see the color of a body's journey, to divine meaning from fascination, even if translated again and again over centuries and multiple languages, becoming if only a whisper, an ideogram splashed across skin. The skin may be accusatory, but like paper, it receives and reflects its text, memory and knowing to be interpreted by the reader. So Sei Shōnagon's deft brush thrust from a silken sleeve through eight centuries to lick the ear of Borges. Thus he would pronounce the name of María, how many mornings and seas, how many oriental and occidental gardens, his Shōnagon, her Genji, his Beatrice, her Virgil, his little stone on a board of chess.

Sei Shōnagon lifted her head from her pillow and spoke in perfect Spanish: "A la otra, a Amelia Nagamine, es a quien le ocurren las cosas." In the book of things that occur to young women, there might have been, had Amelia kept such a notebook, a notation about a Mexicano in the uniform of the American Army, a journalist for the *Stars and Stripes* who covered the Tokyo war crimes trials. Instead it was the journalist and writer Américo Paredes who kept his notebook, musing over the beautiful features of a Japonesa born in Uruguay who also spoke the educated Spanish of a diplomat. Who among the Puerto Rican GIs treated by the Red Cross in those years of Japan's occupation, followed by a war in Korea, hadn't fallen in love with Amelia? But it was Américo, an older though still young man of charm and resolve, to whom Amelia tied her future. And from that moment, I might catch glimpses of Amelia, for the next fifty years always at the side of Américo.

The world of Américo was not a forking garden but a contested border-land experienced in wide swatches: the Tex-Mex border; the American occupation of a war-torn Japan; a Greater Mexico, later perhaps the mythic atlas named Aztlán. The world known to Américo was a rebellious world of men in an endless war, crimes committed by enemy and ally, survival by cunning and happenstance. It would seem Amelia remained fixed at the center of Américo's borderland in Austin, Texas, where she raised her children and kept a modest household and supported her husband's scholarly ambitions. No doubt her gracious ways domesticated this Chicano, compressing Américo's passionate anger beneath a genteel veneer. But by the time Américo Paredes was discovered to be the godfather of Chicano studies, Amelia had discovered a borderland of her own.

Perhaps her borderland began in the four walking blocks between the university and the Lone Star state capitol, its dome looming over the Austin landscape where Amelia beat a mother's fury at the doors of political power. And over time, Amelia occupied the borderland radiating around the Austin State School for the disabled and handicapped, the difficult and nearly impossible terrain of access to independent living and quality of life. I followed but could never fully imagine Amelia's meticulous caretaking, her persistent and obsessive advocacy, the meaning of her life becoming the body and the brains of a child who could not do for herself. But if not the mother, then who? And what of the postwars Amelia had also witnessed, the amputated and disfigured lives of veterans and civilians. She joined to plead the justice of the Fourteenth Amendment: the Rehabilitation Act of 1973, the Education of All Handicapped Children's Act of 1975, the Civil Rights of Institutionalized Persons Act of 1980, the Americans with Disabilities Act of 1990. I saw her there at every turn, whether as commissioned community member or spokesperson or letter-writer or petitioner at the grassroots. But I guess Amelia was too busy to keep any lists.

So Amelia and Américo shared lives across separate though overlapping borderlands, and perhaps over the long years, each chaffed at the obsession of the other, the understood refusal of either to become completely converted to the concerns of the other. I knew this sentiment of pride of partnership, public standing side by side, private guilt and jealousy, but finally death silences the frailties of illness, blesses loyalty, forgets.

Some believe that Américo Paredes, desperately lonely in the border-lands of death, called his beloved Amelia from his grave and that she obediently followed him only two months later. But the border's paths are mysterious, and Amelia and I took the bus out of Austin, headed down the obligatory border, and tossed cherry blossoms into the Rio Grande all the way to Brownsville, pursued by corridos, haunted by Américo's serenade, fierce and tender. *Japonesa, Japonesa,* the song crooned after us. *Que sonriés tu dolor, en tus brazos orientales mitigaré mi destierro.* And from Brownsville, we caught a boat to New Orleans. On a dappled spring morning several Wednesdays after the turmoil of Mardi Gras, we met María with Borges at the Café du Monde, sipping café and chicory, teeth tearing the doughy skin of sweet beignets, lips and chins dusted in powdered sugar. Not until that moment was Américo's Tokio guitar replaced by the insistent sax interlude of King Curtis, John Lennon driv-ing his lyrics, *You gotta live, you gotta love, you gotta be somebody, you gotta shove, but it's so hard.*

Amelia's tender eyes then turned to me, smiled old pain. "A la otra," she began, "la otra called Yoko Ono, is the one things happen to." Our minds wander back to Tokyo, precisely firebombed; we emerged from shelter and rural escape and remember the bewildered face of a young girl, yet a child of twelve, following her belongings in a wheelbarrow, the precarious future to be forged out of rubble and defeat. Twenty years— prestigious schooling, two marriages, and an artistic career attached vari-ously to John Cage and Andy Warhol—later, I stood with her at the foot of a ladder in a gallery in London, watching a wealthy Beatle from Liverpool climb its rungs, awkwardly balancing at the top to decipher a message through our magnifying glass: YES. I suppose that privilege comes back from war with fierce defiance, grabs a fistful of burned earth, an act of reclamation, but in Yoko's fist, a declaration of freedom. Still, that earth could be churned back eight centuries; thus a *Grapefruit* could have the acidic taste and shape of a pillow book. The conceptual MAP PIECE read, *Draw a map to get lost.* And so we did. And then, WALK PIECE: *Stir inside your brains with a penis until things are mixed well. Take a walk.* And so we did.

I followed Yoko into her world made famous by John Lennon, their conceptual country of peace: Nutopia, without land, boundaries, or pass-ports, and if laws, only cosmic. I hung around like one more groupie in their New York embassy in the Dakota, claiming diplomatic immunity. I lived inside the looking glass ballad of John and Yoko, for there was nothing about the intimacy of their lives that was not made public. Two virgins displayed in full-frontal nudity. Honeymoon bed-in in a sea of white sheets to give peace a chance. Among the guests: Timothy Leary, Tommy Smothers, Hare Krishnas, a delegation of the blind. West met East in the Plastic Ono Band, the oriental riff chasing the revelatory experience of first sight: *Oh my love, everything is clear in our world.* Thus John Lennon would call her name, *Oh Yoko, oh Yoko, my love will turn you on.*

In the public's mania for recycling their every movement, Lennon's attachment to Yoko would seem an obsessive submission to his oriental soulmate, his continuing pursuit of answers, fascinations eventually abandoned at the foot of Sergeant Pepper, Maharishi, and primal screaming. And perhaps it was true he had met his match, the knowledge of fatherhood and feminism in which he recreated himself as househusband, breadmaker, caretaker. This was his enlightenment, his peaceful revolution. Who then had submitted to whom? Meanwhile, I accompanied Yoko daily from the Dakota to work, to run the business of being John Lennon and Yoko Ono, unknowingly preparing for the burden of legacy, money, and memory.

And in opposing seasons in Buenos Aires, María finally opened Borges's library to Las Madres de Plaza de Mayo, but having embraced order for so many years, perhaps it was too late.

With his pistol in my hand, I pulled the trigger. I do not know if the man who fell was an elderly man in his eighties or a younger man half that age. I do not know if he was a learned sinologist or a Mexican folklorist or a lyricist of Jabberwocky. I do not know if he could finally see me through his blindness, through the borders, the utopia of his mind. It was his pistol and his pop. The myopic splinter of spectacles. My primal scream caged and yellowed by a judgmental media.

I do not know which of us has written this page.

---

*Special thanks to Frank Gravier, Ryuta Imafuku, and Earl Jackson.*

# Bibliography

Borges, Jorge Luis. *Labyrinths: Selected Stories & Other Writings*. New York: New Directions, 1962, 1964.

―――. *La cifra*. Madrid: Alianza Editorial, 1981.

―――. *Sei Shōnagon: El libro de la almohada*, ed. and trans. María Kodama. Madrid: Alianza Editorial, 2004.

―――. *Un ensayo autobiográfico*. Barcelona: Galaxia Gutenberg/Círculo de Lectore/Emecé, 1999.

Borges, Jorge Luis, and María Kodama. *Atlas*. Buenos Aires: Emecé Editores, 2008.

Henitiuk, Valerie. "'Easyfree Translation?' How the Modern West Knows Sei Shōnagon's *Pillow Book*." *Translations Studies* 1, no. 1 (2008): 2–17.

Lennon, John. *Imagine*. Apple/EMI, 1971.

―――. *In His Own Write*. New York: Simon & Schuster, 1964.

Ono, Yoko. *Grapefruit*. New York: Simon & Schuster, 1964, 1970, 1971.

Paredes, Américo. *Between Two Worlds*. Houston: Arte Publico Press, 1991.

―――. *The Hammon and the Beans and Other Stories*. Houston: Arte Publico Press, 1994.

―――. *"With His Pistol in His Hand": A Border Ballad and Its Hero*. Austin & London: University of Texas Press, 1958, 1973.

Saldívar, Ramón. *The Borderlands of Culture: Américo Paredes and the Transnational Imaginary*. Durham: Duke University Press, 2006.

Sheff, David. *All We Are Saying: The Last Major Interview with John Lennon & Yoko Ono*. New York: St. Martin's Griffin, 1981, 2000.

# Kiss of Kitty

In the typical way we search for lost persons these days, via Google, I try to find Robert Hashima. There seems to be a Robert S. Hashima, born September 24, 1920, died April 2, 2009, and that might be him. The Hashima I'm looking for is the kibei whose stories and opinions informed the work of Ruth Benedict's *The Chrysanthemum and the Sword.* C. Douglas Lummis, a writer and political thinker who lived and taught in Japan, wrote about his interview with Hashima and how Hashima's viewpoints, living as a student in the prewar years of a militarizing Japan, must have influenced Benedict's thinking. If Hashima died in 2009, I've missed meeting him. Well, I've missed meeting a lot of people whose lives mattered to me in ways impossible to know. But back to the Google search; perhaps a photograph of Hashima will show up in "images," but what I find are aerial maps and photographs of concrete wreckage that remind me of Alcatraz. Turns out to be Hashima Island, also known as Gunkanjima or Battleship Island, somewhere off the Nagasaki coast. I scrutinize the photos and recognize the final scenes of 007 in *Skyfall,* in which a blond Javier Bardem faces off with Daniel Craig, who manages to fist fight, hurdle rooftops, and escape bombs and bullets without ever soiling or tearing his pinstripe sharkskin suit. How does 007 fall into that ruined island fortress of a crumbling prison and coal mining facility where Mitsubishi industries forced the wartime labor of hundreds of conscripted Korean and Chinese prisoners? Hell, it's probably not on location but a CGI backdrop. Still, I imagine sooty faces under helmets crouched claustrophobically in narrow shafts deep under the ocean, picking, picking rich black veins of coal. But what has this got to do with Robert Hashima? Nothing and everything.

I think about Benedict's anthropologic extraction of Bob Hashima's experience as a young second-generation Japanese American sent by his parents to be educated in Japan. Hashima made it home before 1941, got incarcerated with all the other Japanese Americans, then became an assistant to Benedict at the Office of War Information. Apparently what impressed Benedict was Hashima's ability to give nuance to an incident in Natsume Sōseki's novel *Botchan*. You have to admire Benedict for never having been to Japan but getting it by reading its literature. Some notes and translations by, and a recognition of, Hashima are cited in Benedict's book. I know my parents read *The Chrysanthemum and the Sword*. There was always a copy of it in our library den. I read it too and thought it was the bible of what it meant to be Japanese, like samurai: beautiful and violent, with intricate categories of duty, obligation, and shame. Until I visited and lived in Japan, I had no idea how all of this might be true but also cockamamie. And until now, I never thought about how Benedict's work was also maybe a mix of literary criticism and fiction. There is something endearing, though likely only for the novelist, about occupying a people with their own fiction. But never mind arguing whether fiction is true or not; it is the speculative aspect of the anthropological project here that intrigues me, how in fact an investigation of culture might predict human reactions and outcomes. Benedict was hired to predict and, therefore, to occupy the future.

Did her work predict, for example, Godzilla? The first *Godzilla* or *Gojira* film came out in 1954, two years after the end of Japan's occupation. Even if you've only watched one Godzilla movie, you know Tokyo or some great cosmopolitan city and its infrastructures will have to be squashed back to Stone Age ruination. This is an absolute must, but when you watch the first *Godzilla*, you realize that maybe you're seeing actual footage of Tokyo during its wartime firebombing, and then you think that every other *Godzilla*, even the cheesiest version, must be a reenactment of that trauma and catastrophic loss. Even after the occupiers are gone, the reenactment is hidden in a movie about a big fake dragon dinosaur.

When the Herman Melville Society convened its international conference this past year in Tokyo, the insignia for that event was a graphic of Moby Dick rising in the same sea with Godzilla. Indeed, in the imagination of the Pacific as imperial frontier and manifest destiny, a century later, Godzilla must be Moby Dick's most terrible and revitalized replacement. The pursuit of the whale was about its blubber refined into oil, while the pursuit of Godzilla signaled the atomic age, our nuclear present. The great leviathan and the great dragon/dinosaur are primeval prehistoric cyphers, paradoxically, for technology and the precarity of human omnipotence and arrogance. Even if Benedict couldn't predict Godzilla as recurring trauma, she, like Herman Melville, followed the enigma of the great white whale to Japan.

Recently, the famous theoretical physicist Stephen Hawking had this to say in a BBC interview: *The development of full artificial intelligence could spell the end of the human race.... Humans, who are limited by slow biological evolution, couldn't compete and would be superseded.* In thinking about this and considering that Japan is likely at the forefront of this technology of AI, or artificial intelligence, I proposed at the International Melville Conference, of all places, that our contemporary Moby Dick turned Godzilla now has a very different and even benign or cute look. The great leviathan has become this: Hello Kitty. And this, I think, is a turn Benedict might have predicted. The end product of Melville's nineteenth-century discovery: a plastic doll. Well, maybe. That is to say, occupying a people under the auspices of chrysanthemum and sword might mean that people play out the chrysanthemum in order not to suffer, again, the sword.

Japanimation, or the animation of the two-dimensional manga world, is a universe of fantastic escape, bizarre or torturous sexual pleasure, magical monsters, romantic immaturity, pederasty, transformer warriors, alternative universes and futures, heroes and ghosts. If your previous world changes forever, if you experience your own extinction, maybe this kind of escape is inevitable. Japanimation is now reproduced for and sold to foreign audiences with binaries of beauty and violence that exceed Benedict's contradictions. Even when the presentations are asexual and plastic, the commodification is not. For example, when performance artist Denise Uyehara created the show *Hello (Sex) Kitty: Mad Asian Bitch on Wheels,* I tried (though not very hard) to procure a Hello Kitty dildo for her in Tokyo, an item I was told certainly existed. While we were buying Sanrio's Hello Kitty, My Melody, and Little Twin Stars in every rendition from erasers to watches (and maybe dildos), our counterparts in Tokyo became living dolls in extravagant costuming from Lolitas to gyarus. The last time I bought a Japanese music CD, it was produced by the girl band AKB48 (for Akihabara with forty-eight singing/dancing girls). If you look closely, they might be girls, but most likely they are young women in their twenties dressed in pink fluff with anklet socks in pink patent-leather Mary Janes. Then come to find out that a principal singer, Aimi Eguchi, wasn't just a virgin but a CGI composite. My friend told me that Aimi Eguchi, despite not being a real person, appeared on television to apologize to her fandom for not being real.

A fake person apologizes. You might wonder about this. At least I do, since I'm always insinuating to my students that they need to be responsible for their writing, even though they can always plead fiction. The author is never dead, and even when you're dead, some critic will come around and say you were a sexist techno-orientalist. O.K., they might say the writing was sexist techno-orientalist, but it's still your dead writing. Can you get off the hook if your character apologizes?

Sometime post 9/11, after the turn of the century, when *Sailor Moon* turned into a live-action television show (that is, from a cartoon to a show with real actors), I drive my mother, Asako, to San Jose Japantown for the summer Obon/Nisei Week festivities. This is supposed to be a Japanese American festival celebrated in August in all Japantowns, Nihonmachis, Little Tokyos, and Japanese American cultural centers, churches, and temples across the country. When we get there, it's afternoon, and Asako is a bit irritated at me for arriving late, and probably we've missed stuff, like the parade and dances. I get her seated at a table near Fifth and Jackson, in front of a stage set up across from the Buddhist temple. Maybe there'll be a karate or kendo demonstration or enka singing or a bonsai class or taiko drums, anything to make Asako think this rare trip out of hippy Santa Cruz to our culture is worth it. I go foraging for food, skipping from booth to booth, and I can't believe it. No Japanese food. No nigiri, no teriyaki sticks, no tempura udon, no unagi donburi, not even Spam musubi. O.K., there are snow cones and strawberry shortcake, but no manjū. I return with plates of chashu bao, pizza, German sausage, and spaghetti, and she looks at me like, *What*? She reminds me for the fifth time, "We came too late." Like you have to get there early (nisei time) for the real stuff; they only make so much, then close down. Kaput. Owari.

I look up at the stage, and there are two high school girls there. One is Latina, the other white. The Latina has on a blond wig, but the hakujin girl has real hair up in long pigtails. Both are dressed like baby dolls, dancing and singing into the mic.

Asako leans over and asks, "What language are they singing?"

I answer, "Japanese."

"No, that's not Japanese." She smirks.

I protest, "No, really, it is. It's from the cartoons."

She shakes her head and chomps on pizza, cheese glutamate coagulating onto her chin.

I look around for taiko drums, but there's nothing in the wings to save me. Instead, a stream of little girls in *Sailor Moon* outfits, maybe between the ages of three and seven, are being persuaded to climb up on the stage. The MC turns out to be the hakujin high school girl in pigtails, who sings in Japanese and speaks in English with a cute Japanese accent: *Haro boysu and garus, eve-ri-budy, comu and joinu usu on stage and retsu dansu togetha.* I want my mother to ask me what language she's speaking now, but Asako's become disinterested. If only those little girls were wearing kimono. The music comes on, and it's the *Sailor Moon* intro, and apparently there's a special dance routine they've all been practicing, sort of. I haven't felt this feeling in years; it's the same feeling I felt when I entered an L.A. sushi bar and discovered all the Japanese clients had turned into white people. Well, that was a long, long time ago. This must be the other end of the end, how everything finally gets swallowed up in a parallel world. When I wasn't paying attention, I'd been erased. I look at Asako for reassurance, but she's never going to be erased. We are just plain late. This is some irrelevant aftershow.

The cute hakujin blathers on in accented English. I listen carefully. Her syntax is perfect. I think it's a fake accent. I'm thinking, if it's fake, this is an outrage. An entire generation of valiant protesting sansei didn't fight for our ethnic rights to be Asian American and the continuation of Japantown for you to pretend to be Japanese. My head goes cloudy, and I imagine my sister, Jane Tomi, there next to us, listening and going crosseyed. *This is f'd up,* she'd sneer. Yeah, I think, we might be old sansei. We might be post-Asian, but we ain't faking it. Jane Tomi and I would instantly become dynamic sansei, back to defend the old ways. *Make up!* We'd meet that cute pigtailed girl backstage and push her against the chain-linked fence of the Buddhist temple playground and make her speak real English. *You wanna fight, Sailor Moon, huh? Try Sansei Moon!* That's right. I want an apology.

But obviously, it's all over. Sailor Moon. AKB48. Hello Kitty. I apologize to Asako for getting to Nisei Week late and for staging an imaginary fight with a Japanimation fan with a Japanese accent. Years ago, I tried turning Japanese, but some things are only possible for another generation, or maybe robots.

The Japanese roboticist Masahiro Mori theorized something called the "uncanny valley," in which he described the moment in which a computer-generated or humanoid robot, as it becomes more humanlike, conjures the sense of the uncanny, which sparks revulsion in real humans. Mori calls it "uncanny," which seems to be a polite way of saying repulsive or perverse. O.K., we real humans would prefer not to engage with unreal mechanical humans. Preferable would be R2-D2 or C-3PO, but then maybe not, since the Japanese are making and selling these very real-looking sex dolls for intimate pleasure. Plus, there's AKB48 and Aimi Eguchi. Or, say you surgically remold the contours of your face: Botox, rhinoplasty (the nose job), and blepharoplasty (double eyelids). Or, perhaps, you go topical and do it with makeup: yellowface. Are you beautiful or uncanny?

But how about the Turing Test, proposed by the computer theorist Alan Turing to evaluate whether a machine might exhibit intelligent behavior indistinguishable from a human's? The Turing Test was in a recent movie, *Ex Machina,* in which the protagonist can't, in fact, tell real humans from robots, cutting into his own flesh to see if he himself might not also be a robot. What surprises, or rather disgusts, the viewer (me) of *Ex Machina* is that all the women, in what turns out to be a Bluebeard's digital castle paradise, are robots, even the mute but dancing Japanese housekeeper/concubine, Kyoko.

Of course, *Ex Machina*'s Kyoko is hardly the first to star as an Asian robot. I would say *Star Trek*'s Mr. Spock and Data are Asian versions of the uncanny logical robot. How about the replicant Rachel in Ridley Scott's *Blade Runner,* whose father is supposedly Chinese? Then there's "Cylon number eight" and her many copies in *Battlestar Galactica,* played by Grace Park. And in the television series *Humans,* check out Gemma Chan as domestic synth Anita. You can read articles about synth actors having to go to uncanny boot camp to act robotic. Or you can visit Hiroshi Ishiguro's website and see his humanoids, who have participated as actors in dramatic plays by Oriza Hirata. Asian cyborgs and clones abound in our media and literature. What happened to Mori's uncanny? It's not just that the robots in movies are human actors. It's now our assumption that humans can, like the cultivation of the chrysanthemum, be perfect. As I depart ANA flight 0172 from Narita, all the matching flight attendants bow with exactly the same gestures, exactly the same smile, the same voices. I could freak out, but it all seems really real.

The uncanny valley, like *Ex Machina*'s digital paradise, is hidden. The Turing Test is unnecessary.

In his book *The Future of the Mind,* Michio Kaku writes that Japanese "are steeped in Shinto religion, which believes spirits live in all things, even mechanical robots." And Masahiro Mori of "uncanny valley" fame wrote the book *Buddha in the Robot,* proposing that robots have the potential to attain Buddhahood. Come to think of it, you can visit Hello Kitty in Sanrio Puroland, where she stands in an altar, a blessing bodhisattva. What would Ruth Benedict say?

What would Bob Hashima say? Searching for Hashima, who could have been my dad's buddy, I find a dead island fortress of ghosts. The next generation of laborers on such an island could be uncanny robots. Will they be programmed with duty, obligation, and shame? Will they apologize for not being real? Will they die when the sword splits their skulls? Will they attain Buddhahood? I'm not sure what this means, except that I feel uncanny. Just uncanny.

# Indian Summer

On 9/11, I flew out of JFK on a 6:00 a.m. flight headed for SFO, ignorant of danger and spared the consequences of the disaster in my wake. Though preoccupied for months later by my narrow escape and devastated by any bad news of friends and old acquaintances, I had long resolved to leave New York for a new start in the central coastal town of Santa Cruz on the northern peninsula of Monterey Bay. Upon arrival, I turned selfishly to unpacking and situating myself in a comfortably clean and furnished rental, bathed in warm, dry winds and swirling heat, hot days interspersed with cool, the fall season intervening in fits and starts. We call these days Indian summer, supposing the Indians had long ago marked our calendar with their climate wisdom. By contrast, having just traveled in Europe from August to September, I was surprised to note, while in Fiesole, the autumn coolness trade away the summer heat, as if on schedule from August 31 to September 1, which made me think the parsing of seasons is a European expectation of time passing.

I had been offered a lectureship in art history on the subject of American architecture and the Arts and Crafts movement. My focus was the design of Frank Lloyd Wright and the architects of his Taliesin Fellowship, and the turn toward and uses of a Japanese aesthetic. On arrival in California, I thought I knew little of this coastal town, but this assumption of ignorance was eventually reversed. My previous forays to California had been brief and directed: for example, a tour of works by Julia Morgan, including Hearst Castle in San Simeon, Asilomar in Pacific Grove, and various YWCA centers and gracious homes in San Francisco and on the East Bay—Oakland and Berkeley. While quaint Victorians, trolleys running beneath bay windows of pastel painted ladies, were charming, I focused on the modern—the use of concrete and natural stone, exposed beams of giant redwood and extended garden landscapes, seaside cypress, crooked and windswept, reaching beyond glass open to natural light, wavering through sunset and fog. I was thus pleased to discover in Santa Cruz examples of the architecture of Aaron G. Green, protégé of Frank Lloyd Wright. In the fifties, Aaron Green had established himself independently in San Francisco and was the West Coast representative of Wright himself. I happened upon a building by Green somewhat by accident, a combination of fortune and misfortune—fortunate for my research and misfortunate in view of my health.

Soon after arriving in Santa Cruz, I was plagued by dizzy spells, and while walking to class across the wooden bridges spanning long gullies that cut through the redwood campus, I experienced a curious sense of vertigo. I would stumble into my lectures, grip the podium for several moments to regain my balance, trying with difficulty to assure myself and any students who bothered to notice my distress that I had control of the situation. I learned that if I directed my concerns quickly to technology, in those years the use of a Kodak carousel projector, I would soon forget my dis-ease and turn to the subject of my lecture that day, whether interior design and craftsman furniture or perhaps the use of water as natural falls, pools, and flowing sound. So it was: I sought medical advice and was directed to a laboratory for a series of blood tests. The laboratory was in a medical plaza of low-roofed structures. As I walked into the waiting room, I immediately recognized the architectural style: the latticed windows just above the seats, built-in couches facing a brick fireplace. While the narrow windows, stained amber, afforded very low light, light tumbled into the waiting room through a central Japanese garden atrium enclosed in glass. Such a waiting room for a medical laboratory seemed entirely out of character, but it was, as I knew, the architectural design of Aaron Green, influenced by Frank Lloyd Wright and built in 1964. I would come to frequent this waiting room numerous times and would note over the years subtle changes that remade and distorted the original intentions of design and aesthetic, but these were changes of time and age and inevitable forgetting.

You walk around the architectural model placed at the center of the large conference table and smile. You note the location of your future office with the insertion of a Japanese garden atrium. From above, you can see an open square in the low roof encasing a miniature maple, stones, and a pond embedded in moss. At the plaza center, a pharmacy is placed

strategically in a pagoda, buildings graced with low eaves and convenient circling parking. You've driven to San Francisco with your colleagues in your maroon Rolls-Royce, enjoying the day and the pleasant
ride along the coast up Highway 1. You exude a sweet confidence, your
dress casual yet smart, a red-and-gold silk scarf tied jauntily around your
neck—your signature stylishness. Perhaps you, your doctor colleagues,
the builder contractor, and the architect will dine in nearby Chinatown.
You order for the group: Chinese chicken salad, roast duck, pork tofu, gai
lan, bowls of steamed rice, beer for your companions, tea for you. Red
lacquer and circling dragons swirl through the dining hall. You see yourself reflected infinitely in the surrounding mirrors, seated next to the
architect as you discreetly suggest you may be acquiring a mountainside
acreage; would he be interested in visiting the site?

Initially I was put off by the laboratory phlebotomist in charge, a commanding woman who seemed to bark orders from behind the desk,
ensconced behind a half door, that served as a check-in station. *Insurance
card? Medicare? No doctor's orders; who is your doctor? Are you fasting? Drink
some water before you leave. What, no urine sample? Can't pee today? Take
this home, and bring me back some pee.* Passing through the half door, I realized she was a one-phlebotomist show—intake, paperwork, and phlebot-
omy all in one draw. That she managed this operation with efficiency and
accuracy was a tribute to the job. She could slap my arm, tighten the rubber strap above the elbow, locate the vein, stick in the needle, and suck out
my blood in five tubes in a matter of minutes. And despite all this, she
remembered all her victims by name and likely our blood types and dis-
orders, and when, in her infrequent absences, I truly missed her, those
replacing her would commiserate with me. *Ah yes, the General is on vacation.*

Despite the General's efficiency, I found myself on that first day sitting
for perhaps forty-five minutes in the waiting room with a pile of student
papers, which I intended to grade in spare moments. Losing interest in
student responses, I drew the parameters of the space. The fireplace had
ceased use, a potted plant in its altar, dark traces of smoke and ashes clearly
smearing the brick within and above. The cubby designed to hold fire-
wood was empty. I walked to the tall slabs of glass panes that served as
the transparent wall to the garden and peered in. There was a pond with
a small fall of flowing water and goldfish surrounded by grass and moss
and flowering azaleas. A small maple shaded the area. And to one side

was a bronze plaque set over a cement block imprinted with five names. Presumably the garden was a memorial to these names. Studying them, I felt an uncanny awakening, a sudden sense of familiarity. I returned to my seat, pressing a nervous palm into a slippery stack of papers and waited for the General to bark out my name.

You hike up an uneven path, the architect behind you. You point out trees and markers that designate the perimeters of the ten-acre hillside you've recently purchased. At some point in your trek, you turn around and look toward the town below and the bay beyond. The view is spectacular that day, sunlight glinting off blue waves, the outline of the bay sweeping with lush clarity across the horizon. The architect nods with sympathetic pleasure, notes the southern-facing direction, and agrees that this is the perfect open vista; no trees need to be cut or removed from this clearing. You will require a survey and structural engineering evaluations, but the architect imagines that retaining walls and foundation pylons to secure the structure to bedrock will pose no problems. The architect understands your intentions to create a home in concert with the living site, low to the ground and unobtrusive, bringing the natural outside into the gracious space of the home. You trade thoughts about your admiration of Frank Lloyd Wright. While living near Chicago, you'd admired examples of Wright's homes; you admit your fascination for his architecture, bicycling through Oak Park and viewing the houses from the street, one by one. But you were a medical student and an intern in those days, and practical matters set you on a course away from your artistic pursuits. Your hobby has been furniture, following a Craftsman aesthetic. Included in the plans, you'd like a carpenter's studio separate from the house, a place to which you can retreat. You and the architect trade thoughts about the work of Isamu Noguchi and George Nakashima, but you're demure; of course, yours is a hobby, something to pass the time away from your busy practice, your boisterous family.

I jumped to the General's command, passed into her quarters, and sat obediently at my designated seat. She peered, skewering her head toward my hanging face, staring into my eyes, and surprised me with her sharp query: *Are you going to faint on me?* I shook my head and woke to attention. I could not succumb to a dizzy spell at that moment if I were to discover the source of my malady. I thought that she must first draw my blood, and then, I could faint. *Look that way*, she ordered, pointing away from her needle, rubber hose, and tubes. I was offended; I had no such problem with the sight of blood. I purposely showed my strength and determination in this matter and caught her every movement with a purposeful fascination. I watched my blood siphon away into the General's rubber hose, filling glass vials one by one. By the last bloody vial, I knew the source of my discomforting memory. The face of a young woman rose in my vision, someone I hadn't thought of in more than twenty years.

Over time, you and the architect form a close relationship. He wants to see your furniture design ideas, incorporate them into the interior, and you've read about Frank Lloyd Wright's Taliesin Fellowship, prompting the architect to talk about his tutelage with the great master. The architect studied with Wright during the prewar years, became a conscientious objector contending that his work with Wright was an important effort for democracy. He explains his keen enthusiasm for Wright's philosophy of organic architecture, an architecture tied to natural space and the education of the individual. He spreads his initial draft plans over your dining table. Architecture with Wright was a calling, but when the war really began in 1941, the architect volunteered for the Air Corps. You bond over the Air Corps; both you and your brother volunteered to fly as well; your brother was a paratrooper in the war. You say your brother survived, came home, got his degree, then got back into training but died only a year later, a jet pilot over Bavaria in '51. You guess the war isn't ever over. Democracy is a hard mistress. Your last stint was in Dayton, Ohio, at Wright-Paterson, in ophthalmology. When that was over, you piled the family, the wife and four kids and three cats, and some of your furniture into a Volkswagen van and drove across the country to Santa Cruz. Camped out for a while at your sister's place, then started your practice. Despite everything—the war, prejudice—you believe America has done right by its people, given you the opportunities your parents dreamed of. You peruse the ground plans surrounding the house—landscaping, swimming pool, garden with a pond and small fall. The architect asks if you know any Japanese landscaper or gardener friend with whom you'd like to work.

I remembered her exquisite beauty, perfect Eurasian features. It was 1976, the year I began my graduate studies in architecture at Columbia. I was in the elevator scaling the Solomon R. Guggenheim Museum to the top.

Through the faces and bodies in that rising box, I spied her in the corner, shy but with a certain nonchalance and happy innocence. I followed her through the elevator doors and wandered after her at a careful distance. I lost track of time and purpose and spent an entire long afternoon in the museum as if smitten. I had originally intended to view a particular Léger and perhaps a matching Picasso, carefully attempt to memorize the structural design of the building itself, and then rush off to my afternoon class. Instead I wandered and lingered in rooms, leaned from various viewpoints to view the hanging Calder—a cloud platter of red blood cells turning silently, ponderously—and followed her slow snail *descent* to the bottom. She wore the jeans of the day, bell-bottoms over boots, covered by an oversized pink Irish fisherman sweater, hand-knitted I assumed. On her head she wore a worn brown leather cap, which at some point she pulled away. I remember gasping at the glorious motion of her thick hair falling in graceful rivers across her face and shoulders. I was at the time studying architecture with an emphasis on historic preservation at Columbia. That moment in the elevator followed by my circling decline through the museum was the beginning of a tumultuous and torturous year in which I seemed to lose all sense of direction.

You follow the execution of architectural plans with the extreme precision of a surgeon. In your line of work, perfection is a requirement. From the structural integrity of the foundation to the application of a subtle shade of paint, you meticulously manage every detail. The architect and contractor are as conciliatory as you are kind. But you are assertive, forming your commands as gentle requests followed by astute observations and independent research. That is to say, before you make your recommendations, you hit the books, study the matter, prepare with knowing. Your assumption of authority has been learned in the military, but of gentleness, trained at the hospital bedside. But there is another veneer not so easily interpreted. You were born into one of the few Japanese families in a small rural town in Montana. Your father came at the turn of the century, labored as a foreman to complete the Northern Pacific—Minnesota to Spokane—and one day made enough to pay for your mother's passage, a picture bride. As you came of age, you and your family represented an enemy from a place you have never known. To compare the small, tight-knit fishing villages of your parents to the rugged, mountainous cowboy town of your upbringing is to imagine a folktale about two distant and exotic lands. If only it were a folktale and not a navigation through territories of hatred. Within months of the bombing of Pearl Harbor, you are aware that less than two hundred miles away, across the border in Wyoming, ten thousand Japanese Americans evicted from the West Coast have been incarcerated in the same spectacular but desolate landscape in which you continue to be free. But it is a perilous freedom, especially for your immigrant parents designated enemy aliens. Thus every movement, every action, every facial expression must avoid trouble, anticipate a precarious future. Like any other kid from Montana, your older brother volunteers for the military. Your mother embroiders a thousand knots into a woven cotton belt that he obediently wears under his uniform, a protective talisman; so he returns only to be killed in peacetime. You follow your brother's path as if to complete what can never be completed, but you are driven to succeed. You skip lunch and drive from your practice at midday to see the rising stone escarpment, 650 tons of quarried Arizona sandstone, flashing a toothy grin toward the Pacific, a gesture of grandeur and place against a precarious future.

I followed her out the museum's glass doors down Fifth Avenue to Eighty-Sixth, where she disappeared underground and caught a train downtown. Impetuously and mindlessly, I hopped on and emerged at Astor Place, following her to Cooper Union and into a classroom I immediately surmised as a drawing course. Conveniently, I removed a drawing tablet from my satchel, sat unobtrusively in the rear, and leafed past my architectural renderings, mimicking other students with pencil or charcoal in hand. To my thrill and distress, I saw the object of my pursuit, now robed, walk barefoot to a middle dais. The white silk kimono slipped from her body, and there she stood, sans pink fisherman sweater, sans jeans and boots and leather cap—my Eurasian Aphrodite rising. I drew frantic, lousy drawings, one after the other, a cubist montage of breast, nipple, waist, shoulder, buttocks, nose, pubis, and eyes, my heart racing, my mind a bubble about to burst, and all my sensations a loaded gun.

You host an open house. The architect calls a few days before, delighted about the invitation. He asks if a writer for *Architectural Digest* might also be invited. The writer would come with a photographer. You generously agree. The day is perfect, though somewhat chilly, but this is Santa Cruz. Guests who arrive early are greeted with the full expanse of the bay and sit on the stone veranda watching the fading sunlight cast a quiet orange glow. Your wife has ordered catering for the event—large platters of sushi, barbecued teriyaki on skewers, elegant pastel petit fours, sake cocktails, and champagne. You've gathered your entire family. Your mother from Montana and mother-in-law from Illinois have both flown in to visit. Your two young sons run in and out of the house with their friends with abandon. Your two daughters, teenagers now, appear and disappear with their cadre of friends, nodding politely when asked about their individual bedrooms, choice of colors and décor. You watch your wife as she becomes visible through the interior light beyond glass doors. The bubble of her blond coif shines in a halo. You fondle the stem of a champagne glass and nod at the comments of the writer, but your mind wanders to the day you first met your wife, your initial insecurity; could you hope to win the heart of such a beautiful girl? It hasn't been easy, the loss of your first son, but she has weathered every difficulty, growing more beautiful as the years pass. You have become the perfect couple, the perfect family, and this house itself is confirmation. The photographer weaves about, surreptitiously it would seem, pointing a Nikon, capturing the house and décor from every angle, backdrop for beautiful people. Transmitted over pool waters, you catch the waves of a distant argument, something about bombing in Vietnam, and you wander in that direction with a wide smile, wanting nothing to spoil this perfect evening. Your very presence dissipates disagreement, a change of subject, compliments about the house, and *you Japanese really understand nature.* You glance again toward the lighted fireplace, where your relatives seem huddled with your mother apart. In another room, your wife is showing off her current project on the loom; she's weaving fibers dyed naturally for throw pillows. You feel your heart might burst. Meanwhile, the architect is telling the story of his mentor Frank Lloyd Wright to a group of rapt listeners. Wright built for his second wife the house he named Taliesin on family farmland in Wisconsin. Tragically, while Wright was in Chicago, this wife and her children and four of his apprentices were murdered by the housekeeper, a man from Barbados who also set the house on fire.

At the break, twenty minutes later, I rushed from the classroom to the toilet, stood inside a stall, trying to calm the shaking in my knees. I threw cold water on my face and stared at myself in the mirror, unsure of my own reflection. During the course of three hours, I did the same at every break, but I could not tear myself away. At the end of class, I lingered, waiting for her to emerge from the dressing room. A young man entered the room, and sure enough, to my sinking heart, he greeted her clothed body, and together they left the building. By this time, it was evening, and a slight drizzle had wet the dark streets. I watched the couple under an umbrella merge and disappear into the crossing crowd among a blur of car lights and neon. Reflecting back on this day, this was the moment at which I should have simply returned to my apartment in Harlem and continued my studies at Columbia, but I was ensnared in a design with a destiny I felt sure I must pursue to know. To be brief about the ensuing year, foolishly, I all but abandoned my coursework and research and was placed on probation. I forgot and lost contact with my friends and colleagues; if they showed concern, I shrugged away their questions and kept my secret consul. I cannot precisely or chronologically relate with any detail what I did or how I lived during this time. All I remember is that my full-time occupation was that of a detective, self-hired and certainly unpaid to know the daily life and moment-to-moment whereabouts of that young woman. I admit that my curiosity was made of infatuation, but it was an infatuation without any idea of finality—that is, of meeting or consummating a relationship. Late into the early mornings, I pulled sheet after sheet of architectural drafting paper over my drawing table and feverishly designed structures of every sort, engineered houses in lilied valleys or on craggy promontories, next to astounding waterfalls, under snowpack, among bamboo groves, in tropical and desert climates. As much time as I spent as a detective, I was also enmeshed in geographical, climatological, and environmental studies, always concerned with aspects of natural space and local materials. I was astounded by the beauty of my designs, the organic, interwoven nature of place and structure, and always, she hovered ghostly above myriad drafts, rising perfectly from a white silk kimono.

The last time you speak with the architect is over the phone. The architect's voice tremors, then retrieves his confidence with an edge of anger. He wonders what Frank Lloyd Wright would say if he were alive. The Marin County Civic Center was Wright's last project; he died in 1959 and never lived to see the final inauguration of the building. It was the architect who completed the work. Every aspect of the center—its spacious elegance, skylight roof over interior gardens, arched windows framing the

soft rise of distant hills, innovative jail design, the carefully studied con-
figuration of the courtrooms themselves—honored Wright's desire for
democratic space. But this: first, the hostage-taking in the center's courtroom and the shoot-out, the deaths of the prisoners and the judge, and
now, bombing the courtroom. You've read in the papers that some group
called Weathermen say they are responsible. You commiserate with the
architect's sense of confoundedness and outrage. Everything the architect and you believe in is being contested and turned upside down.

At first I thought she led a charmed life, prancing around the city from
art to dance class to photo shoot. For example, I managed to follow her
into the New York art scene—art receptions and openings where the
likes of Yoko Ono, Isamu Noguchi, Nam June Paik, or the young up and
coming, such as Theresa Hak Kyung Cha, might be the featured artists or
emerge among the invitees. Despite her youth, she moved with an easy
grace among celebrity. Always fashionably attired, she wore designs both
chic and elaborate with a casual body language that said, *Of course.*
Modeling for art classes turned out to be a side job she did occasionally as
a favor to her former teachers at Cooper Union. Professionally, she worked
with a prominent agency, and I was able to catch glimpses of her strutting
the runway for Ralph Lauren, Yves Saint Laurent, Hanae Mori, and
Stephen Burrows, to name a few. Despite her success, I followed her weekly
to the office of a psychiatric therapist. I waited patiently for the hour to
end and tried to discern the results of each session; I comprehended nothing. I clipped her photographs from *Vogue* and *Elle,* taping them to every
inch of my small one-room studio. In the night, sleeping on an old futon,
I could hear the tape peeling away with the bad paint job, the magazine
photos fluttering to the floor like autumn leaves. One particularly snowy
night, I entered my cold apartment, banging on the old lever of the radia-
tor, and finally noticed gashes of blood-orange paint beneath the powder
blue, scarring the walls, her colorful images scattered. I saw my breath in
the cold air of that horrid old apartment and wept.

You stare at the man with the gun, who can't be much older than your
eldest daughter, who is thankfully safely far away, studying art in New
York. He accuses you of crimes against the environment. You think you
recognize him, a long-haired fellow, but they are all long-haired these
days; even you are letting your hair grow out stylishly. Perhaps he came

to the office with a case of pink eye. He told you how much he liked the garden in the middle of the office, never seen an office with a garden. His eyes were so infected they were almost glued together with gunk, but he could see the garden. But, he said, you can't live in a little garden like that; maybe the Japanese could, but anyway he lived in the forest up there in the mountains, lots of room and close to God, he said. Nothing artificial. You nodded in agreement. Japanese gardens are artificially natural, miniature vistas to create the sensation of distance and expanse. Gardening is an art. You were thinking about your father's garden in Montana. He thought about this and said he liked his art original, wild. No stunted bonsai for him, but of course he'd never been to Japan. Neither had you, except for a short R&R at a base in Okinawa before returning to the states. Looking at your watch and into the crowded reception room, you knew you didn't care to reply. He had no insurance, no money to pay. You waved him off, told the receptionist to make an exception. She looked up, and her eyes said, *Another exception.* As the fellow left, the mail arrived, and your receptionist handed you a box with a small card. You opened the card: *Doc, a small token of thanks for your handiwork on my cataract. Sure is great to see clear again.* You handed back the box of See's candies and pointed to the reception room, gesturing, *Pass it around.* Perhaps it is not the same long-haired fellow, but you, your wife, your two sons, and the receptionist will die today.

One day late in October, I scanned the Halloween paraphernalia decorating shop windows, the proliferation of jack-o'-lanterns, witch hats, black cats, and skeletons along my route. I had affected a disinterested manner, gazing with feigned interest in odd directions, at window treatments or sidewalk displays. At this particular shop, I pretended interest in a skeleton mask, knowing she was passing on the sidewalk behind me. In all the time I followed her, our eyes never met, and I supposed she never knew or felt my presence. But this time, for some reason, she turned back to look my way, and our eyes met through that mask. I saw her disgust and terror. She stumbled away, walking hurriedly if not running into the underground. I abandoned the mask and followed with trepidation, chasing my sightline for her white trench coat, the slip of a red-and-gold silk scarf trailing in the overheated draft of our descent. Surfacing at Eighty-Sixth Street, she walked quickly toward Fifth Avenue, fall colors of Central Park sparkling beyond. I slowed my pace, knowing her frequent destination.

It was her habit to visit Magritte's *False Mirror*, staring into that surreal sky eye. I should have anticipated this day, but I was obsessed with my own arrogance, my manic certainty of my own artistic genius, poet and prophet. That day, only I looked upward from the rotunda into the last rays of that October day streaming through the glass dome and saw her body tossed from the top of Wright's magnificent nautilus, her white trench coat flapping, windswept black hair separating in silky strands, red-and-gold scarf fluttering along, passing the silent Calder, imposing an unusual commotion on those glorious clouds of vermilion.

Even though you were buried Catholic, you wander the past as a Buddhist. There is no extinguishing your anguish. The beauty of this place has betrayed you. After the murders and the fires, they rebuilt it all completely new again, but unlike your wife and your children, it returns no love, a temple of permanent and radiant beauty. A real Japanese has been hired to keep the gardens in a state of eternal beauty, constantly trimming and replanting, leaves and fading blossoms fluttering onto rock and still water to form exquisite traces, never rotting. Koi flap about, red and gold and white, turning their bodies in chaos or moving gracefully in liquid silence. The bodies of you, your wife and children, and your associates lie beneath in the dark shoals where your blood pools like lead. One night in Indian summer, I climb the hill to your house and meet you there. In the tepid night, I see you shape-shift between father and lover, doctor and architect, artist and prophet. I guide you to the Rolls-Royce, and together we siphon gasoline, spread it gallon by gallon at the most vulnerable corners of your beloved architecture.

Note: *This is a work of fiction based on true events.*

*With gracious thanks to Frank Gravier, bibliographer for Humanities at UCSC McHenry Library; Paul Shea, director of the Yellowstone Gateway Museum in Livingston, Montana; and Lucy Asako Boltz, research assistant.*

# Colono:Scopy

You are a sansei. You used to be feisty and youthful and, quite frankly, intolerable. You might still be intolerable, but now they pretend to tolerate you because, well, you're old. When you turn fifty, they give you an over-the-hill party with black balloons and taunt you about the last half century, but this is just the beginning of the second half of your century, which you decide to embrace because, what the heck, maybe you can finally say anything you want and even speak for your generation since you might outlive them all. But then you realize what the Brazilians call *the merda* that happens boils down to three significant things: 1. You need reading glasses; 2. You find out you're the "sandwich generation," meaning you're the baloney between your needy, illogical kids and your needy, illogical parents; and 3. You'll need a colonoscopy.

Number 1 is a minor bummer because you already had lousy eyes, Coke-bottle goggles in the fifties until contact lenses came around and your high school buddy became an optometrist. Number 2 is what your parents were trying to prepare you for: oyakoko; maybe you missed the lesson in which they explain if it's the egg or the chicken first, but now you know it's a deviled egg, and that the egg-chicken conundrum is beyond the point. Stuck between adolescent angst and elder dementia, you might accept the justice of this return to your sansei attitude and the memory of the Quiet Nisei stuck in repeat mode. After all, this is America. Life isn't a donburi. Trust me, number 3 might be the real turning point.

Your experienced elders give you the lowdown on the liquid diet and the enema prep, and when they say don't leave the toilet, they don't mean don't leave the *vicinity* of the toilet; they mean DON'T LEAVE THE TOILET. Bunker in with your books and magazines, your iPhone, laptop, and Netflix, and be glad you don't have to share a communal potty without partitions. Now the bogey word *evacuation* takes on a whole new meaning.

The gastroenterologist asks if you want general anesthesia or conscious sedation; that is, do you want to be knocked out or semialert for the investigative procedure? Someone with experience who stayed awake says it was like watching *Fantastic Voyage*. You vaguely recall the 1966 film with a crew of microastronauts voyaging through blood cells, though all you really remember is Raquel Welch. To have Raquel swimming around your large intestine doesn't seem like such a bad idea, especially since you've really cleaned it out just for her. O.K., you accept the challenge.

The gastroenterologist, who is clearly not yet fifty, eyes you with a mixture of pathos and amusement and assures you she has performed hundreds of routine colonoscopies. The pathos is connected to the possibility that a cancerous polyp might be detected; the amusement is connected to your desire to swim with Raquel through your own butt. Raquel Welch, the gastroenterologist queries, is she still alive? You think about all the current gorgeous Hollywood pretenders who are pale copies of Raquel, the original hot cavewoman gunslinger who conquered the West plus the world Before Christ. O.K., as a feminist, you were never into Raquel, but is she still alive?

From your left side, in a semifetal position, a flimsy blue cotton gown indecorously flapped open down your back, you peer at the gastroenterologist in her scrub cap and face mask, and, in your semisedated dream state, she appears to be an indigenous person with tribal affiliations. Forget Raquel. Think Sacagawea. She launches the colonoscope into your rectum. The colonoscope is a four-foot-long tube with a camera and light source at its tip. It could be la Niña, la Pinta, or la Santa María. Let's go find India.

You stare at the monitor, watching the colonoscope snake into your unknown, unmapped territory. Your plumber guide nods with approval at the clean, shiny pink walls, congratulating you on a flushing job well done. The camera spelunks with slow precision. In the dark distance, you see a tiny slim figure in slacks. As the light positions itself, you see a woman with graying hair walking a dog. It's Donna Haraway. O.K., the dog isn't a dog but a companion species. Donna points with wonder to the walls of your cleaned-out gut, normally a microbial ecosystem of a thousand species of critters with whom you coexist. And you just spent the previous day shitting the critters while incarcerated with your toilet. You apologize to Donna, but she's a scientist, no apologies required; just remember who shares this precious space with you. Suddenly, the shepherd companion herds Donna into the tube, and they tumble away like Alice down a rabbit hole. What happened? The doctor plumber articulates some directive to your dream team. Apparently a polyp. We'll take a biopsy and let you know. If it's any consolation, it looks benign.

The procedure plods on, gently turning the corner. Oh, lookee here, di-ver-tic-u-lum. Diverticula are pouches in your colon where stuff collects and settles and can cause diverticulitis. Have you been eating your vegetables?

I'm Asian, you protest. We grow it; we practically invented the stuff.

The camera points and shoots. Your diverticulosis is recorded. You lookee there and blink in disbelief, because the stuff in your particular diverticulum looks like a bunch of nineteenth-century white guys on locomotives. You squint, and it's the meeting of the Central Pacific with the Union Pacific and the completion of the Transcontinental Railroad on Promontory Summit in Utah. Wait, you protest, where are the Chinese who built that railroad?

Right, says Dr. Sacagawea, on native land, all stolen.

But, you continue to protest, where are the Chinese critters?

Sacagawea points and shoots from another angle. You wanna be in that picture too? An accomplice to indigenous genocide? Be my guest.

Wait a minute, I'm not Chinese.

So much for solidarity.

Check out Google Maps and go to central Utah. Right there, Delta, Utah. My people were incarcerated in a concentration camp.

Boohoo, says Sacagawea. You had no business being concentrated there in the first place.

My folks were hauled from their homes based on racism and fear with not a single incident of espionage or sabotage to justify their imprisonment.

We've heard that loyalty bullshit; you're the models that make everyone else's lives miserable. Considering the path you're headed down, this diverticulum will eventually assimilate, neoliberalize, get inflamed. You're in for a lot of pain.

Look, you say, I eat vegetables, but I diversify my diet. Diversity against diverticulitis! You put up a weak but defiant right fist.

Sacagawea replies drolly, It might not be your diet. These days, multicultures are overrated, if not cliché. Might just be your genes.

One diverticulum, two diverticula. Another pouch? Ouch. This one looks a lot bigger, but Sacagawea is unimpressed. There are some human tribes whose colons are truly impressive, pristine environments.

Pristine?

No foreign-settler inhabitation. Sacagawea takes the camera in for another shot. Yours is, well, twisted and acculturated.

You scrutinize this second picture and observe what looks like a battleship sinking into your diverticulum. Oh no, you've got to be kidding. Isn't that—?

The USS Arizona.

Pearl Harbor?

Look, we didn't invent this infamy. Depose Liliuokalani, set up a plantation system, install the military, start a war.

What, the war is my fault?

A high-fiber diet might have prevented this. You know that Spam musubi you love so much?

Wait, this is my colon. My colon!

That's what they all say. Face it, you've been colonized. When are you going to take responsibility for this mess? Your habits have destroyed the habitats of hundreds of native cultures.

You look back again and notice Daniel Inouye in full dress uniform with all his purple medals, waving his one arm from the sinking Arizona. Sayonara, Dan. And through the black smoke and sirens, you can see a small floating vessel, a lifeboat with the demoralized faces of yes-yes/no-no Tule Lakers, MIS guys, and go-for-brokers, Nisei artists with communist antifascist affinities, Frank Chin in an inner tube splashing behind it, all drifting out of that pearly harbor in search of the promised land, which is certainly not in your big, capacious colon.

Finally the colonoscope chugs into cecum Dodge, the beginning of your small intestine and, you think hopefully, the end of the line. This could be India, land of gold and spices. But there on the platform, you see it: a blooming mushroom backlit in a pink aura. Walter Cronkite's authoritative present-tense voiceover booms through the talking cecum, and you see the Cold War frantically spin around the mushroom. Like Walter says: and you are there.

It looks like we've a got a live occupation! Sacagawea scrutinizes the situation. In the future, she announces, we'll have nanodrones to take care of nuclear waste like this. But for now, we'll be old fashioned and do some preemptive surgery. Remember? You signed that treaty, a binding contract that allows us to proceed with impunity.

You ask, *Why me?*

Too much Kool-Aid. Refined plantation sugars. You're an accomplice, collaborator, and coconspirator in your own destiny.

You watch the surgical removal of your polyp morphing into serial versions of Godzilla, dumped memories and revised history screaming into the tube's void. Never mind that Sacagawea has ripped out the last polyp of your precious dignity; maybe she's saved your life for another half century. Why settle for less? Good luck. She snorts through the disposable face mask. I recommend a strict diet of native grasses, acorn meal, pine nuts, foraged blackberries.

The colonoscope backs out, retracing its path with the same intensive scrutiny. No diverticulum, adenoma, or cancer will go undetected. The good news is there's a four-foot limit to this tether, and it's anchored to nothing except that camera and Sacagawea's judgment, which you'll just have to trust. Sacagawea recommends a repeat procedure every five years. If you live another fifty years, that means Sacagawea will have ten more chances to whip you into shape before you die.

# KonMarimasu

Your relationship to popular culture and its discontents is on a need-to-know basis. This isn't because you've risen above it, but because you're too busy with the past (history) and the future (speculation) to pay attention to the present. What you don't know about the past is an endless forking back road, but it might give clues to the future, so you continually run back there to catch up, and it's impossible to catch up with today. O.K., this might be a big lie. Generally speaking, you're clueless and always lagging at least a decade behind. You tell your son you're on season two of *The Wire*. "That's great, Mom," he says with encouragement. You say, "I'm skipping to the last season. I get it; it's about drugs. *French Connection* in Baltimore." He says, "No, no, each season is different, a whole new cast. You have to see them all, or it won't make sense." "Oh." You pause, then say, "It's a little dated," and look for the date on the DVD box. 2002. He probably wants to say, "Duh," but he doesn't. He's a nice kid, and this was his generation's version of your generation's first generation of *Star Trek*. Even then, you didn't really watch *Star Trek* when it was *Star Trek*; you let it seep into your conscious present at the time because otherwise you'd have looked really dumb when everyone else was beamed up.

So when your sister comes over to your house and finds you cleaning and discarding stuff, she mentions something about Marie Kondo and hoarding. You query, "Marie who?" "Kondo," she says, and you think about how maybe you knew a sansei named Kondo way back when. But then she says, "You don't know who she is?" And to rub it in, "She's translated into maybe forty languages, published all over the world." When did this happen? "Geeze, it's gotta be a couple a years ago." She doesn't say, *Where have you been*? She could, but she knows. You've been right here all this time with all your junk.

Your sister opens a *New York Times Magazine* and points to a cute Japanese woman on a pink background in a pose with her finger pointed up and her foot raised behind her in a small kick. It's the J pose, translated as "joy." You both imitate what you figure is the pose for the kanji: joy. You scan the article. A book on tidying? "It's great literature." You smirk. "Say," your sister reminds you, "that woman is laughing all the way to the bank." Right; when have you ever laughed on your way to the bank? So you ask, "You've read it?" "Yeah," she says, "picked it up in a pile at Costco for nine forty-nine."

*Three million copies sold. A* NYT *Best Seller.* You size up the title: *the life-changing magic of tidying up: the Japanese art of decluttering and organizing.* Everything is in lowercase, like it's in hiragana, except the J in *Japanese.* *Translated from the Japanese by Cathy Hirano.* Where have you been? While you were dozing, the Japanese invented the art of tidying. And it's not just an art; it's a method. The KonMari method. Like the Suzuki method. Or Kumon, the math method. It's like Zen and the art of fill-in-the-blank, except Kondo was a Shinto shrine maid. You think about Shinto shrines completely rebuilt every twenty years. Why not? A complete package for transformation. In the first pages you discover that satisfied clients of the KonMari method have realized dramatic changes in their lifestyle and life perspective, every sort of transformation from the loss of ten pounds to divorce. You read that the average amount of stuff discarded by Kondo's clients can be from twenty to forty-five garbage bags per person. In a family of three: seventy bags. At some point she writes that the sum of all the stuff discarded by her clients would exceed twenty-eight thousand bags and the number of items, over one million. Knowing garbage (gomi) collection in Japan, this staggering number of garbage bags makes you reel. Where did it all go? Into the Tokyo Bay?

You glance at the corner of the study that could be your Tokyo Bay, boxes filled with letters, photographs, artifacts, and piles of supporting documentation—a massive dumping place of the thing called your family archive. Since the death of all your dad's siblings, your cousins have been KonMari-ing the last effects of saved memorabilia into boxes and mailing them to you. You open boxes that exude the musty air of basements and flutter up dust that could be a hundred years old. On page 115, Kondo writes, "People never retrieve the boxes they send 'home.' Once sent, they will never again be opened." Of photographs, she suggests you remove them from their albums, look at each one by one, then toss. You handle the crumbling spines of old fashioned, obsolete albums, and you understand the urge to never open these boxes, but it's your own fault. Didn't you agree to this noble preservation of family history? Besides, there could be treasure in them there boxes or the missing code to some family secret. You collate by date the old correspondence, handwritten letters often five pages long, and read through that period when your folks were shipped off to concentration camps with only what they could carry. Kondo says, "Letting go is even more important than adding," but you know no one said, *Thank you for bringing me joy* or *I love you* before saying sayonara to all the rest of the stuff they couldn't carry to camp.

So you fly into Providence, Rhode Island, where your niece Lucy has packed seven humongous UPS boxes of her possessions acquired over eight years for send-off to L.A. The back of her Honda Fit is packed with more stuff, including a hand-built crate with a painting, an official USPS plastic box of sewing material, and a giant stainless steel bowl for kneading bread. You don't ask about the KonMari spark of joy thing, but you figure, if you hold the bowl, you will feel it. There is some room left in the Fit for your rollerbag, backpack, rice cooker, and you. Your sister has charted a course across the country through seven of the ten Japanese American internment camps. The goal is to bring the Fit and Lucy home, but you're calling this "the incarceration road trip."

First stop: DC. You meet Noriko Sanefuji, museum specialist at the Smithsonian National Museum of American History. Noriko will curate the *Executive Order 9066: Japanese Incarceration & WWII* exhibit scheduled to open in 2017 on the Annual Day of Remembrance. She shows Lucy and you the room and corridors, currently displaying an exhibit on guano, that will house the incarceration exhibit, explaining the complications of limited space, flow of information, and the politics of presentation. Then, you get special entry into the back rooms and basement of what's known as America's Attic. Noriko has arranged a small array of objects on a table she hopes to put on display. She pulls on black gloves and carefully caresses the pink crochet of a child's dress, aged by wear and years. This dress was handmade by a mother in camp, and it is accompanied by a portrait photograph of a little girl in the same dress, standing with her extended family arranged formally in their barrack home. Noriko pulls forward another object, a cotton cloth embroidered with a thousand red knots, nickel and dime secured in the threads, and the words *God Bless.* An issei mother made this sen nin bari for her soldier son to be worn around his waist to protect him in battle. Each item is handled with gloved care and stored with protective cellophane in acid-free paper and boxes. You remember the ceremonial observance of Kondo's method, plus her practical advice for storing the stuff you don't toss: Don't hang; fold. "Folding is fun." She writes on page 74, "Japanese people quickly grab the pleasure that comes from folding clothes, almost as if they are genetically programmed for this task." You note the sen nin bari, each fold remembered in a yellowed tinge, the sweat and grime of battle, the unspoken story of a soldier's survival, a mother's prayer.

On the way out of DC, as you traverse the verdant Virginia highlands, Lucy exclaims out of nowhere, "Hey, I wanna know who's going to go on a road trip with me when I'm sixty-five!" Maybe she's interrupted your NPR podcast or the audiobook reading of Tony Horwitz's *Confederates in the Attic,* or maybe you're stopped on some ridge comparing Google Maps to your sister's highlighted AAA map. You laugh though you feel that Lucy's anxiety is real, but what the heck. Who wrote that song "When I'm 64"? Good grief, is it all about getting old? Lucy's only twenty-six. The road trip, you guess, is one of those vestiges of your generation. When Lucy is sixty-five, you can't speculate what would replace it; probably something virtual. What twenty-six-year-old in the next forty years is going to want to go on a road trip? Like, are we there yet? One thing you realize is that Lucy is a stickler for the truth of history, and what you do anyway is fiction. Seeing might be believing.

Your first incarceration stop: the southeastern edge of Arkansas along the Mississippi River and McGehee, the local town that's converted its old train depot into the Jerome-Rohwer Interpretive Museum and Visitor Center. Susan Gallion, the museum's curator and host, greets you with Southern hospitality and stories of Jerome and Rohwer internees and their descendants who've preceded Lucy and you to this moment. Lucy will probably remember the precise context of Susan's southern phrase "God doesn't make junk," but you'll only remember the phrase that will follow you like a GPS satellite on that long road trip, the probing matter of human-made junk left behind in camp museum after camp museum. At the Rohwer site, you walk around the remake of a mini guard tower on a gravel road rising in a field of cotton and push buttons on the placards to hear the disembodied voice of George Takei (aka Mr. Sulu) tell you about life circa 1942 and his boyhood relationship to the present desolation of the landscape and the snakes and mosquito-ridden bayou cleared by inmates. You think, you could be beamed up now, please, but you walk on down the gravel road, trying to ignore the oppressive and scalding humidity, looking for the cemetery. Stone monuments mark bodies left behind and bodies sacrificed in battle, and outside the human burial perimeter, a dog named Papy. You imagine the deep, surreal voice of George Takei departing in his starship to that final frontier where no man has gone: *God doesn't make junk.*

For over a decade, you've been collecting your family junk with some idea it might be useful research material for another book. You didn't know what book or what story, but that's the way writing is. If you knew, you wouldn't bother. By the time you propose the road trip to Lucy, you've mostly finished the book. The road trip is an excuse, a kind of finishing up of the project—realizing and experiencing what had been read in letters and seen in photographs. Maybe if you'd done the road trip before, the book would be different, but circumstances make the archive real and the real places surreal. Or perhaps the contemplation of the past and its memory is the work of the written book, and the realization of being at locations of incarceration finally visceral and unwritable.

Literally and figuratively getting out of Dodge, you and Lucy make your escape in the trusty Fit, then saunter over the Kansas border into the quiet town of Granada on the eastern edge of Colorado. The Amache Museum is a small house on the corner of Goff Avenue and Irwin Street, across from a grain silo. You peruse the "Preserve America" information signs outside the museum, and Lucy calls the number on the door. Five minutes later, John Hopper pulls up, and the Amache Preservation Society turns out to be John Hopper and his crew of high school students. John arrives sans students (it's a school day), but he's like a one-man show: the principal, the coach, and the AP teacher of the local high school, a former city councilman, and the director of the Amache Preservation Society. The museum began as a high school project; then, John got on the city council to secure the ninety-nine-year land lease for the Amache internment site. John says the students do everything except run the tractor to mow the brush and maintain the roads. "Too dangerous," he says. He does that work himself, so he's the maintenance man as well. If the site goes over to the National Park Service, they'll handle all that. Big loss will be the students won't have hands-on access to the collection, but, says John, "I need to retire." Considering his energy, you don't quite believe him.

Inside, the small house is packed with what John says is the largest and most varied collection of Japanese American internment artifacts of any of the camp sites. Usually John's students run the museum, trained by John and university scholars to guide visitors, curate exhibitions, participate in site archeology. He opens a box with a recent acquisition, a dark-green 1944 Amache high school sweater. Some collector contacted John and wanted $1,000 for the sweater, said if John didn't take it, he had a WWII collector waiting to buy it. John said he didn't have that kind of money, offered the guy $35. The students got mad; they wanted it for their planned exhibit on high school in camp. Eventually, as John suspected, the seller came around for reasonably less. But everything else is donated. "We don't turn anything down. If they send it to us, it has a story and meaning." You observe a glass jug that could be any glass jug except that it held sake distilled locally and consumed by internees; you snap a photo.

Riding north, two days later, at the Heart Mountain Interpretive Center, you meet Darlene Bos, who tells you and Lucy her story of growing up in nearby Cody in one of the camp's repurposed barracks, reshaped into an L-shaped ranch-style homesteading home. You think you've spotted these barracks, likely scattered all over the region as shotgun houses and barns, and maybe haunted, well, haunted with old history since Darlene became curious and studied that history, eventually volunteering to work at the Heart Mountain site. Now she's the center's marketing and development manager. From childhood, she says she argued with her father, a U.S. military veteran. When the interpretive center finally opened, and both her parents had also volunteered their energy to build the meditation garden, her father finally said to her, "You were right." She admits she's always on the lookout for visitors like her dad, hoping to change their minds. She says, "I love my work."

The Heart Mountain center is impressively curated, packing history into a small and concentrated space, deeper layers of documentation and oral histories for visitors who care to take the extra time. In the foyer, a windowed outlook to the meditation garden, visitors have strung, Tanabata-like, on a barbed-wire fence replicas of the internee name-tags, leaving behind messages of their impressions and wishes. As you leave, you note the box of Kleenex discretely placed on a bench.

What the road trip reveals is the broader nature of your family archive, its being subsumed into one museum project after another, curating and deciding the stories of the past. Every museum and its collection is different and yet the same—same in the urge to preserve, to historicize, to teach, to place values, and to entice you to enter. To you, books and museums are much the same. Your road trip, like every other account of a road trip, is an open and physical book. You retrace the steps of others, stand in the places of their discovery, loss, and misery. Books and museums curate stories, a version of events and truth.

Two days after Heart Mountain, you come through Yellowstone to visit Minidoka in Idaho. Then, you and Lucy take the Fit south into Utah to a town called Delta and the camp site named Topaz, the jewel of the desert. It's a desert all right. The clear blue sky sweeps the horizon, sun and hot wind unrelenting. You squint across a landscape of salt desert shrub and greasewood and follow your guide Jane Beckwith's sure steps, sinking into the parched and cracked crust of soil that churns into fine dust. Jane is a retired teacher who, like John Hopper, taught history through Delta's local stories, storing internment artifacts in her house until she founded, with the passionate efforts of a lifetime, the Topaz Museum. Jane points to the outline of rocks and stones that mark the garden and threshold of barrack 6-3-F in block six and ushers you through an imaginary door. You walk around the twenty-by-twenty-four-foot perimeter of your family's confinement, home to thirteen people from 1942 to 1945, and scuff around in the remains of rusty nails, wood scraps, broken pieces of cement foundation. Jane picks up rocks and identifies them geologically. What you learn is that every rock and stone had to be brought to the area by the internees to create the gardens that have since disappeared. Every rock and stone. You want to find a piece of pottery or perhaps the rusty hardware of your family's abandoned waffle iron, but even if you found it, you'd be prohibited from taking anything from the site. All that past broken and discarded stuff, every rock and stone, belongs to the place, to be left untouched, scorched by sun, weathered, and returned to the earth, an archeological site whose desolate surface memory is now a sacred memorial. Kondo's admonition that clutter is the failure to return things to where they belong, her insistence on simplicity and minimalism, all this only reminds you of what you assume is the Japanese American motto: "Leave it cleaner than you found it." Kondo writes, "No matter how wonderful things used to be, we cannot live in the past. The joy and excitement we feel here and now are more important," but you have the deep urge to exchange the word *wonderful* for *awful* and sit in that spot and weep.

To be fair to Kondo, she could be your daughter (O.K., unfair), a yonsei raised in a capitalist consumer society with great privilege (no war, no refugee boat, no exile from genocide, no Trail of Tears, no Underground Railroad, no Great Depression, no eyes on the prize), but she is still a product of the long postwar. You wonder what people in what forty languages have required Kondo's advice. Can the trauma of the hoarder be undone with the methodic and ceremonial movement of clothing, books, paper, miscellany, and sentimental value rendered into honorary trash? She says, "The question of what you want to own is actually the question of how you want to live your life." This could the most succinct clarification and synthesis of Buddhism and Marxism, the revolution you've been anticipating. Voilá.

Kondo might say that this stuff in your family archive and this stuff in all these internment museums were parted with to launch them on a new journey. You cogitate the joy spark thing, and you think about simple furniture made from wood scraps, the pink crocheted dress, the sen nin bari, the green high school sweater, the jug of sake, and the waffle iron you know your family smuggled into camp. You know your family had to gather precious eggs, milk, butter, flour, and syrup, and they convened in the ironing room for access to an electrical outlet that wouldn't blow the barrack fuse. All this for a small celebration made special by probably the only waffle iron in camp.

Jane Beckwith pauses with a last story. She remembers bringing a class of children to visit the Topaz site and one boy who was particularly rambunctious, jumping and noisily running about. A girl his age admonished her classmate, "Be quiet." She advised him, "Don't you know? They are here."

You will finally also visit Manzanar under the Sierra Nevadas, between the desert towns of Independence and Lone Pine. You reflect as you enter California that you and Lucy have traveled through those red states and communities that will vote for the current president and his race- and religion-based mandate against immigrants and refugees, but that in each of those remote sites of Japanese American incarceration, there are monuments, interpretive centers, museums, and real people, volunteers and docents, that all decry the racism, hatred, and fear that unjustly imprisoned citizens and honest, hardworking immigrant families. These sites and their caretakers stand as places of evidence, accountability, resistance, and hope.

You and Lucy are home now. Lucy opens the garage door and is greeted by the seven humongous UPS boxes, plus, on the porch, a narrow box containing her bicycle. She announces that one of her next projects is to go through the stuff in her family storage unit. You return to your personal Tokyo Bay, a landfilled space of junk you can't abandon. You know you can't hold each item and feel for the spark of joy, kick your foot back and point your finger up in the joy position. If there is joy, it's a painful joy. You ponder the thought that Lucy has beamed up most of it into digital space and reorganized it into a website story. A new journey. You reflect on the lives of Jane Beckwith and John Hopper and every other curator and keeper of history along your incarceration road trip, and you think that keeping the stuff, saving it, might also be a way of transforming your life.

# Sansei Recipes

### Karen Mayeda's Furikake Popcorn

Mix ½ teaspoon of shoyu into 3 tablespoons of butter. Toss over bag of popcorn with furikake mix and spicy sembei. Watch a movie and eat.

### Teresa Yokoyama's Sesame Shoyu Philly Cheese (J.A. Brie)

Pour ½ teaspoon of shoyu over a slab of Philadelphia cream cheese. Sprinkle sesame seeds. Heat in microwave 1 minute. Serve with crackers and gossip.

### Garrett Hongo's Volcano Poke

Combine best-quality diced tuna or marlin, minced white onions, chopped scallions, and pickled seaweed. Splash in shoyu; squeeze in wasabi; drizzle sesame oil; sprinkle with salt. Toss, and serve with sake and beer. Play cards.

### Tosh Tanaka's Mexican Bao

Mix up bao dough (package of yeast in 2 tablespoons of warm water, 3 cups flour, 1 cup water), let rise one hour, and punch down. Sauté chopped onions and salt in lard or oil, then mash in cooked beans, adding water to keep smooth consistency. Place dollops of beans with grated cheese into four-inch flat rounds of dough, gathering into bundles. Steam and eat warm.

## Buddhahead Spam Musubi

Cut rectangular slices of Spam and fry until browned. Place Spam slices with sesame seeds between rice and wrap with nori. Use a plastic musubi mold for best results.

## Paul Yamazaki's Natto-don

Heat up a can of chili. Sauté chopped green onion with cubes of Spam. Stir up a portion of natto with shoyu and Colman's mustard. On a hot bowl of rice, layer in order: chili, sautéed Spam and onions, natto, raw egg. Garnish with fresh chopped onions. Eat this when Sara isn't home.

## Jane Tomi's Avo/Cottage Cheese and Natto

Layer cottage cheese, slices of avocado, and natto mixed with raw egg, Colman's mustard, and shoyu. Eat like that. For real.

## KT's Crab Miso Bake with Egg

Having saved the crab shell with miso guts, crack an egg into the shell and bake until egg is soft cooked. Eat with spoon. Offer to guests to test their Asian quotient.

## Jonny Grandson's Asako Signature Tofu-You

Sauté chopped onions and sliced ginger with bite-sized pieces of pork. Mix funyu with shoyu, water, and cornstarch, add to sautéed pork, and cook until thickened. Add block of chopped tofu and simmer. Garnish with chopped green onions. Serve with rice.

## Carole Ono's Baked Sushi

Mix ½ cup of mayonnaise with 1 cup of sour cream. Stir in crab, chopped shrimp, chopped hydrated shiitake mushrooms (soaked and cooked in mirin and shoyu water), chopped green onions, chopped water chestnuts, and slivered cucumber. Spread this mixture over a casserole of rice sprinkled with furikake. Put under the broiler about five minutes until bubbling. Garnish with beni-shōga and serve with nori, as cone makizushi.

## Asako's Nihonmachi Corned Beef and Cabbage

Make corned beef and cabbage as usual, boiled in water, adding potatoes and carrots. Serve in bowls of salted soup with rice and Colman's hot mustard. (Discarding soup would be mottainai.)

## Tamio Spiegel's Miso/Mayo Salmon

Lay half filet of salmon over oiled pan skin up. Broil until skin bubbles and chars. Turn over and slather miso and mayonnaise (one-to-one) mixture over salmon and broil until top begins to char. Serve with rice.

## Finally, that Layered Jell-O Potluck Casserole

It was usually green, in several complicated layers, and had cottage cheese in it.

# A Selected L.A./Gardena J.A. Timeline

| Year | J.A. Events* | American Generations | J.A. Generations | | |
|------|------|------|------|------|------|
| | | | Issei | Nisei/ Kibei | Sansei |
| 1868 | Meiji Restoration | | Early years | | |
| 1882 | Chinese Exclusion Act passed | | | | |
| 1884 | Shigeta Hamanosuke (Charlie Hama) opens first restaurant on First Street in neighborhood to become Little Tokyo | | | | |
| 1887 | First Japanese boarding house opens in Little Tokyo | | | | |
| 1896 | Japanese Methodist Episcopal Mission of Los Angeles founded | | | | |
| 1902 | Kamesaka Oda buys one acre of strawberry fields in Moneta (Gardena) | GI/Greatest 1901–1927 | | | |
| 1903 | *Rafu Shimpo* newspaper founded in L.A. | | | | |
| 1903 | Fugetsu-Do confectionary store opens in Little Tokyo | | | | |
| 1903 | Tsuneko Okazaki becomes first state-licensed Japanese midwife in California | | | | |
| 1904 | Russo-Japanese War | | | | |
| 1905 | First Buddhist temple (later named Hongwanji) established in L.A. | | | | |
| 1905 | Momoji Yanaga buys five acres of farmland in Gardena Valley and introduces Klondike variety of strawberry | | | | |

* selected with emphasis in L.A./Gardena and with apologies for omissions

| Year | J.A. Events* | American Generations | J.A. Generations | | |
|------|-------------|---------------------|------|------|------|
| | | | Issei | Nisei/ Kibei | Sansei |
| 1905 | Jinnosuke, Yujiro, and Kamekichi Kobata (brothers) buy land in Gardena for floriculture | GI/Greatest (cont.) | Early years (cont.) | | |
| 1906 | Moneta Strawberry Growers Association organized in Gardena | | | | |
| 1906 | First sushi bar opens in Little Tokyo on Weller Street | | | | |
| 1907 | Gentlemen's Agreement restricts Japanese immigration in exchange for desegregating San Francisco schools | | Middle years | Early years | |
| 1908 | Ten Japanese students recorded attending University of Southern California; two at California Institute of Technology | | | | |
| 1910 | Rafu Judo Dojo established in Little Tokyo | | | | |
| 1912 | Southern California Flower Market founded | | | | |
| 1912 | Moneta Gakuen Japanese language school founded in Gardena | | | | |
| 1913 | California Alien Land Law prohibits ownership of land by "aliens ineligible for citizenship" | | | | |
| 1914 | Gardena Valley Baptist Church founded | | | | |
| 1917 | Tagami brothers build White Point Hot Spring Hotel resort in San Pedro | | | | |
| 1918 | Japanese Union Church founded in L.A. | | | | |
| 1918 | Fukui Mortuary founded in L.A. | | | | |
| 1918 | Southern California Japanese Fishermen's Association hall opens on Terminal Island | | | | |
| 1920 | Los Angeles Nippons semipro baseball club founded | | | | |
| 1922 | Cable Act promises citizenship to women regardless of marital status | | | | |
| 1922 | *Ozawa v. U.S.*—Supreme Court rules Japanese are not white | | | | |

| Year | J.A. Events* | American Generations | J.A. Generations | | |
|---|---|---|---|---|---|
| | | | Issei | Nisei/ Kibei | Sansei |
| 1924 | Immigration Exclusion Act ends immigration from Japan | GI/Greatest (cont.) | Middle years (cont.) | Early years (cont.) | |
| 1925 | Umeya sembei company founded in L.A. | | | | |
| 1929 | Japanese American Citizens League founded | Silent 1928–1945 | | | |
| 1929 | Japanese Hospital opens in Boyle Heights | | | | |
| 1930 | City of Gardena is incorporated | | | | |
| 1931 | *Kashu Mainichi* newspaper founded by Sei Fujii | | | | |
| 1932 | Tōyō Miyatake establishes photography studio in L.A. | | | | |
| 1934 | First Nisei Week festival held in Little Tokyo | | | | |
| 1937 | League of Southern California Japanese Gardeners forms | | | | |
| 1941 | Pearl Harbor bombed—U.S. enters WWII | | | | Early years |
| 1942 | Executive Order 9066 authorizes forced removal and incarceration of all Japanese Americans on the West Coast | | | | |
| 1945 | Hiroshima/Nagasaki atomic bombing; WWII ends | | | | |
| 1946 | Matoba family opens Atomic Cafe in Little Tokyo | Boomers 1946–1964 | Late years | Middle years | |
| 1946 | George Aratani launches international trade business, All Star Trading (Mikasa and Kenwood) | | | | |
| 1948 | Japanese American Evacuation Claims Act passed | | | | |
| 1948 | Sei Fujii purchases lot in Boyle Heights to test California Alien Land Law | | | | |
| 1950 | Grace Pastries Shoppe opens on Jefferson Boulevard in L.A. | | | | |
| 1951 | American occupation of Japan ends | | | | |

| Year | J.A. Events* | American Generations | J.A. Generations | | |
|---|---|---|---|---|---|
| | | | Issei | Nisei/ Kibei | Sansei |
| 1952 | McCarran-Walter Immigration and Nationality Act passed, formally ending Asian exclusion and removing race as a basis for citizenship | Boomers (cont.) | Late years (cont.) | Middle years (cont.) | Early years (cont.) |
| 1953 | U.S. Refugee Relief Act passed | | | | |
| 1953 | Kokusai Theatre opens on Crenshaw Boulevard in L.A. | | | | |
| 1955 | SK Uyeda Department Store reestablished in Little Tokyo | | | | |
| 1955 | Southern California Gardeners Federation founded | | | | |
| 1956 | Kaz Inouye opens Kashu Realty in L.A. | | | | |
| 1957 | John Okada's *No-No Boy* published by Charles E. Tuttle | | | | |
| 1957 | Miyoshi Umeki wins Academy Award for *Sayonara* | | | | |
| 1957 | Sessue Hayakawa is nominated for Academy Award for *Bridge on the River Kwai* | | | | |
| 1957 | John Aiso appointed to Los Angeles Superior Court | | | | |
| 1958 | Holiday Bowl founded on Crenshaw Boulevard in L.A. | | | | |
| 1958 | Pat Suzuki releases recording of "How High the Moon" | | | | |
| 1959 | James Shigeta stars in *The Crimson Kimono* | | | | |
| 1959 | South Bay Friends of Richard basketball club founded | | | | |
| 1960 | Nissan (Datsun) Motor Corporation U.S.A. subsidiary established in Gardena | | | | |
| 1961 | Keiro senior health services founded in L.A. | | | | |
| 1961 | Little Tokyo Community Redevelopment Advisory Committee forms | | | | |
| 1961 | *Flower Drum Song* musical is adapted for film | | | | |

| Year | J.A. Events* | American Generations | J.A. Generations | | |
|------|--------------|----------------------|------|------|------|
| | | | Issei | Nisei/ Kibei | Sansei |
| 1962 | Seibu Department Store opens on Wilshire Boulevard in L.A. | Boomers (cont.) | Late years (cont.) | Middle years (cont.) | Early years (cont.) |
| 1962 | Merit Savings and Loan founded in L.A. | | | | |
| 1963 | Fair Housing Act passed | | | | |
| 1963 | Japanese American Community Services–Asian Involvement (JACS-AI) established in Little Tokyo | | | | |
| 1964 | Paul Terasaki invents microcytotoxicity test at UCLA | | | | |
| 1965 | Immigration Act abolishes national origins quota system | Gen X 1965–1980 | | | |
| 1965 | East West Players founded in L.A. | | | | |
| 1965 | Watts Riots | | | | |
| 1966 | Term "model minority" first appears in the *New York Times Magazine,* by sociologist William Peterson | | | | |
| 1966 | George Takei cast in *Star Trek* | | | | |
| 1967 | Mako nominated for Academy Award for *The Sand Pebbles* | | | | |
| 1967 | Thomas Noguchi appointed chief medical coroner for L.A. County | | | | |
| 1967 | *Loving v. Virginia* strikes down all state laws banning interracial marriage | | | | |
| 1968 | Yuji Ichioka coins term "Asian American" | | | | |
| 1968 | Last of 4,978 J.A. renunciants restored to citizenship after two decades of litigation by Wayne M. Collins, attorney | | | | |
| 1969 | Harry Kitano publishes *Japanese Americans: An Evolution of a Subculture* | | | | |
| 1969 | Storefront, Third World activist collective, opens on Jefferson Boulevard in L.A. | | | | |
| 1969 | Yellow Brotherhood founded in West L.A. | | | | |

| Year | J.A. Events* | American Generations | J.A. Generations | | |
|------|-------------|----------------------|------|------|------|
| | | | Issei | Nisei/ Kibei | Sansei |
| 1969 | Asian American Studies Center established at UCLA | Gen X (cont.) | Late years (cont.) | Middle years (cont.) | Early years (cont.) |
| 1969 | *Gidra* newspaper founded | | | | |
| 1969 | First organized Manzanar Pilgrimage | | | | |
| 1970 | Visual Communications founded | | | | |
| 1970 | Tritia Toyota hired as radio reporter for KNX-AM | | | | |
| 1971 | *Roots: An Asian American Reader* published by UCLA Asian American Studies Center | | | | |
| 1971 | Amerasia Bookstore founded in Little Tokyo | | | | |
| 1972 | East Wind, Marxist-Leninist political collective, formed in L.A. | | | | |
| 1972 | Ken Nakaoka elected mayor of Gardena | | | | |
| 1973 | Paul Bannai elected to California State Assembly | | | | |
| 1973 | Jeanne Wakatsuki Houston publishes *Farewell to Manzanar* | | | | |
| 1973 | Little Tokyo People's Rights Organization founded | | | | |
| 1973 | *A Grain of Sand: Music of the Struggle of Asians in America* released | | | | |
| 1974 | Band Hiroshima forms | | | | |
| 1975 | Jack Soo (Goro Suzuki) cast in *Barney Miller* sitcom | | | | |
| 1975 | Wendy Yoshimura Fair Trial Committee established | | | | |
| 1976 | Westin Bonaventure hotel owned by Mitsubishi Trading and John C. Portman Associates opens | | | | |
| 1976 | S.I. Hayakawa, from California, elected to U.S. Senate | | | | |
| 1976 | Robert Takasugi nominated to serve as federal judge to Central District of California | | | | |

| Year | J.A. Events* | American Generations | J.A. Generations | | |
|---|---|---|---|---|---|
| | | | Issei | Nisei/Kibei | Sansei |
| 1977 | Iva Toguri d'Aquino pardoned by President Ford | Gen X (cont.) | Late years (cont.) | Middle years (cont.) | Early years (cont.) |
| 1977 | Wakako Yamauchi's play *And the Soul Shall Dance* awarded L.A. Drama Critics Circle Award for best new play | | | | |
| 1978 | Japanese Village Plaza built in Little Tokyo | | | | |
| 1980 | Commission on Wartime Relocation and Internment of Civilians formed, followed by public hearings | | | | Middle years |
| 1980 | Japanese American Cultural and Community Center building in Little Tokyo opens | | | | |
| 1980 | Duane Kubo and Bob Nakamura direct film *Hito Hata: Raise the Banner* | | | | |
| 1982 | Vincent Chin killed after being mistakenly identified as Japanese in Detroit | Millennials 1981–1996 | | | |
| 1983 | Coram Nobis cases: Gordon Hirabayashi, Fred Korematsu, Minoru Yasui | | | | |
| 1984 | Pat Morita stars in *Karate Kid* | | | | |
| 1988 | Civil Liberties Act HR 442 signed | | | Late years | |
| 1989 | Richard Sakai is one of original producers for *The Simpsons* | | | | |
| 1990 | Redress apologies and payments begin | | | | |
| 1991 | Steven Okazaki wins Academy Award for documentary film *Days of Waiting: The Life & Art of Estelle Ishigo* | | | | |
| 1991 | Hisaye Yamamoto's short stories adapted as *Hot Summer Winds* for PBS American Playhouse | | | | |
| 1992 | Japanese American National Museum opens in historic site of Nishi Hongwanji Buddhist Temple in Little Tokyo | | | | |
| 1992 | Los Angeles riots | | | | |
| 1994 | Mikawaya confectionery shop creates mochi ice cream | | | | |

| Year | J.A. Events* | American Generations | J.A. Generations | | |
| --- | --- | --- | --- | --- | --- |
| | | | Issei | Nisei/Kibei | Sansei |
| 1995 | Judge Lance Ito presides over O. J. Simpson trial | Millennials (cont.) | | Late years (cont.) | Middle years (cont.) |
| 1999 | Tuesday Night Café mic series lauched in Little Tokyo | Gen Z 1997–2009 | | | |
| 2001 | September 11 | | | | |
| 2005 | Cynthia Kadohata's *Kira-Kira* wins Newberry Award | | | | |
| 2007 | Naomi Hirahara's *Snakeskin Shamisen* wins Edgar Award | | | | |
| 2008 | Warren Furutani elected to California State Assembly | | | | |
| 2010 | Karen Tei Yamashita's *I Hotel* becomes National Book Award finalist | Gen Alpha 2010– | | | |
| 2011 | Julie Otsuka's *The Buddha in the Attic* becomes National Book Award finalist | | | | Late years |
| 2013 | Kevin Tsujihara becomes CEO of Warner Bros. Entertainment | | | | |
| 2014 | Hello Kitty exhibit debuts at Japanese American National Museum | | | | |
| 2015 | Vigilant Love formed to combat Islamaphobia | | | | |
| 2019 | Supreme Court overturns *Korematsu v. U.S.*, but upholds Muslim travel ban | | | | |
| 2019 | Tsuru for Solidarity successfully protests use of Fort Sill to detain migrant children | | | | |

# II. Sensibility

## Author's Note

The following stories were published posthumorously and are dedicated to my sister, who, due to her powers of projection, thankfully destroyed all our correspondence prior to my despondence, making conjectures about our personal lives impossible. What we did and said is none of your business. That said, the fictional lives of the characters exposed here represent the minutiae of sansei life as it once existed in a small provincial island in an armpit of postwar sunshine.

Respectfully,
J.A.

# Shikataganai & Mottainai

Mukashi, mukashi, as they used to say in our little world of teahouses and dainty gardens of pine bonsai and azalea, dappled in puffy mounds of lime-green dichondra, lacquered bridges expanding serene ponds of fat polka-dot koi resting in the shadows of water lilies, leaning red maple and purple wisteria, the click-clack of bamboo on rock. The clatter of geta over wood and the swishing of silk were the happy undertones of the chatter of the two young sansei sisters who appeared on the bridge to scatter round pellets of koi food from a small handwoven basket. A flutter of banana-yellow butterflies seemed to swirl from their bright kimono and scatter over the pond, when suddenly a gigantic white koi broke the surface, its large albino lips and gullet open and flaring, and handily gulped down the largest of the butterflies, though perhaps only the impudent size of a baby canary. The sisters watched the delicate wings fold and crush and the koi's pink eye blink and disappear.

"Oh!" said Marianne, the younger of the two Dashimori sisters. "You've seen for yourself. He's done it again!" She pouted and banged her geta into the bridge, the sudden noise sending the koi below to scatter. "I'm telling John tonight to catch that old monster and serve him for sashimi."

"I'm not eating that. Besides, Moby Dick is Harry's favorite. FanFan will never allow it."

But let us pause to explain this early example of sansei life, an idyll of small-town Japanese Americana ensconced and undisturbed in suburban sunshine. Dr. John Dashimori Senior had opened his optometry practice as soon as he could return to the West Coast in the postwar and, being the only optometrist in a town of Japanese Americans all genetically disposed to myopia, had quickly become prominent and prosperous. His son, John Junior, conveniently followed his father professionally, and eventually inherited the business. Early on, the first Mrs. Dashimori died, and in time Dr. John Senior married his secretary, added two daughters to his brood, and gradually left the clinic to his son, retiring to cultivate an expansive backyard Japanese garden with a teahouse attached to a seven-bedroom, five-bathroom ranch house with a pool, a dojo, and lots of sliding glass doors.

About the time of this opening scene, the second Mrs. Dashimori was still mourning the death of Dr. John Senior, who was discovered collapsed with his arms flung over the abundant garnet clusters of a massive rhododendron bush. And Dr. John Junior was in the kitchen nursing a Scotch, watching his kid, Harry, build a Tinkertoy castle, and listening to his wife, FanFan, discuss how it was time for him to ask her stepmother-in-law and those two half sisters to find their own place to live.

"But," said Dr. John Junior, "I promised my dad."

"Promised?"

"O.K., it was a conversation. About, you know, being head of the family. He wasn't about talking much. It musta meant something."

"Something maybe, but no promises were in his will." FanFan studied her pink nails and continued, "It's your business that makes their way of life even possible."

"Elinor and Marianne take turns at the desk. They're good with the patients."

"They don't need to stop working. They just need to be," FanFan paused, trying to find the right words and puckering the gloss over her lips, "more independent."

Dr. John Junior took another swig of Scotch, watched the ice clunk and reposition in the amber glass, and changed the subject. "Did my shipment arrive?"

"I had them put it in the garage." FanFan waved.

Dr. John Junior made a quick escape. In the safety of the garage, he pried open a large wooden crate and carefully pulled back the shredded paper to reveal a complete set of nineteenth-century samurai armor. He set the helmet to one side and pulled out the cuirass and the rest of the protective gear, as well as the shoulder pads and leggings, smelling and fondling the pieces and spreading them on a large blanket like a puzzle. All day he went back and forth from the garage to the teahouse, carting the armor, polishing and dusting, and arranging each piece on a lacquer armature. When the thing was complete, he went to find his son, Harry, who was tooling around on a tricycle. He had to pry the kid away from his playacting by promising a special treat, and even then, Harry dragged his sneakers unwillingly.

"See?" announced Dr. John Junior, pointing proudly at the seated warrior wearing a horrific grimacing mask, tall horns rising from its helmet.

Harry took one look and ran away, screaming hysterically.

Along the dirt path came FanFan's younger brother, Eddie, with a friend. Harry tore by, stubbing his toe against an exposed tree root, and, tossed into flight, was caught by Eddie's friend, who fell backward with the boy in his arms. Harry grappled with the young man, punching him as if fighting an imaginary enemy, both yelling, "Hey buddy! Hey buddy!"

Eddie bent over and pulled Harry's flailing body away. "Harry! What the hell?"

By this time, Dr. John Junior and FanFan had both arrived, converging at the bridge. FanFan gave her husband the look and took Harry by the hand, escorting her crying child away to the house.

Eddie shrugged and pointed in the direction of FanFan. "That was my sister." He looked at Dr. John Junior, who was pulling up the fallen man. "Willie, this is my brother-in-law."

"Dr. John," said Willie, rising and brushing off small pebbles and leaves. "Pleasure."

After this, Eddie and Willie were at the Dashimoris' every day in the afternoon, hanging out at the pool with Sapporo beers, in happi coats and hachimaki. FanFan would appear with bowls of sembei, plates of makizushi, or skewered chicken teriyaki. Initially, the guys were there to wait for and watch the two Dashimori sisters emerge from the glass doors and slip out of their kimono; Elinor, in dark shades and with a large bottle of Coppertone, would slather and sun herself and retreat into a book, and Marianne would dive into the blue waters without a splash and move across the pool like a sleek seal. As the days lingered on, there were pool games, pinball, miniature golf, and card games. Or the sisters would amuse themselves by attending a kendo or judo match in the dojo. Even though the guys spent a great deal of time working these matches into complicated performances, the sisters pretended to be impressed by the display of faux calisthenics. Elinor wondered to Marianne when they were going to start breaking two-by-fours and bricks. "Don't you dare suggest it," Marianne worried. "Willie has such beautiful hands."

In the background, Mrs. John Senior came and went in her diesel-fueled gold Mercedes to her widows'-club activities. The widows' club had helped her tremendously, she said, to transition to a new life. And weekly, Baba-sensei arrived at the house to give Mrs. John Senior lessons in flower arrangement. She and Baba-sensei could be seen walking around the garden, making comments about or taking cuttings of flowers and plants, and eventually spending an hour in the teahouse arranging a stylized presentation. These arrangements were taken over to the optometry office and remade to grace the ocular frames in the street side window, or posed elegantly at the reception desk. Dr. John Junior said nothing, but FanFan reported that one receptionist was allergic to flowers, and clients couldn't see the receptionist through what she called "all the bushes."

One day, FanFan brought home two young women: Lucy, a Eurasian brunette, and Sophia, a strawberry blond, acquaintances who were traveling from far away, over there in the valley. FanFan introduced them to the household as if they were foreign-exchange students, which perhaps they were, but Dr. John Junior thought she must have some other plans in mind. Something about if a household were crowded, make it more crowded, then see if that wouldn't make her stepmother-in-law and her daughters move out.

"You know, John," said FanFan, "I see there's a cute house for sale on Catalina, that quiet little cul-de-sac near the high school. It would be perfect."

Dr. John Junior was carting another acquisition out to the teahouse, this time a samurai sword in a handsome scabbard. He would add it to his growing collection. "Right." He nodded. "I'll look into it."

Eventually, with the daily visitations of Eddie and Willie, FanFan hosted a lively crowd of six teenagers, and the girls seemed to get along splendidly, eventually all camping out in the same room, watching *The Twilight Zone* in the dark and destroying pillows in the requisite fights of fluff. Lucy said, "Oh Elinor, it's so darling that you eat rice with chopsticks and wear kimono." And pretty soon, she and Sophia were traipsing around in zori and kimono too. And the guys were also traipsing after.

Marianne said to Elinor, "I have a funny feeling, Ellie. Willie has been acting strange. He won't neck with me in the car anymore."

"Ewww."

But one day Lucy put her arms around Elinor as they walked to a bamboo seat near the koi pond. "I have a secret I want to tell you," she confided. "You can't tell anyone."

Elinor blinked.

"It's about me and Eddie. We met at Christian camp two years ago and pledged ourselves to each other under a rugged cross just behind the campfire. It was so meaningful and romantic. That's why I'm here."

"What?" Elinor's throat constricted, and her heart fell into her stomach.

"You're going to be, like, like, my sister," Lucy exclaimed. "I'm so happy."

Elinor lifted the edges of her lips with difficulty, a bad attempt at a smile, then hesitated. "Is there a similar arrangement with Willie and Sophia?"

"Oh no, but Sophia has got Willie to teach her judo. Haven't you noticed? It's a contact sport."

"Right."

Lucy chattered on, "I'm going to tell FanFan because I think she likes me even though I'm hapa. Eddie's afraid, but with FanFan on our side . . . What do you think?"

"FanFan?" Elinor said nothing more, and when, the next morning, she heard screaming from the kitchen, she figured Lucy had tested her false assumptions on FanFan.

Elinor shook herself from sleep and wandered to the front door to see FanFan chasing after Lucy's convertible red Mustang and aiming a teacup at the taillights. Bingo, a hit. The last thing she could see was Sophia trying to yank her yellow hair from the hastily shut car door, her screeches bouncing off the shiny metal of the chrome bumper, like a tin can tied to a wedding car. Of course, thought Elinor, FanFan wasn't racist or anything, of course not.

That afternoon, Eddie came storming in to see FanFan. They yelled at each other for about twenty minutes. Meanwhile, Marianne ran out and stood outside the passenger side of Eddie's blue Datsun with her fingers straining blue and close to bleeding against the edge of the window, which Willie had tried to roll up. Elinor could see Marianne peering through the window slit and tearfully imploring Willie, who stared stoically forward, tapping his foot and drumming his fingers on the dash. "Come on, Eddie," Willie mumbled impatiently.

"What did you say?" Marianne choked.

"About what?" he croaked back.

"About us."

"What about us?" Willie tried to sound quizzical.

Marianne screamed and ran past Elinor into the house as Eddie came storming out. He paused next to Elinor. "Sorry, Ellie, it wasn't going to work out."

"What do you mean?" she asked placidly but not without pain.

"Well, you're just too smart. Smarter than me. When I got an A-, you'd get an A. If I finally got an A, you'd get an A+. It just wasn't going to work out, you know what I mean?" And he strode in mock confidence toward the blue Datsun, gunned the motor, and the guys were gone.

FanFan ran to find and wail at her husband. She found Dr. John Junior in the teahouse dressed in the full regalia of his samurai warrior getup and her son, Harry, in a mini version of the same armor. As she sprang onto the tatami mats, she found them sparring off with their swords. "Are you crazy?" she yelled.

"Mommy," Harry yelled through his mask, "we're samurai!"

Distracted, Dr. John Junior turned clumsily toward her while Harry plunged his sword into an opening in the armor near his thigh. "Call an ambulance!" the doctor cried.

For the next three days, Marianne shut herself in her room with the curtains drawn. Elinor came in regularly with a tray of food, which reappeared variously untouched or half-eaten in the hallway, as if they were running a hotel or something. On the fourth day, Elinor went into the room, flung open the curtains, and pulled wide the glass doors. All the soggy air in the room gushed out, and Marianne sat up with bloodshot eyes. "It's over," Elinor said. "Get over it. And by the way," she stood outside the sliding door and looked out at the guy cleaning the pool, "John's o.k. Cut through an artery and lost a lot of blood, but he's home now." As if to prove it, Dr. John Junior hobbled by on crutches. Elinor walked back in and handed Marianne a postcard. "It's from Mom. She left."

Marianne shuffled into the kitchen and rummaged in the freezer. FanFan was at the kitchen table leafing page by page through *Life* magazine and pretending to be oblivious. Marianne found a box of ice cream and scooped out two scoops into a glass bowl. FanFan looked up and said, "Someone is at the door. Can you get it?"

Marianne appeared at the door, disheveled and with the bowl of ice cream, and recognized Baba-sensei, who had a bucket of chrysanthemums and a basket of clipping tools, spiky pin frogs, and other flower-arranging accoutrements. She handed Baba-sensei the postcard from her mother. He turned it over and looked at the photograph of Caesars Palace in Las Vegas.

> *Girls:*
>
> *You won't believe it, but Ich and I were married. We won't be back for a while. Going to the Grand Canyon for our honeymoon. Don't worry.*
>
> *Love, Mom*

"Well," said Baba-sensei, "maybe nisei can learn to be spontaneous. Couldn't hurt."

"Do you want some ice cream?" she asked, spooning the melting stuff into her mouth.

"Sure."

Baba-sensei picked up his stuff and followed her. They sat with their feet dangling over the side of the teahouse ledge, eating ice cream. "Mint chocolate chip. My favorite," she said, pushing her finger into the bowl to scrape the green cream clean and licking it with satisfaction.

"Mine too. Have you been to 31 Flavors?"

Marianne shook her head. Glancing at Baba-sensei's bowl, she asked, "Are you going to finish that?"

Elinor carted a plastic lounge chair from the swimming pool to a shady place near the koi pond. She could see Baba-sensei directing Marianne's hands to correct the placement of each chrysanthemum. She settled into the lounge chair with a pocket book, something by an English writer named Ian Fleming. She'd just finished *Doctor No*, about some evil Fu Manchu character on a Caribbean island. She cracked open this new book, *You Only Live Twice*. James Bond was British, a secret agent, and a real man.

But before she could slip into Fleming's first sentence, Elinor was distracted by a tiny frog leaping. She waited for it to plunk into the water, but instead Moby Dick rose to the surface, snatching the green thing into its pugnacious jaws and plunging into the dark, murky reaches of the old pond, effortlessly, silently, the slightest ripple hardly evidence.

# Giri & Gaman

The truth of the matter is that despite what you may think, sansei do have a sense of humor. O.K., let's not be grandiose about it, but we always see you in groups laughing about something. What are you laughing about? What *is* there to laugh about? As for nisei, they do have a sense of humor; they just never laugh. It's hard to test this theory because most nisei these days are well over eighty, and after eighty, 1. You've pretty much heard all the jokes; 2. You can't hear, or you hear what you want to hear; 3. Dementia screws with the funny bone; 4. If you laugh, you'll pee; and 5. Nothing is funny. But, would you laugh if you found out life was some kind of endurance test for which you sacrificed yourself to an abstract idea of duty? And what if that abstract idea was based on the nostalgic idea about your people being samurai? Truth is that maybe that blood theory would account for one real drop; the rest of you are lousy peasantry or third-class merchants. That's right, you've all been lying, because once you escaped from debt, drudgery, poverty, and the laws of primogeniture by crossing the Pacific, you too could become a born-again samurai. But let's face it, all sansei have one drop; it could be one fake drop, but all we have to do is give you swords and hachimaki and watch the transformation. But enough pontificating. Back to storytelling.

Mukashi, mukashi, it was said that Darcy Kabuto II (the second) was God's gift to sansei women. The thing about gifts from God is they're complicated, because you've got to wonder if you deserve them, and anyway, what's the catch? Well exactly: Darcy was the catch. To be simplistic, Darcy was the captain of the football team, class vice president, and voted best looking, which meant he looked like he was the son of Toshiro Mifune. To complicate matters, Darcy's best friend, Benji Lee, walked to school in zori and a Mao jacket and looked like and pretended to be Bruce Lee.

When young men of this caliber present themselves to the aching hormones of sansei girls, you'd think there'd be some commotion, but for the most part, no one seemed bothered. After all, this was a suburb gerrymandered by nisei real estate brokers turned politicians; it was, well, let's say, postcamp, a safe place where sansei had the opportunity to grow up in camp without being in camp. Darcy and Benji were, though not a dime a dozen, nothing special. Benji was an accommodating kid who excelled in gymnastics since there was no kung fu team in those days. Other than pretending to be Bruce and excelling in gymnastics, he was mostly interested in getting straight As. And Darcy was so perfect, he was just plain boring.

The only women who were smitten by Darcy Kabuto and Benji Lee were the principal of the school, Miss Catherine Borg, and the president of the PTA, Mrs. Benihana. To be clear, neither of these older women had any romantic interest in the young men; their interests, however, were still selfish. In her other secret life, Miss Borg, writing under the pseudonym C. Borg, was a YA author doing what she thought was undercover research. The school library had a complete set of the C. Borg series, though no volumes were ever checked out. Mr. Collins, the school librarian, occasionally stamped the books with random dates in case Miss Borg came in to check, and no one was the wiser. As for Mrs. Benihana, she was the mother of five teenage daughters, and she remembered how much fun she had in camp at dances, and when, in her day, had there ever been such cute beaus? If she were blessed with five daughters, then she would live their youth vicariously. A second youth outside the barbed wire! Mrs. Benihana touched her hand to her heart and sighed. More importantly, no one in this new generation, Mrs. Benihana had said enthusiastically to her husband, would have to suffer the nisei consequences of sacrifice and spinsterhood, absolutely not.

The newest and most anticipated book by C. Borg was going to be set in Japan. Miss Borg was amazed that after all these years she had not thought of this. Not that she had ever traveled to Japan or anywhere in the Orient. She'd been right here in this little city dotted with gardens trimmed to perfection by dozens of Japanese gardeners, ensconced within its Japanese language school; its cultural center, complete with flower arranging, go, origami, and abacus clubs; its noodle restaurants; and its temple with summer festivals. And to complete the wonder of it all, most of her students were Japanese Americans. She had been the principal of a petri dish begging to be examined. At lunch, Miss Borg excitedly discussed her ideas with Mr. Collins, who was the only other person who knew anything about her other identity.

"Mr. Collins," announced Miss Borg, "there's no time to lose." She paused, dunking her tea bag in and out of the cup, and eyed the librarian conspiratorially. "I could use some assistance."

"Catherine," Mr. Collins put down his bologna sandwich and addressed Miss Borg with haughty affection, "I am always at your service."

"It may involve some, shall we say, research. I want this to be authentic, you see. The challenge is the setting. Don't you see? Recasting the story in Japan."

"Catherine, with great deference for your art, but you've been using these kids as fodder for your books for years. Whatever do you mean?"

"Oh, I'm tired of writing about American children."

"So now you will write about Japanese American children?"

"Of course not." Miss Borg blew the surface of her tea. "Who would read such books?"

From that moment, Miss Borg and Mr. Collins moved into high-gear research, diving into the library resources to sniff out Japan as backdrop. "Oh Mr. Collins, look at this charming garden." Miss Borg pointed to the wisteria hanging in ponderously plump, luscious clusters over a path of rocks pressed into dappled green moss. "It's settled, this is where they meet!" And meanwhile Mr. Collins completed the scene with living characters in what he called, with a titillating flutter of intrigue and danger, human espionage. Mostly this meant Mr. Collins snuck around the school with a notepad surreptitiously recording teenage conversations.

"Catherine," he exclaimed, handing over his notes carefully concealed in an envelope marked CONFIDENTIAL: GARDEN SCENE, as if it were a *Mission Impossible* dossier, "I never knew what fun this could be!"

"Now," said Miss Borg, "that sister of Benji Lee. What was her name?"

"Caroline, I believe."

"That's right. She's the prettiest of that in-crowd clique of bubble-headed girls. She and that Kabuto boy," continued Miss Borg, "would make a lovely couple, don't you think? It must be already evident to them. After all, the brother and he are best friends."

"Catherine, how perceptive you are. But you do know the Lees are Chinese, the parents in the restaurant business. An anomaly in the community; that is to say, they are not Japanese."

"Oh, Chinese, Japanese, who can tell the difference?" Miss Borg waved her hand and turned the pages of Heian prints of the *Genji Monogatari*. "Now what we need is a dance. The prom would be perfect, and Caroline would be chosen queen, of course."

"And Darcy Kabuto her escort," Mr. Collins surmised. He was getting the hang of this stuff.

"Well," she looked at Mr. Collins, "what are you waiting for?"

"For you to write the scene?"

Miss Borg sighed. "Mr. Collins, we are building conflict. The scene will write itself."

Mr. Collins went off, presumably to stuff the prom queen ballot box, and Miss Borg met with Mrs. Benihana about the matter of the PTA funding a live band for the prom. Miss Borg put it to Mrs. Benihana directly: "How many cake sales would it take?"

Mrs. Benihana's thoughts stumbled back to big-band jazz in camp, Glenn Miller and Tommy Dorsey re-creations, and how she could cut a rug in the day.

Miss Borg stared at Mrs. Benihana, who listened to some memory and sat with a faraway internment look, an odd expression of confined freedom and pathos. "Mrs. Benihana?" Miss Borg prompted her from reverie. "The students have chosen a band from Los Angeles, and we are way over here in the boonies." She waved her arms indicating freeway distance, then continued as if Mrs. Benihana had protested. "Yes, I know, but they say this band is very popular. I know nothing of these things, but I'm always for the students. It would be a shame to disappoint them. Otherwise, it will be LP records on the PA system as usual."

Mrs. Benihana jostled herself from the past and said, "Yes, a shame to disappoint. However, PTA funds are usually for activities of academic substance." She used Miss Borg's own key words.

"Or," Miss Borg inserted, "activities that enhance access to opportunities outside of the students' reach."

Mrs. Benihana went home, immediately made a dozen calls, and went into PTA baking action. She was in a high state of happy anxiety thinking of her daughters. Miss Borg's suggestion that her girls had been denied access to opportunities beyond their reach resonated within her psyche. The bake sale might be a deciding factor in their young teenage lives. Though she would never ever say so publicly, of all the sansei born in those years, certainly her girls were the most deserving. There was the oldest, a senior named Janey, the sweetest and kindest; next Lizzy, also a senior, having skipped a grade, therefore studious and the smartest; and then there were the three cheerleaders: Mary, Kitty, and Liddy. She called the last three her "chirpies," and they came in and out of the kitchen to lick the chocolate frosting from the spoons, whips, and bowls and to do cheer routines while Mrs. Benihana tossed sprinkles on cupcakes and wrapped giant chocolate chip cookies in saran wrap.

Mr. Benihana came up from his basement workshop smelling the air. His protective goggles were pushed up on his forehead.

"Mr. Benihana," Mrs. Benihana exclaimed, pointing to his dusty goggles. "That porcelain dust must remain outside my kitchen. We can't poison our buyers."

"Why not?" Mr. Benihana grabbed a cookie and began to return downstairs.

His wife relented. "Oh, now that you're here, why don't you enjoy a cup of coffee with me and a piece of cake." She pointed to a lopsided lump on a plate. "The chirpies were jumping around. That one plopped, but the ingredients are the same."

"Later." He continued away. "I want to finish."

Mrs. Benihana thought he meant finish a bridge or a set of false teeth, which was after all how he paid their bills. But while he polished, he'd been listening to audiotape number three of a Harvard lecture series on American philosophy, and he was puzzling over transcendentalism. Mr. Benihana worked and mostly lived in his basement, with false teeth in various stages of repair and creation, contemplating the ethics of knowing. Drafted out of camp, the army utilized his artistic skills in the fine crafting of prosthetic replicas of teeth; soldiers needed teeth to fight. Given other opportunities, he'd have been a sculptor or a philosopher. Given five daughters to raise, he was resigned to being both, sort of.

About the same time Mr. Benihana pressed the Play key on his tape recorder, Mr. Collins had checked out a similar Sony model from the projection equipment room. He slipped a blank tape into the receiving caddy. "Testing, testing?" After this, the Sony was left strategically under desks, in bathroom and shower stalls, in empty lockers, under lunch tables and athletic benches, and in cozy spots under stairwells and known kissing cubbies. Much of it was useless drivel and noise—banging of metal lockers, thumping of books, munching and peeing, and some bits of moaning and smooching, but he faithfully transcribed everything and handed it regularly to Miss Borg in the manila envelope marked CONFIDENTIAL. However, as his investigations intensified, he discovered the shocking truth: these children were doing everything he thought had been fictionalized in the C. Borg YA books. He felt it his duty to warn Principal Borg.

"Catherine, I should bring it to your attention that after lunch, Caroline Lee and her cohort secretly smoke in Bathroom B."

Miss Borg was nonplussed. "Mr. Collins, is that the best you can do?"

Mr. Collins's shoulders sagged, as these were well-behaved Japanese Americans as featured in *Time* magazine, still corralled in a cultural bubble that C. Borg meant to appropriate before the onslaught of pot, reds, LSD, sex, and rock 'n' roll.

Mrs. Benihana smiled to see the handsome Darcy Kabuto and his Chinese friend Benji Lee approaching the PTA cake sales table outside of Meiji Market. It was the extroverted Benji who sauntered over in his flip-flops and greeted her. "Hi, Mrs. Benihana. How are sales going? Let me make a contribution." He pulled out a dollar and bought some peanut butter cookies, handing one to Darcy, who only nodded. Benji munched on the cookie as if it were some kind of ambrosia. "Mrs. Benihana, can we be of assistance?"

Darcy looked puzzled.

Mrs. Benihana was quick to pounce on this opportunity. "Oh yes, yes. I have to pack all this up and bring it back to the house. Can you?" She pouted with a needy look. "I could use your muscle."

"I bet you could use Darcy's pickup," said Benji.

Darcy shrugged his marvelous shoulders and strutted over to his parked Toyota, a polished black deal with big tires. And that was how Darcy and Benji got into the Benihana household, straight through the front door.

Mrs. Benihana sat them down for more cookies and Cokes, and the chirpies greeted them in their cheerleading outfits, bouncing around and running away to giggle. Benji looked delighted and elbowed Darcy, who only drank his Coke and stared at a wall covered by large framed photographs of the five Benihana daughters, all lined up in matching dresses in yearly portraits.

Moments later, Janey and Lizzy ran through the door, Janey with the car keys and Lizzy complaining, "Mom, where were you? We went to pick you up, and the table was completely gone!"

Mrs. Benihana smiled. "Oh, I had some help," she said, and she nodded at the boys, seated with their cookies and Cokes. "Do sit down, will you? We have guests."

Benji waved. "Hi."

Lizzy pouted at the two guys and went to the fridge, pretending to look for something, but Janey smiled and said, "That's a relief."

By then, Mr. Benihana had made his reappearance and decided to find out why there were young men in his house, which might be an interesting change (that is, the company of men).

Benji reached over and shook Mr. Benihana's hand firmly. Darcy followed his example. Benji, who worked at his father's restaurants, was all about customer satisfaction. "It's a pleasure to meet you, Mr. Benihana," he said warmly.

"Catherine," Mr. Collins cleared his throat to make his report, "it seems the Benihana girl and Benji Lee are a thing, shall we say."

"That reminds me, I should call Mrs. Benihana and see how much money she's raised." She turned from her typewriter and asked with exasperation, "Which girl? There are five of them."

"The oldest. The angel, Janey."

"And how is the Darcy–Caroline alliance proceeding?"

"Well, not at all. It seems he just follows Benji around and hangs out at the Benihana house every afternoon." Mr. Collins scratched the back of his neck. "When do they do homework?"

"Oh, this will never do." She ripped the page from her typewriter and tore it angrily into little pieces.

Mr. Collins crept away from this unseemly display of author hysteria, and taking advantage of fourth period, snuck over to the lunch benches in the senior court and duct-taped his Sony to the bottom of a bench.

After a while, it had become routine for Benji and Darcy to sit at that bench and wait for the Benihana sisters to walk by with their paper lunch bags and thermoses. "BLT today," smiled Janey, sitting between the guys and offering half to Benji. Lizzy stood in front of Darcy, who didn't move or say anything. He wasn't getting half a BLT anyway. Lizzy tugged a crisp piece of bacon from her sandwich, stood and munched, and said to no one in particular, "*Oedipus Rex*. Did you finish?"

Janey turned to Darcy, who actually nodded. Janey's lips turned up in subtle pathos, and she handed him a cookie.

"Thanks," he said.

Benji's sister, Caroline, rambled by with her chatty companions, all claiming no doubt the tallest ratted hair in the entire school, eyeing Janey and ignoring Lizzy while making eye-rolling movements, most of which were impossible because their lids were actually taped open. Caroline walked over, said hi to Benji, and conspicuously handed Darcy a folded note.

Darcy took the note, shoved it into his pocket, and said nothing as Caroline and her crew gaggled on.

Benji finished the BLT in five bites, then got up and grabbed Janey's hand. "Let's get in the ice cream line while it's short."

Lizzy sat in the now-empty part of the bench, but, trying to keep her distance from Darcy, her hand toppled Janey's thermos. Darcy jumped to avoid the spilling juice and followed the tumbling thing as it rolled under the bench. "Hey," he said in a monotone. "What's this?"

Lizzy crouched to look at what seemed to be a package taped beneath the bench. "Maybe it's a bomb," she said with a smirk.

Darcy pulled the tape away. "It's recording," he observed. He replayed their conversation, which amounted to "What's this?" and "Maybe it's a bomb."

Lizzy commanded, "Erase that and put it back."

Darcy and Lizzy hung around after the bell, hiding around a blind corner, and watched Mr. Collins pretend to walk nonchalantly to the bench and rip away the Sony.

About a week later, Mr. Collins handed his usual confidential dossier to Miss Borg, suggesting she should listen first to the tape itself. "Mr. Collins, what on earth? What language are they speaking?"

"Japanese."

"Oh, they don't speak Japanese. Not even their parents. Preposterous."

"Haven't they all gone to Japanese school? I've been going myself in the evenings at the cultural center." Mr. Collins pulled out a dictionary and announced with great pleasure, "It took some study, but I've managed to translate everything."

Miss Borg read the translated transcript:

*Darcy: I swear by the moon.*

*Lizzy: Don't swear by the moon. It's always changing.*

*Darcy: What should I swear by?*

*Lizzy: Don't swear. Everything is happening too fast. We need to slow this
down to see if it's real. Good-night.*

*Darcy: Are you going to leave me so unsatisfied?*

*Lizzy: Just what sort of satisfaction do you need?*

*Darcy: Your promise that you'll be my girlfriend.*

*Lizzy: But that's a given. I already promised you, but now that I think
about it, I'm going to take my promise away.*

*Darcy: What? Why take it away?*

*Lizzy: To promise you again and again. My love is deep and boundless as
the sea. Oh I'd better go now. Bye.*

Mr. Collins smiled and exclaimed, "Sweet isn't it? The part about the
moon, can't you use it?" Mr. Collins paused to reflect. "Odd how that
Darcy kid even speaks Japanese in a monotone."

Miss Borg shook her head. "Mr. Collins, I think you've been had."

The prom came and went, but these were the highlights: Janey Benihana
was voted prom queen. Mrs. Benihana, who volunteered to be a chaper-
one for the event, was absolutely thrilled and wept through the entire
crowning, the sash thing, the bouquet of a dozen red roses thing, and the
first dance. Miss Borg looked quizzically at Mr. Collins, who shrugged.
Maybe he had been the only one to vote numerous times for Caroline Lee.
Caroline didn't seem to care; she had the biggest hair in the ballroom,
and the lead singer of the L.A. band the PersuAsians jumped from the
stage and danced with her most of the night. Miss Borg was pleased anyway with the live band, her slyly orchestrated invasion of urban sophistication into this world of suburban provincialism. These band boys were
obviously a bad lot, with their slicked-back hair, black leather, and shiny
pointed shoes. Between sets they were guzzling something from unla-
beled bottles and smoking pot in the parking lot. The three backup croon-
ers charmed the crowd with their timed routines—turns, hip swivels,
and jumps—and Miss Borg noted that Mrs. Benihana's chirpies were
right there in perfect coordination. Eventually, one of the chirpies, Liddy,
would venture to L.A. and hook up with one of the backup singers, a kid
named George Wakama. From there, Liddy went rogue, so to speak, disappeared into an underground collective and did all the usual stuff like
sex, drugs, and radical politics. Mrs. Benihana would weep to her husband, "My youngest chirpie has gone off to be a hippy." Well, it was Miss

Borg's payback. She pressed a thick envelope into Mr. Collins's arms and said, "It's done. Intrigue. Tribal conflict. Cliques. Adolescent rage. Hormonal experimentation. But," she shook a pointed finger, "stylistically oriental."

Mr. Collins bowed. "Catherine, I'm sure it's a masterpiece."

On the night of the prom, Mr. Benihana came up from his basement to find his wife and daughters in a titter of pastel chiffon and satin, nylons, pointed heels, hair spray. He greeted each of the young men, all awkward in stiff suits and ties, who came to take his daughters away, but only Benji Lee offered to shake his hand with that firm grip of his. When everyone seemed to have disappeared and left the house in peaceful calm, Mr. Benihana saw Lizzy on the sofa with a book. "What are you doing here? What about that Darcy kid whose dad is always talking about serving in the 442nd?"

"He took his sister to the prom."

"Oh yeah?" Mr. Benihana seemed to think about this but said nothing. "Let's go to a movie," he offered. "I heard about it on the radio. *The Graduate*. Sounds real," he added, looking at the tossed book on the sofa. "Forget Salinger."

# Monterey Park

Mukashi, mukashi, Mario Wada, with a diploma from Cal State L.A. in business and culinary skills learned on a summer cruise ship, met, on that same ship, the vivacious and very prosperous Tammy Wuya and fell impossibly in love. The impossibility of their love had to do with Tammy's requirements for partnership, which were defined by what she called her triple whammy, something she tested on Mario with, well, success. Did he have a superiority complex? Check. And yet, did he feel insecure about his assumed superiority? Check. And three, could he control his emotional and physical impulses (that is, to have sex with her)? Check. He was the very model for ethnic American success. And he was also very handsome, tall, muscular with his shirt on or off, and an excellent chef and sommelier. By the end of the cruise, the two were married and very soon after had nested into an expansive, fully furnished in feng shui hillside house in Monterey Park. Although the nomenclature didn't exist at the time, Mario Wada settled quite comfortably into his role as a trophy husband for the rest of his life. In time, Mario sired with Tammy four children: Tommy, Eddy, Mariko, and Julia. When Mario's sister Francie, abandoned by her Caucasian husband, found herself suddenly a single parent with two children, Mario offered to house the younger child, a shy little girl of ten years, until Francie could find a job and stable living. To add a fifth child to the existing four, in addition to a half-dozen Chinese pugs, seemed of no consequence to anyone except the shy ten-year-old newcomer, Fanny Rice.

Mario ran his kitchen like a cruise ship diner, offering anything on the menu from grilled cheese to ceviche. When not in the kitchen or tending to his pugs, he shuttled his kids around in a vw van, depositing and retrieving them at various private schools, but more importantly, to endless activities scheduled by Tammy: tennis, violin, piano, fencing, ballet, equestrian training, landscape art, archery, language lessons, to name a few. No Wuya-Wada child was allowed to participate in what Tammy considered precivilized traditions like the gamelan, Filipino tinikling, ukulele, Peruvian panpipes, or congas. These folksy music traditions, she declared, might be mesmerizing but only because of their unstructured simplicity and repetitive nature, nothing close to the complexity of Debussy; it was the difference between a grass shack and Notre Dame. Similarly, arts and crafts like origami or pottery were sure to lead nowhere, although Tammy might've made concessions for tea ceremony or calligraphy; this stuff, however, was for old people, and therefore never came up. Furthermore, no Wuya-Wada child was allowed to participate in plebeian communal street sports like basketball, soccer, football, boxing, or even the national pastime, baseball. Kung fu was the singular exception; still, Tammy expected the attainment of black belt and the subtle ability to vanish. Each child was assigned a language in which to be fluent: French, German, Italian, and Russian, but everyone had to learn Chinese. Tammy considered Spanish a no-brainer since they lived in California on the border of Mexico; and besides, Mexicans spoke it. If this sounds shockingly elitist, it was, and Tammy made no bones about it. She justified her matriarchal position as the continuation of a long line of Chinese mothers. Chinese mother after Chinese mother had succeeded in molding the soft clay of their offspring into the best and brightest professionals of their generation, and now it was Tammy's turn. There would be no coddling, no Dr. Spock nurturing of the individual. It wasn't about self-esteem; once a child was good at something, self-esteem would follow. Her children, by the very fact that they were Chinese and Japanese, were superior to others, and in an unequal and historically racist world, they would surpass all expectations. Of course, they would have to work at it, succeed, and be the best in whatever "it" was. Failure was of course out of the question, but being second best was also not an option. As for Mario, he was an accessory to these matters and possibly enjoyed raising his pugs more than accompanying the intense competition and excruciating trauma his children experienced daily. And then there was Fanny.

Fanny seemed to come after the pugs and along for the ride. What Fanny did was of no concern to Tammy, who surmised that at age ten, it was probably too late to fix the damage of a public education, dysfunctional parenting, and an unfocused life purpose. The Wuya-Wada children came variously to complain about Fanny. "Mother," Julia complained, "she has no knowledge of simple geography. Can you believe it? She couldn't locate Asia Minor."

Tammy sighed and replied, "Julia, how can you compare your education with hers? You knew all the world capitals by the time you were in the first grade."

Mariko came to add her frustration. "Mother, shouldn't Fanny be doing calculus by now?"

Tammy replied, "Oh Mariko, I know you were doing set theory at age five, but set your sights lower in Fanny's circumstances. Perhaps you could give her your old algebra books?"

And Tommy queried, "Why can't Fanny speak Mandarin?"

"Tommy, by the time you were three, you knew one hundred Chinese characters. But, tell me," Tammy eyed her son sternly, "what about your German? Have you gone on to Book Seven?"

Only Eddy said nothing and quietly introduced Fanny to the grand piano. "Try this scale," he suggested. "See the notes?" He pointed to a practice book. "A solid note for one beat each. The notes rise like this." He played the keys. "Easy." As it turned out, for Fanny, it was easy. She was some kind of human sponge, and as the years passed, willy-nilly and unnoticed by anyone, Fanny either caught up or surpassed her cousins. It was just what she was supposed to do.

Despite Tammy's tiger fist, Fanny noted that the Wuya-Wada kids eventually all had ways of coping or escaping. Given the opportunity now as teenagers, they scattered from the hills of Monterey Park to the streets, to the beach, to the desert, to the mountains. What they did out there could only be surmised, and this drove Tammy crazy, but she wouldn't lose control. For example, when Tommy and Mariko returned from a weekend excursion, Tammy interrogated them.

Tommy explained, "We drove out to the Mojave."

"What for?"

"To see the wild flowers," replied Mariko.

"Flowers?" Tammy sneered.

"Desert ecology," Tommy said. "Scientific research. We brought back samples."

"Right," asserted Mariko. "Geologic rock samples plus flora and fauna."

"I got a dead lizard." Tommy wiggled the stiff thing in front of Tammy's face.

Tammy screamed.

Eddy was more honest, being unable to lie. "Hollywood," he said. "Whiskey a Go Go."

"You're too young to drink!" Tammy cried.

"I didn't drink. We just listened to music."

"What kind of music?"

"The Doors," he suggested and added, "of perception?" since saying "rock" seemed like a bad idea.

Tammy was flabbergasted. From Suzuki violin to the Doors? It had come to this?

"What if," Eddy pleaded with soft eyes, "it makes me happy? Don't I get to be happy sometimes?"

Tammy was scornful. "The right to happiness is an American idea."

"But we're in America."

"Not inside my house."

Julia admitted, "I went to the beach to see the ocean."

"So, if Tommy and Mariko went to do desert ecology, you were doing oceanic studies?" Tammy chided.

"No, I just wanted to feel the sand under my bare feet and to hear the sound of waves. I wanted to see the sun set over the Pacific."

"Is that so?"

"I think I'm depressed."

Tammy rolled her eyes. "Depression is a psychological disorder that only exists in the West."

It was pointless to argue. Julia pouted. "I need to go west."

Fanny wondered at these occasional lapses and escapes from the regimen, but her cousins all played their roles as excellent overachievers with their sights on the Ivies. The world order confined by Tammy's Monterey Park seemed uncontested. Being the youngest, no one confided in Fanny. She could only imagine what they imagined. Only Eddy came occasionally to share his thoughts with Fanny, for they were bound by their love of music. Eddy brought Fanny LPs and tapes. "But what will Tammy say?" protested Fanny.

Eddy shoved the prohibited LP into the cover of Beethoven's *Fifth*. "Dah dah dah dahh!" sang Eddy.

Then, one day, two more teenage cousins, Merry and Harry, were deposited in Monterey Park at the Wuya-Wada household. This time, these were the kids of a second cousin of Tammy's in Manila. Their parents had sent them away, hoping to prevent them from getting any political ideas and before President Marcos did anything preposterous like declare martial law. Mario welcomed the addition of two more to his brood of five, plus the pugs, and used their arrival as an excuse to hire a sous chef and a driver. Fanny marveled that Merry and Harry, unlike herself, settled easily into the comforts of a large household with a housekeeper, tutor, driver, gardener, and sous chef. Merry and Harry were used to doing nothing for themselves. But they came with excited stories of violent protest, bloody assassination, and Marxist-Maoist revolution and spoke of themselves as exiles. Fanny felt genuinely sorry for them. At least her mother was on the other side of the city in Gardena, in a two-bedroom apartment within walking distance of her favorite Italian delicatessen, Giuliano's, and her brother was studying law at UCLA.

Tammy listened to these accounts of political turmoil, made a quick assessment of her offshore holdings in Asia, and booked a plane ticket to Manila. In Manila, she had inherited a plastics factory from her grandmother. Years ago, Tammy's grandmother had started the business by supplying cheap toys like kewpie dolls for curio shops. Tammy had repurposed the factory machinery to produce molded plastic bases for Bic lighters. These disposable lighters were selling like hotcakes among American soldiers in Vietnam. No revolution, unionizing, or anti-Marcos politics were going to disrupt her lucrative operation. If necessary, she'd move the entire operation out of Manila to Singapore. In the larger historic picture of the global economy, she would raise her children in America, where the profession of democracy, pluralism, and tolerance would open avenues to their obvious superiority. But when it came to her money, tight-fisted intolerance and homogeneity were absolutely necessary.

Business trips of this sort weren't unusual, and the Wuya-Wada kids could be sure that any trip meant detailed instructions about work progress, with hell to pay if it wasn't completed to Tammy's satisfaction upon her return. A business trip was business as usual. However, as soon as the door closed behind Tammy, the deCuervo cousins were immediately disposed to test this assumption with the cliché that it was about time to turn the Wuya-Wada house—with its twinkling hillside view of L.A., its kidney-shaped swimming pool, its tennis courts, expansive gardens, professional kitchen, dog kennel, and spacious rooms—into the best party ever. That evening, Harry appeared at dinner in a bow tie and white jacket, announcing, "I think we should dress up for dinner. After all," he bowed deferentially to Mario, "it's a way of honoring the chef."

Mario smiled over a platter of barbecued teriyaki chicken, staring at Harry's outfit and thinking back to his days as a cruise ship waiter. "If you get this shoyu sauce on that, it could be a problem."

"Uncle Mario," Merry explained, "Harry wants to be James Bond."

Could've fooled Mario, but he wasn't one to squash youthful dreams.

"Double-o seven," inserted Mariko, in case her father didn't know.

"Actually," replied Harry, "my dream is to make movies."

Julia jumped up from the dinner table. "Yes, Harry's right. We should dress up," she exclaimed. "I'll be right back."

Suddenly there was a scurry away from the table past Harry, past Mario and his chicken. Only Fanny and Eddy were left seated, confused and hungry.

"The food will get cold," Mario said predictably, serving the rice.

Like quick-change artists, the three girls and Tommy returned in the fancy, uncomfortable outfits, elegant gowns and suits they wore at recitals and weddings.

Mariko looked at Julia and said, "Next time," she pointed at Julia's bare neck, "we've got to complete your look with a necklace and earrings."

Harry said, "Diamonds."

Merry drawled with emphasis, "Dia-monds are for-ever."

By the end of the evening, it was decided. They would stage a 007 casino night with a dance band. The three-car garage would be cleaned out for the casino, and they'd roll out the grand piano to the pool and plug in the equipment for the rock band on the tennis courts.

Fanny watched the cousins spin into high gear, Harry directing everything from the lighting to the rental of sound equipment and tables. Tommy was busy learning magic and trying to invent a way to disappear one of Mario's pugs. Fanny rescued the poor pug from the compartment in Tommy's contraption, and Tommy wandered around amazed that his magic actually worked. Mariko practiced her blackjack and poker moves, though Fanny assumed she was probably counting cards. Harry came around to stage a practice round. "Mariko," he praised her, "you're a natural dealer."

"The correct terminology is *croupier*," Mariko sniffed haughtily as Harry put his chips down.

Eddy was inspired to take his electric guitar out of hiding and plug it into a speaker system. Then, he and Merry came looking for Fanny in the study, and, prying her away from Tammy's workbooks, got her to play the piano while Eddy improvised chords and Merry belted "Goldfinger." Fanny played watching Eddy play while watching Merry sing as if she were Shirley Bassey. At some point, Julia entered in gold tights and a shimmering gold chiffon skirt, providing her dance interpretation, which amounted, Fanny thought, to slinking and rolling around histrionically over the floor.

Even Mario became enthusiastic at the possibility of creating canopies, fruit and ice sculptures, and exotic tropical (he assumed virgin) drinks to complete the atmosphere.

Predictably, Tammy finished her business in exploiting cheap Filipino labor earlier than expected and arrived on the very night of the grand 007 extravaganza. Her limo pulled up to the house and competed with dozens of cars emptying kids in prom outfits into her front doors. She wandered into her house, which had been transformed by low lighting, rotating strobes, and lava lamps, and meandered through crowds of girls with thick makeup, exposed bosoms, and martini glasses posturing haughtily and moving lasciviously to the live music pumping from the rock band playing on a platform at the far side of the pool. She could see Eddy on guitar, random other kids on drums and bass, and Merry belting vocals into a handheld microphone, modulated through a sound system Harry controlled on the other side. And through the glass doors, Tommy, dressed like Dracula, was lit up on an inside stage placing a pug in a black box and tapping it with his magic wand. Fanny, looking up from the keyboards, was the first to see Tammy. Julia was barefoot, dancing precariously on the diving board over the deep end, and when Tammy screamed her recognizable scream, the shock tossed Julia into the pool. Splash. That, Fanny would remember, was the beginning of the end. The final blow to Tammy was to find Mariko in the garage in the middle of an intense and cheering crowd, presiding over a table of blackjack.

Most immediately, Merry and Harry were sent packing. Fanny watched them leave with trepidation over their courage, but anyway, they were already exiles. Merry left merrily for San Francisco to be, she said, a poet, and Harry tipped his hat to the Wuya-Wadas and headed for Las Vegas to begin his career in show business. Soon after, Mariko followed Harry to Las Vegas. Fanny discovered that Mariko and Tommy's excursions to the Mojave weren't really ecological desert investigations. From the Mojave, Mariko crossed the California border into Nevada to test her exceptional math skills, and Tommy raced cars on the salt flats. When the deception was finally revealed, it turned out Tommy had been keeping a car in a friend's garage, street racing and hanging with low riders for the past two years. With Tammy shouting epithets like "ungrateful," "spoiled," "worthless," "failure," and "bum," Tommy got in his car, and once he started driving, he didn't stop.

One day, as usual, Eddy came to confide in Fanny. "I really miss her, Fanny," said Eddy.

"Merry?" Fanny heaved a sigh. She missed her too.

"I'm going to leave in a few days. I've made up my mind. My only concern is you."

"Me?" asked Fanny.

"Are you going to be all right here by yourself?"

Fanny didn't answer.

"Look," Eddy said. "I'm going to leave you with my entire collection of LPs. It's all yours. You know where they are. Just don't let Tammy know, or she'll throw them away." He kissed Fanny on the cheek and left with a duffel. Eventually he'd find his way to SF, compose songs, and do backup for what would become the Merry Gang.

As for Julia, she simply danced out of the house. Presumably she traveled south along the coast with a surfboard, then west across the Pacific. Occasionally Fanny received postcards from surfing spots as far away as South Africa or Australia or Asia Minor.

Fanny had nowhere to go except maybe Gardena, but her mother's new boyfriend had moved in with all his golfing equipment. So Fanny continued to faithfully produce her workbooks for Tammy and enjoyed the spacious house with all its amenities, even as it was emptied of everyone except herself and the pugs. On the fateful night of the 007 disaster, Mario had made detailed arrangements for catering and cleanup, then took his pugs, sans the one trained for Tommy's magic show, and left for a quiet rental cottage on Catalina. When everything cooled down, Fanny telephoned him to let him know the coast was clear, so to speak. Mario represented, after all, the perfect triad of arrogance, insecurity, and self-control. That is to say, he felt himself to be too brilliantly endowed and too ambivalent to be involved, and nothing Tammy said made him lose his temper. Similarly, Tammy, Fanny, and Mario formed a model unit, the triple whammy Tammy had so embraced. And as if to prove Tammy's theory, Fanny Rice excelled at tennis and fencing, went on to win accolades as a concert pianist, got into Harvard, then MIT, did postgraduate astrophysics research in France and Germany, spoke five other languages, including Chinese and Japanese, wrote a best-selling fictional immigrant memoir, and from time to time had the subtle ability to vanish.

# Emi

Mukashi, mukashi, Emi Moriuchi, intelligent, headstrong, privileged, and cheerfully positive, came of age in the sixties. O.K., no big deal. You boomer sansei all came of age in the sixties, give or take a decade. And intelligent, well, that was a given. Headstrong, meaning stubborn and outspoken, you could certainly be; that's what nisei complained about. Privileged depends on what you mean; slipping past the barbed wire of wartime incarceration into the third generation could be construed as privilege, especially since no one told you the truth until much later. That might be the reason for Emi's cheerfully positive attitude. Never mind the Cold War. The world was her bubble.

Henry Moriuchi left the dead and tattered belongings of his life in camp behind and returned, a broken but still determined father with three daughters, to his childhood farm in the southern and then still rural reaches of Southern California. Returning to his father Old Man Moriuchi's place had been neither his nor the old issei's plan, but the war changed everything. One day Henry found his father kneeling with his bare, rugged hands against a large granite boulder he'd been trying to arrange into some semblance of a garden in that desert nowhere. Henry would never forget the sad supplication of his father's last stance and breath, the filigree of dust already peppering his white but still moist brow. Only a day earlier, Henry and his wife had taken in the young daughter of his best friend, Tad Fukuya. Tad's wife had been hospitalized outside camp for tuberculosis, and when she died, Tad left to fight and die in Europe. Henry and his wife adopted the Fukuya daughter, Anne, and began to raise her in camp with their own little Isabella. But just as the war was ending, Henry would also bury his wife next to his father, below the immovable outline of the Sierra Nevadas, snow-peaked and cutting across cold blue skies. Anne, who was only fifteen at the time, spent every day in the camp hospital learning to swaddle and feed the newborn Moriuchi baby, Emi.

The story was that Old Man Moriuchi came to California and made his money panning gold. Maybe this happened, but Henry really didn't know. However the old issei made his fortune, he was able to buy a small tract of farmland before the California alien land law of 1913. He must have been one of the few issei who owned his land fair and square, as he said, but in unfair times with no equal sides. Henry came home to restart his life with three girls in a ramshackle farmhouse, but owning the land, Henry discovered, was everything. As metropolitan L.A. claimed the landscape with its slow urban sprawl, Henry churned his verdant plots of flowers and strawberries into suburban lots and a construction and real estate business with a preference for nisei families. Old Man Moriuchi's place was finally whittled down to a pretty Japanese garden and park that Henry gave to the city and had dedicated, on a plaque, to the old man.

One August afternoon, Emi and her sisters, in cotton summer yukata, posed with matching parasols around the inauguration of Old Man Moriuchi's plaque, smiling into posterity for the cameras. Henry leaned into his cane, watching this scene, and blinked back tears. Emi, now fourteen, looked for her father and yelled, "Daddy, you should be in this picture too!"

Henry shook his head, but a young man stepped forward. It was George Kishi. George's younger brother, John, was newly engaged to Henry's daughter Isabella. "Mr. Moriuchi, Emi's right. Please." He guided Henry to a place between his girls. George then hopped out of the frame and waved to John, who steadied his Nikon for the shot. "One, two, three, cheese!"

Reporters and photographers for the local city and two Japanese American newspapers cornered Henry for stories. Emi stood by her father and listened with interest. Someone asked Emi, "Do you remember your grandfather?"

"Oh no, I wasn't born yet. You'll have to ask Izy or Anne."

"Were you born in camp?"

"Camp?" Emi chewed her lip in some confusion. "I guess so."

George Kishi walked from the shaded picnic table where Anne and Isabella had arranged a spread of teriyaki skewers; musubi; makizushi; fruit skewers of melon, pineapple, and strawberries; mochigashi; cookies;

and tea. He offered Emi his selection of picnic food. She picked up a teriyaki skewer. "I'm so hungry, but this obi thing is killing me. It's too tight."
Emi pushed her fingers under the wide belt. She ripped off a piece of teriyaki with her teeth, rubbed the sauce from her mouth, then asked, "George,
was I born in camp? And what's that?"

Anne Fukuya was both big sister and surrogate mom to Isabella and Emi.
Even when in college across town, Anne was back at home every weekend
taking care of her adopted sisters, shopping for them or following their
homework. After receiving her teaching certificate, she found a job at a
local elementary school and continued to live with the Moriuchis. Henry
had long ago relinquished his maternal responsibilities to the young Anne,
not only because she took them on with stalwart energy and great affection but also because for a time, he didn't know why he had survived the
war and not his father, his wife, or his best friend. It wasn't a surprise Emi
didn't know the circumstances of her birth. And while Isabella was a more
sullen, shy child, filled at times with unaccountable fear, Emi was always
happily content, and Anne made sure nothing interfered with Emi's enthusiasm and curiosity for her world. She knew Henry's well-being depended
on Emi's joy. But one day, Anne announced her plans to leave the household and to finally marry.

Henry complained to Emi, "First Isabella, now Anne."

"Gee whiz, Daddy, aren't you happy for Anne? You called her an old
maid."

"Gee whiz," he mimicked her. "I never said such a thing."

"*Spinster,* the word was *spinster,*" Emi corrected. "And by the way, you
can call me a spinster too, because I'm never getting married. Marriage is
simply overrated."

"Is that so?" Henry smiled a crooked smile.

"By the way," she tapped his elbow, "Izy is coming over this afternoon
with the kids."

Henry groaned. "The pool is off limits. It's too cold today, and besides,
you and Isabella jabber on and don't provide proper supervision. Much
too dangerous."

"Oh Daddy, really."

But it wasn't Isabella who arrived with her tumult of five boisterous
kids; instead they came with their uncle George. "Mr. Moriuchi!" George
greeted Henry, who sat at the kitchen table with his coffee and newspaper.

Henry observed the kids rush past in a blur of skin and bathing suits, zori slapping the linoleum, beach balls, plastic blowup tubes, snorkels, and masks dragging behind. A fait accompli, but then George had come along. Henry nodded with guy approval.

George explained, "Isabella needed some downtime. Got a migraine."

"What's she taking?" Henry queried. "There's something new on the market. Works better than plain aspirin."

George looked at the blanket over Henry's knees. The temperature was in the eighties, though maybe ten degrees cooler inside. "Izy just needs some rest." Outside, they could hear the splash of diving bodies.

"What about suntan lotion?" The thought dawned on Henry. "I was just reading an article about sunburn."

George jumped up. "Don't worry, Mr. Moriuchi. I've got it covered."

"Daddy!" Emi dashed in and out of the kitchen. "They're here!"

"Don't worry," Henry said to no one, pulling up another section of the paper. "George has got it covered." He peeked over his reading glasses and watched Emi toss off her hat and towel and jump into the fray to celebrate another summer with her five nephews and nieces. How old was she now? Almost out of college, but still a kid too.

Toward the end of the afternoon, Emi came out with giant slices of cold watermelon, and George got all the kids to sit in a row to see who could spit the seeds the farthest.

George watched Emi chomp greedily on ripe watermelon. "I haven't seen you in a while. How's college?"

"Taking a summer class."

"Oh, doing makeup?"

"Makeup? I'll have you know I'm doing this for extra credit. I got straight As."

"Impressive. What's the class?"

"History of War."

"Let me guess. You're doing a paper on the internment."

"How did you know? Would you read my paper, please? Usually Anne would do it, but have you heard the news?"

"Anne's getting married to that guy Nishida who owns the tackle shop on the pier in Hermosa."

"Dad's very sad. Nobody's supposed to leave his nest."

"And you?"

"I miss her." Emi was gnawing on the white part of the melon.

George turned to study Emi's eyes, red from chlorine but maybe not.

"But you know," Emi sniffed, "gotta move on." Then, "George," she said abruptly, "I'm against this racist war. I know you're in law school, but if you ever get drafted, you have to go to Canada." She got up, collected melon rinds, then announced to the kids lolling in the grass, "O.K., how about we go watch *Mister Ed*?"

By the time of Anne's marriage, Emi was completely conversant in the circumstances of her birth and its historical context. It's surprising how historical context can give the matter of an inconsequential birth an unexpected gravitas. When George saw Emi again, she was one brides-maid among five in a flutter of matching pink chiffon, but he could distinguish her by the happy lilt in her voice even as she said, "Anne's father volunteered for the 442nd and died saving the Lost Battalion. He was my dad's best friend." Emi puckered glossy lips on the rim of her champagne glass, then, recognizing George, smiled brightly.

George eyed Emi skeptically, but she countered conspiratorially, "George, my birthday was yesterday. It's official, but it's so insulting."

"Should we be singing 'Happy Birthday'?" he wondered.

"No." She pouted and sipped champagne. "I haven't even been carded."

"O.K., I'm carding you."

She produced her California driver's license from inside her bustier, and George busted out laughing. "What's it doing there?"

She frowned as if it should be obvious.

George read the pertinent information. "Born in Manzanar, California."

"Say, let me see that." They'd been ignoring the young man whom Emi had been educating about Japanese American history. It was Frank, the groom's son by a previous marriage. "Where's Manzanar?" Emi and George rolled their eyes in opposite directions while Frank adjusted his bow tie. "I was born in Philly."

Across the ballroom, the band crooned the Righteous Brothers: *Without you, baby, what good am I?* Emi led George to the dance floor, saying, "I swear, George, there is so much work to be done."

"What are you talking about?"

"Well, there you have it." Emi nodded back to Frank.

"You're going to work on Frank? I might be wrong, but I think he likes you."

"Don't be ridiculous."

The next time George saw Frank was on a panel with Emi at a local church function. Mrs. Esa, one of the church matrons, thought it would be interesting to hear the sansei point of view on the internment. Emi had rustled up two more panelists, Phil Furumachi and Augusta Taka. Frank was busily opening folding chairs and lining them across the church gymnasium floor.

"How's Frank doing?" George asked Emi.

"Very helpful."

"And who are the other two?"

"Phil and Augusta." She nodded at a couple getting in a last smoke at the open entrance of the gym. "Very articulate and outspoken. They were in my summer class on war, remember?"

Mrs. Esa approached the mic and said enthusiastically, "We are so pleased tonight to have with us five sansei members of our community who have agreed to share their ideas with us. These young sansei are the bright future of our community, and we have an opportunity to hear them speak their minds."

Emi opened with, "Thank you Mrs. Esa for inviting us here to speak our minds," then launched into, "The nisei have been complicit in the erasure of our history. The history of the Japanese American internment is one paragraph, if it exists at all, in American history texts. Imagine our surprise to even read that one paragraph since you, our parents, have refused to talk about the injustice done to our people."

Frank said, "I'd just like to say I believe the term *internment camp* is incorrect. It should be *concentration camp.*"

And Phil said, "The Vietnam War is a continuation of racist wars against the Asian people, and we need to make the connections between how Japanese Americans were treated during World War II and the current genocide of Asian people by the American military in Vietnam."

And finally, Augusta polished it off with, "Nisei have been described as quiet Americans, and this is bullshit. We're not going to be quiet anymore. The JACL needs to apologize for leading you nisei into camps like sheep."

George sat in the audience and felt the shock of the nisei shuffling uncomfortably in their chairs.

Mrs. Esa fumbled for her composure. "Yes, yes, you've spoken your minds, and this is very good for us all to hear." She looked out on her fellow nisei, who either glowered back or looked down at the floor in silence.

Someone said under his breath, "Bunch of ungrateful brats." A few got up looking as if they had to go to the bathroom.

Mrs. Esa asked, "Well now, any questions?" No one said anything, so Mrs. Esa tried, "The relocation was a very difficult time for those of us who lived through it, and it's been very difficult to even talk about it because, because . . ." She paused, her voice trembling. "We lost so much, and—"

Emi interrupted with gusto. "Yes, precisely. That is why we are advocating for the next step, that is, to demand redress for the injustice of wartime relocation."

Mrs. Esa looked at the diminishing audience and then at the sansei panelists. "Oh my." She recuperated her composure. "I guess our time is up."

As the crowd left the gymnasium, Mrs. Esa said almost cheerfully, "Emi, that was very interesting. You are a very . . ." She searched for the right word. "Outspoken group." Then she changed the subject. "I want you to meet my niece, Jane." Mrs. Esa motioned to a young woman sitting in the back. "She is so in need of friends. She's just come from Japan."

George came up to greet Mrs. Esa, who exclaimed, "George, I'm so happy to see you. Have you met Jane?"

Later, George drove Emi home. Emi chatted on triumphantly, as if she'd won the evening, but George said nothing. "You're awfully quiet," she quipped.

"You guys were pretty harsh over there," he said. "Was that necessary?"

"What do you mean? We told it like it is."

"It was really brave of Mrs. Esa to invite you. Her sister married a no-no and renounced her citizenship with him and left for Japan. That's where Jane was born. But then, her sister died and the husband committed suicide, so Mrs. Esa asked for help to bring Jane home. I helped with the repatriation case. It took years. What she was trying to tell you was that her family was separated, and no one talks to her because her family was no-no."

Emi closed her eyes. "I screwed up big-time."

Henry hobbled into the kitchen and sniffed the air. "Chocolate chips?"

"Daddy, I'm having a meeting here tonight."

"What for?"

"We're plotting the revolution."

"Good luck."

The doorbell rang, and Emi left to answer it. "Harriet, you're here early."

Henry looked over his shoulder, quickly stole a plate of hot cookies, and snuck away to hide in his den.

"I wanted to talk to you about something personal. Get your advice." Harriet Kajiya worked as a secretary at Moriuchi Real Estate. When Emi worked for her father's business during the summers, the two became close friends. All Harriet ever talked about was guys, so Emi suggested she might expand her horizons—that is, come to meetings.

Emi pulled a sheet of cookies from the oven, shoved a spatula under the soft cookies, and listened.

"You know Bob?" Harriet asked.

"Bob Torii."

"Right. He asked me to marry him."

"Oh, well, congratulations." Emi frowned at one cookie that had folded over itself. "But I thought we were working on Phil or Frank."

"I haven't said yes or no yet." Harriet stuffed a warm cookie into her mouth and muttered through the dough, "What do you think?"

"You have doubts? I mean, why ask me? I'm never getting married."

"Never?"

"Let me ask you this: What are Bob's politics?"

"I have no idea."

"Maybe he'd like to join our group."

The ringing bell ended the conversation. In sauntered the crew that was supposed to start the Japanese American revolution: Frank, Phil, Augusta, and now Mrs. Esa's niece, Jane Kikami, as well.

They sat on the big sofa and zabutons around the coffee table, munching on cookies.

Phil cleared his throat and began. "We've been trying to define our goals over the last month now, but I think we need to first do some deep study." He pulled a book out of his satchel. "Confining our thinking to narrow nationalism isn't going to cut it." Phil put the heavy book on the table. Everyone stared at the cover: *Capital* by Karl Marx.

Augusta piped up, "I agree with Phil. We need some direction."

Frank asked plainly, "What's narrow nationalism?"

Phil said, "It's the business of defining ourselves as Japanese when the real problem is to recognize our class differences."

"Exactly," agreed Augusta. She pulled out a cigarette, lit it, and puffed.

"But I'm not Japanese," Frank pleaded.

"O.K., Japanese American," Phil inserted.

"But"—Augusta puffed and waved her arm around the spacious Moriuchi living room, its Japanese prints, vases, shag rug, and teak furniture—"have you examined your position vis-à-vis the bourgeoisie?"

Emi watched Harriet's mouth moving with silent exaggerated elocution: booge wa zee. Emi hoped Augusta couldn't see this and, as a distraction, poured more tea, saying hopefully, "But I thought we agreed that we'd research books and articles about Japanese American history, start a bibliography, and go from there." She pushed an ashtray toward Augusta, along with a sheet of paper with a typewritten list. "I spent all day in the library yesterday."

Phil picked up Emi's typewritten sheet. "Admit it: there's nothing out there about us."

"O.K., then," Emi countered. "We're going to have to write it ourselves."

Harriet flipped through *Capital* and whined, "I don't know if I can read this."

"What do you mean?" Phil's voice rose as he pointed to Marx. "The revolution is inside that book!"

Harriet and Jane, sitting on either side of Phil, both jumped.

Frank said, "I liked the idea of doing oral histories, going out with a tape recorder and collecting stories. That was Jane's idea."

Jane looked away and shrugged shyly, pressing her knees together and shrinking into the couch.

Frank caught sight of Henry Moriuchi across the room sneaking away with another plate of cookies. "Mr. Moriuchi can be our first interviewee. I've already learned so much from Emi about her family's sacrifice." Frank's gaze lingered on Emi, whose cheeks glowed.

Harriet nodded supportively, but Phil thrust a finger into the air. "I believe we've spent enough time circling the problem, and it's obvious that we require an ideological basis for our process and actions. If we're serious about this, we need to study the theory that's made revolutions possible. We need to take our thinking to the next level."

"Oh," Harriet murmured with wonder, "yes, of course, the next level."

Augusta blew her smoke into the room and drew a Z with the tip of her cigarette over the chocolate chip cookies. "Making a revolution isn't like making a tea party."

Emi watched the ash from Augusta's cigarette snow over her cookies and tried, "Well, maybe Phil and Augusta can read *Capital* and report back?"

Augusta rose regally and said, "Oh good idea, don't you think so, Phil?"

Phil grabbed his book, stood with Augusta, and marched out with her. The door closed with a bang behind them. Emi looked around, but no one's eyes met.

Breaking that wake of silence, Frank jumped up and said, "Jane and I were thinking of going to a movie tonight. Want to join us? If we leave now, we can make the 9:00 p.m. showing."

Harriet asked, "What's playing?"

*"Planet of the Apes."*

"Oh, I've seen it already." Harriet waved them on. "Bob took me. Enjoy." She started to remove the teapot, cups, and cookies, then saw Emi slouched on the couch in confusion. Harriet consoled Emi. "Well, I'm looking forward to that book report, because I certainly wasn't going to read that entire book."

"Right."

Harriet returned from the kitchen and cozied up to Emi. "Emi, I know you're disappointed. I know you invited me to these meetings because you wanted Phil to like me. Don't get me wrong; he's smart, but he's kind of a prick, and anyway he should be with someone like Augusta. And then you wanted Frank to like me, but he likes Jane. It's not your fault. Don't be depressed. You've been really super." Harriet squeezed Emi with a hug and got up. "Hey, I'll see you at the next meeting. Bye."

Emi could hear the phone ringing. If it had been today, it would have been ringing from her iPhone, and she would have been able to see the caller ID or read a text: George Kishi. Henry Moriuchi wouldn't install an answering machine for another decade. The vagaries of communication in the day made life less predictable, but you still had to talk to each other. The phone gave up. She picked up a cookie, brushed off the ash, and bit into it. Obviously, the revolution wasn't going to start in the Moriuchi living room, but maybe they could take it to the next level.

# Japanese American Gothic

In this story, you get to be the sansei heroine because you are like a lump of narrative Play-Doh, and the less self-awareness you possess, the more you can be poked, prodded, and punched into possibility. You are the heroine because we follow your adventure even if other characters might have better adventures and more interesting lives, because your adventure has moral authority, and because it's a trick. This is not said to make you feel special or bad or even tricked; the real story is there, just not necessarily in your exact direction.

Mukashi, mukashi, Cathy Ozawa grew up a tomboy, but then around adolescence got it together to pretend to be a girl. In those years, girls did a lot of pretending. Let's pretend Barbies. Pretend your Barbie and my Barbie live in castles right next door. Pretend that Ken lives with your Barbie one week and my Barbie the next week. There's only one Ken, so they take turns. Sometimes your Barbie and my Barbie live in the same castle, which is way more fun. Sometimes our Barbies leave Ken all alone in your castle wearing your Barbie's clothing because Ken only has one set of clothing, even if it's glitter pants and a jacket, but the shoes never fit. The only way to make the shoes fit is to screw Ken's head onto your Barbie's head or vice versa. O.K., if you let your imagination run, you get the pretend picture.

Cathy grew up in Fullerton with white people who had escaped the darkening inner city. As it turns out some J.A.s, too, escaped into the burbs of scattered cities across the U.S., since returning from concentration camps to the confinement of ghettoed J-towns didn't seem like an option for the future. And if J.A.s just spread out all over the country, maybe the next time around, it would be harder to find them. Besides, Mr. Ozawa had served America honorably during the war, using his language skills for military intelligence, interpreting and breaking Japanese codes, linguistic and cultural. Not that anyone knew this; it was a secret. Those white neighbors who chafed at having to live next door to the only Japanese family within miles could wonder at their luck, but Mr. Ozawa conducted himself with a mixture of friendly and aloof dignity, because he had the upper hand of conscience that patted him on the invisible stars of his kibei shoulders. By the time he was known as Ol' Man Ozawa and had trained several generations of white karate kids, even his own kids were surprised to read their dad's obit. Jim and Cathy Ozawa went through childhood and adolescence like it was normal to be white, until one day Jim left for college to study Asian American studies at UCLA and Cathy drove her mother's elderly friends Mr. and Mrs. Ishi to a dental appointment in Little Tokyo.

Mrs. Ozawa said to Mrs. Ishi, "Cathy just got her driver's license." She searched for a plausible excuse in case it turned out to be a bad idea. "She's never even been to Little Tokyo."

"Oh," replied Mrs. Ishi, "I'm sure she's a very safe driver. Never been? Oh my."

"Tosh and I go. You know, funerals and maybe Nisei Week, but we never bring the kids," Mrs. Ozawa replied defensively, but the kids weren't kids anymore.

Mrs. Ishi pouted, then recuperated her natural optimism. "It will be an adventure. You know, I never learned to drive the freeways, and Woody's eyes just aren't trustworthy anymore. Cataracts." She blinked for emphasis and sighed. "When we moved out here"—she waved her hand around like it was all Disneyland in a Midwestern cornfield—"we changed all our doctors, but we just couldn't change dentists. Am I wrong, Mary? Living out here all these years, you probably don't have a Japanese dentist, but I couldn't trust just anyone inside my mouth." Mrs. Ishi moved her lips over her crooked teeth, sported an apologetic smile, then continued, "And besides, we like to eat in Little Tokyo and stock up on provisions." By provisions, Mrs. Ishi meant Japanese foodstuffs: Calrose rice, shoyu, rice vinegar, miso, sake, nori, bancha, ajinomoto, etcetera. "Don't forget to send Cathy with your list."

Mrs. Ozawa put a list into her daughter's hands, not without noticing the black fingernail polish and the blood-ruby ring attached by a delicate chain to an ornate black lace bracelet. As usual these days, Cathy was dressed in black—boots, jeans, tee. Mrs. Ozawa queried her daughter's face, and Cathy reassured her, "I didn't apply it that thickly today, Mom.

Don't want to scare the Ishis." Cathy was really the sweetest young woman, and Mrs. Ozawa prayed everyone would see her daughter through that dark outfit.

Cathy resisted the urge to turn on KROQ and drove the Ishis' gray Buick with conscientious attention, darting eyes checking mirrors and merging like a cab driver, Mr. Ishi at shotgun and Mrs. Ishi in the back seat and chattering nonstop with great particularity about the Lakers—the players, their positions, averages, heights, injuries, scoring patterns, prospects for the semifinals, and on and on.

When Mrs. Ishi seemed to be catching her breath, Cathy turned to her husband. "Are you a fan, too?"

"Oh yes, but she's the expert. I just took her to her first game."

Mrs. Ishi pounced back in, leaning forward into the gear shift. "That was when Woody could drive. UCLA versus USC. From that moment on—" Mrs. Ishi paused rather romantically.

And Mr. Ishi finished as if responding to a song, "It's all history."

"My brother Jim is at UCLA," Cathy offered.

"What's he studying?" Mr. Ishi queried.

"Sociology, I think."

"Smart kid," Mr. Ishi remarked.

"That game at UCLA," Mrs. Ishi returned to her subject. "I first saw Lew Alcindor . . ."

"Kareem Abdul-Jabbar," Mr. Ishi corrected.

"It was like," Mrs. Ishi searched for the right word and landed on, "ballet."

Meanwhile, Southern California whooshed by until they descended an off-ramp into that iconic cluster of downtown high-rises hugged by a floating donut of smog. As Mrs. Ishi had promised, it would be an adventure.

As instructed, Cathy dropped Mr. Ishi off at his dentist on First Street, then proceeded on to Third with Mrs. Ishi, who wanted to visit her friend Mrs. Murata at the Hiroshima Café. "I'm surprised your folks didn't at least bring you here," Mrs. Ishi remarked to Cathy as the door opened and chimed behind them. "Min and Mitoko are old friends. Opened this place right after the war." She strutted over to a booth in the corner, settled into the red Naugahyde, and leaned over the table, whispering to Cathy conspiratorially, "Chashu ramen."

A young woman with a pad sauntered over to the table and exclaimed, "Mrs. Ishi, where's mister?"

"Bella." Mrs. Ishi smiled exaggeratedly, showing her canines. "Woody's doing his teeth."

Cathy's eyes traversed the Hiroshima hostess Bella, who sported a red happi coat over a leather skirt and fishnets, her hair ratted in every direction. "Tsk tsk." Bella shook her finger at Mrs. Ishi. "Too many sweets."

Mrs. Ishi nodded back and forth like it was her fault. "Bella, this is Cathy."

Bella took a step back and glared appropriately through mascara and thick eyeliner, moist red lips articulating, "How do you do?" emphasizing the *do*'s.

"Uh," Cathy stumbled. "I don't. I mean—"

Bella turned and left the table, yelling over the counter into the kitchen, "Momma, guess who's here?"

Mrs. Murata emerged from the kitchen rubbing her hands on her apron and scooted into the booth next to Mrs. Ishi. Cathy watched the ladies turn into little girls again.

"How's Min?" Mrs. Ishi asked.

"Not so good. Can't talk hardly. Can't use his right side."

"My brother had a stroke too," Mrs. Ishi commiserated.

Mrs. Murata pushed gray hair under a stretchy net. "I've got to go home and feed him now." She looked around the café. "Bella's taking it over."

Without bothering to ask, Bella came around with bowls of chashu ramen, then walked over to the jukebox and punched in what Cathy recognized as Siouxsie and the Banshees. She scanned the walls plastered with band posters and concert flyers, picking out her favorites. She couldn't believe her luck. What sort of café was this? There was no such place in Fullerton. Fullerton was a cultural desert. The door chimed in tune to Siouxsie's oriental song, *Hong Kong Garden,* and they all looked up. Mr. Ishi appeared dejected.

Cathy knew all the words: *disoriented you enter in / unleashing scent of wild jasmine.*

"Woody," Mrs. Ishi suggested, "show us your smile."

"Got to come in next week again. Root canal."

Cathy couldn't help herself. "No problem at all!"

Bella's eyes caught Cathy's. Bloody lips parted in a cruel grin, message sent and received. *Slanted eyes meet a new sunrise / a race of bodies small in size.*

Cathy shut her eyes and sucked in, one egg noodle sliding between her teeth, salty wet tail disappearing into a puckered *O*.

The summer started like that, back and forth for Mr. Ishi's teeth, provisions, and chashu ramen. The Hiroshima Café was, let's say, an eclectic dive, where all sorts of human beings happened along: the regulars from the local community, retired migrant workers looking for a cheap meal, aging beatniks and deadbeats, day laborers, local yakuza, and now Bella's cohort of activist anarchists, jivers, musicians, and, lately, punks, post-punks, goths, or whatever the scene was that outdid the previous, plus scattered unsuspecting tourists. Eventually Bella proposed to Cathy, as if an afterthought, waving a cigarette, "We could use some help. I can pay you by the hour, but . . ." She paused to think. "If you do your eyes bigger and badder, you'll probably make more in tips." A job sounded legitimate, but Mrs. Ozawa was suspicious, because who goes to work plastered in makeup with fishnet stockings and spiky hair? So she sent Cathy's older brother, Jim, on forays to Little Tokyo from UCLA. "Mom, relax. Relax. Don't you know the Muratas? I go to school with the son, Jonny Murata." What he didn't tell his mom was that he was soon also dating Bella, if whatever relationship they were in could be called dating.

Whenever possible, Jim and Jonny were at the café, usually for lunch or dinner. "Beats dorm food."

"I bet. You might at least," Bella smirked, "leave a tip."

Jim looked at Jonny. "What say we unionize the workers here?"

Jonny sneered. "Minimum wage, bullshit. Who do the Muratas think they are?"

"Putting you through college, dope." Bella rolled her eyes.

Jonny pranced around, shouting, "On strike! On strike!" He returned to the table and shoveled down a plate of egg foo yung and said to Jim with his mouth full, "I could use this place in my paper about Asian family restaurants, child and cheap labor. Be an exposé. Hey, I lived this shit."

"Jonny, you never lived no shit." Bella's eyes drilled into her brother's. "I live this shit."

Jonny grumbled at Bella's behind as she walked away, but Cathy returned with a tray of glasses and two cold bottles of Budweiser.

"Cathy," Jonny began, "when do they give you a break? I got my Supra right here beyond that door, waiting. Purring. You know what I mean? The meter's ticking. If you wait too long, I could get a ticket. Tick tick tick. Make up your mind. I can take you away from this chungking ichiban fast."

Cathy smiled. "If you drink that Bud and drive away, you can get a ticket too." She stepped away to the next booth.

Jonny raised and knocked his glass on Jim's and took a slug of Bud. "Talk to your sister. I know she likes me."

"She doesn't like you, Jonny."

"No, Jim. She's falling fast. Any minute now."

"Forget it. She's in high school. Way too young."

"Egg fool young! You're doing Bella. Do I say anything?"

"That's different."

One day, Cathy walked to a booth, its table covered with intricately and realistically painted watercolors of fruits, vegetables, and flowers. A young man was turning the paintings in his hands, then placing each carefully back into a folder. "These are great, Nora," he said sincerely to the young woman across the table. "When did you paint them?"

Nora shifted in the seat, and Cathy thought she answered, "In the can. Except"—she pointed at another group—"for these. I did them lately." She looked up at Cathy, who, pad in hand, was quietly observing.

"Oh," said Cathy, "I can come back later."

"No, thank you, we're ready." The young man pulled out a menu from under the paintings.

Cathy looked the couple over with interest. They were local sansei, dressed casually in jeans, probably Jim's age. This was their territory, Cathy thought enviously. They had grown up knowing this place and each other. The woman wore no makeup. There was a tough, determined, but sad air about her, a quality Cathy admired in Bella. Nora could have been Bella without all the makeup.

"Henry," Nora said, "I'm not that hungry. Choose something, and I'll eat some of it. Anyway, I got to get back and do that class."

Henry nodded and ordered the chicken chow mein and tea.

Cathy nodded. "Sure." She looked back at the table, Henry's black ponytail swirling down the back of a worn T-shirt over the words *Manzanar Pilgrimage.*

Returning to the table with tea, Cathy ventured shyly to Nora, "You're so talented."

"Thanks."

Henry suggested, "Nora's teaching classes at the cultural center. Interested?" He handed a flyer to Cathy. "Maybe you could put this up?"

When Cathy handed the flyer to Bella, Bella said, "Nora Noda is back."

"What's that mean?"

"Means she's on parole."

"Oh."

"You wouldn't know, but Nora went underground doing shit like building bombs to start the revolution, and then she got arrested, and now she's doing community service. We're her community." Bella smiled her nasty smile. "Nora's my heroine. If I could do what she did . . . but who has her guts? Easier to do this." She waved her arms around the café. "Oh, and since you seem interested, that sweet sansei guy Henry is her brother. He chauffeurs Nora around to keep her out of trouble." She puckered her lips. "Toot sweet for me."

That evening, Cathy stuck around to do the evening shift because Jim had promised he could drive her home late. Bella got herself into full costume with a black-and-red bodice hugging her breasts and everything showing lasciviously. She handed Cathy a bag. "You need to dress up for the night."

Cathy rummaged through the bag: black gloves, black lace cascading from a tiara, crucifixes, a whip. She pulled out a jar.

"Oh that." Bella pointed a pointed nail. "You're gonna love it. Genuine kabuki face paint."

The café filled up with all these white kids in leather, lace, safety pins, and chains, maybe from Fullerton, dressed to kill, and Cathy felt ecstatically important, maneuvering with trays and plates, until some guy made a pass at her, cooing, "China girl, you don't even have to dye your hair." A rumor spread that band members from Christian Death were there, interrupted by a second rumor that Sid Vicious was there. Then someone yelled, "You idiots! Sid Vicious is dead!" The entire café erupted into the chant *Sid Vicious is dead! Sid Vicious is dead!*

Bella strutted to the jukebox and sent the anthem charging through the café speakers: "Bela Lugosi's Dead." Bella pranced back into the aisle and screeched, "BELLA!" to which the entire café crowd responded in unison: *Lugosi's dead!*

"BELLA!"

*Lugosi's dead!*

Then, *undead, undead, undead!*

In the midst of this, Cathy saw Henry Noda arrive with another guy who could have been his twin. "You're back." She smiled.

"We never got introduced," Henry said, though considering the new layer of kabuki makeup, she could have been anyone.

Bella came by. "Hey Fred," she addressed Henry's companion.

"Hey Bella."

"My brother, Fred," Henry said to Cathy, watching Fred walk away with Bella.

Henry sat by himself, and Cathy came back and forth between serving patrons.

"I've never been here late," admitted Henry.

"Me neither." Cathy shrugged.

"Really? I thought you were the kabuki girl."

"Oh, that must be Bella." She looked up to see her brother, Jim, arrive and frowned to see Jonny.

Jonny swaggered over to the table. "Hey Cathy, working tonight?"

Cathy shot up from the seat and left quickly. The guys slid into the booth.

In the kitchen, Bella and Fred were frantically making out, groping and tugging, tragically on the verge, boiling broth spilling over the pot. The cook had probably left for a smoke. Cathy tiptoed away, even in platform boots, and said to Jim, "Maybe you should take me home now."

"Yeah," he answered. "But let me talk to Bella first." Before Cathy could object, Jim had left the table to look for Bella. Predictably, a crash of plates and pans and shouting came from the kitchen, though no one could hear it over the jukebox.

Leaving to assess the situation, Jonny sauntered back almost victoriously and announced, "Cathy, it seems Jim is a bit, shall we say, indisposed, but I can drive you home to Fullerton. No problema. Turbo horsepower at your service."

But Henry said, "Jonny, you're drunk," and pushed him.

To Cathy's surprise, Jonny fell over.

"Come on, Cathy."

At midnight, the freeway was a dark eternity into starry headlights, eighty miles an hour, a swift blur through white and red. "I love the night," she said.

"I work the night," he said. "I don't see daylight."

"But I saw you at lunch today."

"Helping my sister."

"And your brother?"

"Can't help him. Messed up. Ever since he returned from Nam. Stupid stuff like tonight."

"What work do you do?"

"Produce market with my dad. Get the stuff to market before the morning."

She chuckled. "I thought you might be a vampire."

"You wanna interview me?"

"Did you read it?"

He laughed. "If I lived way out here, I'd be reading Anne Rice too."

"But you know the book?"

"Do you want a reading list? I read everything. Keeps me from going crazy." He drove awhile in silence, then asked, "Why do you want to be the kabuki girl?"

"What do you mean?"

"Bella I get, but you?"

o.k., so we got our heroine and hero in a car at night cruising the L.A. freeways, talking about life's choices. The hero's sister chose the revolution, but it never happened. The hero's brother chose the military, but that too never happened, well, like he expected. Turned out he was mistaken for the enemy, and it was true; the enemy looked like him. After he killed people who looked like him, he came home, and no one thought he was a hero, least of all himself. Meanwhile, the hero stayed home to take care of his widowed dad, a silent and bitter man who felt shunned by his community. And with kids like that, he thought, what was the point? Then there was the heroine's brother, who went after chashu ramen like he was going to get the chashu but only got stuck with the white pepper dregs at the bottom of the bowl. And the heroine's new friend, who chose to try to save the family business, and her brother, who wouldn't know a choice if it were placed in front of him. As for the heroine, catching her own flashing reflection in the dark windshield, she touched the chalky, super-white surface of her cheek and began to wonder on that midnight drive home if she were not still pretending.

Toward the end of summer, Nora Noda had a small art show with her students in the gallery space of the Little Tokyo cultural center. Cathy drove the great gray Buick and Mr. and Mrs. Ishi into town to see the show. Henry was busy taking photographs.

"Oh," exclaimed Mrs. Ishi, "such a lovely display." She was especially appreciating the drawing by a second-grader of a basketball player in a jump shot. "Woody." She tapped her husband on the elbow and pointed. "There's Katz Noda. We haven't seen him in years. He never comes to anything. He must be so proud of—well, relieved over Nora's success."

Mr. Ishi hailed Mr. Noda. "Hey there, General. It's been years."

Mr. Noda nodded.

Mrs. Ishi pulled Cathy over. "Cathy, you should meet the General. Oh, he's not a real general. They just call him that because he runs the produce market. He's just a gruff sort. Don't be afraid. He's an old friend of your dad's. He'll be delighted to meet you." Pushing Cathy forward, Mrs. Ishi announced, "Katz, you should meet Cathy, Tosh Ozawa's daughter."

The General seemed to blanch, his face turning visibly sour. Before Cathy could speak or stretch out her hand, he turned, walked away, and left the gallery.

"Oh dear," said Mrs. Ishi, but Mr. Ishi only shook his head.

Henry, having witnessed the scene, came over to make small talk, but Cathy wondered what Bella would have done. Cathy had toned down her makeup, put on a semblance of normal clothes, removed her lip ring, all for nothing. Oh well, the summer was ending, and so would this episode in her life. She could go back to her normal life and leave these J.A.s to theirs. Obviously she didn't fit. She walked over to a table strewn with square colored papers. Nora was there with a group of children. "What are you working on?" she asked.

A girl looked up. "Paper cranes. Nora says we need to make one thousand."

"How many have you made?"

"Two. Can you help?"

"Sure." Cathy picked up a crane and examined it with curiosity.

"Don't you know?" The girl made a small huff of exasperation. "So first you fold it this way."

But there was one last night at the café. Well, you were there, so you should know what happened. Bella was in high form, queen of the night, and by now she had switched her affections to Fred, who generously divided his drugs with her, so they were continually in a zone. Jim wasn't

there; he'd retreated to school and scholarship, headed futuristically
for his PhD. Jonny was there playing craps in the summer night with
the punks on the sidewalk outside the café. Inside: the usual commotion of chop suey, white skin, black hair, and dilated pupils. This was
going to be Cathy's sayonara night. She was still an innocent high
school girl observing the scene sober like one day she would write
about it, but some idiot in the third booth yelled at her. "Fuck this egg
fuk yung!" and flung a piece of it her way. She picked it out of her bodice and mashed the egg hash into his pimply face. Maybe it was her fault.
And that's how it started. Egg foo yung flying this way and that. Noodles
colliding in air with Buddha's delight and fried rice. When Cathy crawled
out of the chaos, she could see Bella splashing tea and beer into faces
and dragging the fools out. Cathy slipped around in grease and soup and
managed to get out the door. Outside, Jonny was pacing around and
screaming about his Supra. His beloved Supra, the only thing he really
cared about. He'd lost it to craps. Predictably, just at that moment, our
hero arrived.

Henry grabbed Jonny. "Where's Bella? Why don't you answer the
phone in there?"

Cathy stumbled forward, slapping bok choy from her shoulders, and
Henry stared at the noodles laced through her spiked hair. Well, that was
the night Min Murata had a second stroke and died.

Like Mary Ozawa had admitted to Mrs. Ishi, she and Tosh only went
to Little Tokyo for funerals and, maybe, Nisei Week. But this time, their
kids, Jim and Cathy, came along, though folks must have glanced side-
ways at Cathy's version of formal black funeral attire. The family sat sol-
emnly in the front pews and followed all the rituals, listened to all the
stories about Min and his wife and the Hiroshima Café. And that's when
Cathy found out that Min Murata, Katz Noda (the General), and her dad,
Tosh Ozawa, were all kibei educated in Hiroshima before the war, that
the three had been close buddies who banded together to ward off bullies
because they were considered neither really Japanese nor really American.
When they returned to America just before Pearl Harbor blew up, each
made different decisions that changed their lives forever. Min Murata
left for Montana and opened a Chinese café, avoided camp. Katz and Tosh
got hauled off to camp, but when the loyalty questions came up, Katz
checked *no* and Tosh checked *yes*. The two got into a heated argument
and never spoke to each other again. Katz renounced his citizenship and

went to Tule Lake, and Tosh signed up for service, got sent to Fort Snelling, and prepped to be an interpreter in the Pacific.

After Min's funeral, folks gathered at the café. After forty years, Katz and Tosh sat together, an uneasy truce, deep in a red booth next to the jukebox, Min's old enka music dropping in one forty-five after another. A draping spray of black origami cranes cascaded from the ceiling above. They looked out at the J.A. crowd, all eating chow mein and fried rice between what Mrs. Ishi called "Bella's Halloween posters."

Katz broke the silence and nodded at Jim and Cathy. "Nice kids."

"Sanseis," Tosh muttered. "Think they know better."

"Rebels." Katz took a sip of tea. "I should know."

"Yeah." Tosh knew. He read the *Rafu*. "Henry turned out."

"Should have left after the wife died. Thought he should take care of me. I can take care of myself."

"Fred survived the war."

"That's saying a lot. I told him not to go, but you know that argument. Stubborn like you. Said he wasn't going to be a coward like me." Katz's eyes filled.

Tosh closed his eyes and spoke into the table. "Didn't know what he was talking about. Don't be so hard on him. He saw stuff. It doesn't leave the mind. I should know."

Mitoko Murata came to the table, dressed in a simple but stunning black silk shift, white pearls hugging her neck, elegant and still beautiful. The men rose. She put her hands into theirs and squeezed.

So pretend for a moment you're American. Pretend you're Japanese. Pretend you're nisei. Pretend you're kibei. Pretend you're sansei. Pretend if you mix and shake it up enough, no one will know the difference, that even you won't know.

# The PersuAsians

Eight years is a long time. In eight years, you can get married, divorced, and end up being a single parent with an eight-year-old kid. In eight years, you can get into college, drop out, go to prison, turn it around, and still get an advanced degree in the history of consciousness. In eight years, you can go from being a clueless colored kid to protesting and getting arrested for occupying the third floor of Arts & Sciences to subsequently joining a communist collective and preparing for the revolution, then coming up for air to get a law degree and run for public office. In eight years, you can start a band, cut a single but mostly do covers in clubs, bury the drummer from an overdose, regroup, change your name and musical genre, go on the road as the opening act, get a contract, make one LP only to discover (years later) that your music topped the charts in some town in the former Yugoslavia, where youth held on to freedom because of your words.

So what do you do when your old boyfriend shows up after eight years? It's so much water under that bridge, like metric tons, like megawatts, then possibly drought, sewage, gray water, dead bodies, environmental disaster. In eight years, you figure every cell in your body, principally the surface ones that, as far as you're concerned, count—your skin, your hair, your nails—could have been, a thousand times over, reproduced and exchanged. What could possibly be left of the old you? Of course, when you're eighteen years old, you don't take the long view, but then again, not even when you're twenty-six, pushing thirty.

On the other hand, mukashi, mukashi, a nisei pushing Medicare, Walter Kikukatana traced, not literally but perhaps metaphorically, his lineage back to the sun goddess Amaterasu Omikami, inspired by reading Joseph Campbell's four-volume opus, *The Masks of God*. Walter was a widower who had made a lot of money in the import-export industry, a business his entrepreneur wife ran, and when she died, he was left with a profitable business that he passed on to his cousins, not without keeping for himself a respectable nest egg that he proceeded to spend. The Kikukatanas enjoyed a kind of high-society life, being the benefactors of almost every J.A. event or institution in the community. They were always on the pages of the *Rafu Shimpo,* looking glamorously gracious and bejeweled, standing next to George Takei or Daniel Inouye or James Clavell. Liz Kikukatana, Walter's first daughter, a former Miss Nisei, was especially photogenic and, after her mother died, accompanied her father to all public appearances, dazzling the traditionally bland (truth be told, properly boring) J.A. crowd. The youngest daughter, Mary, married Charles Nezuyabu, and had the most expensive and fabulous wedding anyone could remember in recent J.A. history, if you were lucky enough to get an invitation. Mary and Chuckie quickly had a bunch of kids, and everyone forgot about the wedding.

Finally, we get to the middle daughter, Anne. Ah, Anne. *Ooo baby, baby.* So when Anne was three years old and her mother died, quite immediately Mrs. Kikukatana's soul sisters—Mrs. Aka, Mrs. Ekubo, and Mrs. Nendo, not necessarily related—all stepped in to fill the void. Mrs. Nendo actually moved in and started to cook and clean and change diapers. Maybe some people thought that there was some hanky-panky going on between Mrs. Nendo and Walter, but that was all nonsense. Actually everyone thought that after a reasonable mourning period, Walter would marry Mrs. Aka, but Mrs. Aka knew better. She liked her own house, perfectly clean, perfectly quiet. And anyway, she'd been married before. If Mrs. Nendo cooked and cleaned, Mrs. Aka raised the three little girls, got them into music lessons, Japanese language school, followed their homework assiduously. Mrs. Aka was the boss. Mrs. Ekubo dropped in from time to time with mochigashi and See's candy and expensive toys and frivolous apparel, and everyone had to run around and make tea and small talk about her last trip to Japan to keep her happy, but that was about it for her contribution. Anne got raised by three nisei moms. If the original Mrs. Kikukatana was a businesswoman who would've had little time for her daughters, this was perhaps a fortunate change, although Anne would never know.

The soul sisters were a clutch of childless aunties who called themselves the Girls. They were accomplished women who weren't going to let Walter fritter away the chances of Elizabeth's daughters. As for their actual chances, the oldest, Liz, was simply beautiful; the aunties sent her to modeling school, where she learned to walk, do her hair and makeup, and wear expensive clothing. Anne, by comparison, was pretty, but in the family that meant plain, plus she was a nerd. In the day, no one said "nerd," but the family called Anne "the brains," as if they could put her on *Jeopardy* for some quick cash. Older sis Liz's life and accoutrements came to Anne like hand-me-downs, and Anne mixed and mismatched all those marvelous outfits. By the time all this—high fashion and elevated knowledge—trickled down to Mary, she was just plain spoiled.

Mrs. Aka convened the Girls. She called Mrs. Nendo, who called Mrs. Ekubo, and they all met at Marie Callender's for lunch. Mrs. Aka squeezed the sliver of lemon and stirred two lumps of sugar into her iced tea. "We have, shall I say, a situation?"

Mrs. Nendo looked over her bifocals, querying, "Situation?" then back at the menu. "Oh, I can't decide. Pot pie or pot roast?"

"Michi, pot pie. You always do the pot pie," observed Mrs. Ekubo.

"Girls," Mrs. Aka interrupted, "we have a situation." Her eyes drilled into her soul sisters as if this could be the Bay of Pigs.

So, a little background on the so-called situation. Fred Fuyuchi and Harvey Senshi grew up buddies since grammar school. Additional buddies were Jimmy Mameda and Kenji Nojo. They all lived within a five-block radius spiraling from the then-center of Japanese America, which means we're talking inner city. If they had angrier political bents, they might've been another colored formation of the Panthers. If more delinquent, an Asian gang. But they were your B+ sansei, staying cool but out of trouble. They addressed each other like badass pirates. Fred was the Captain. Harvey, who had a bum leg crushed in a car accident, was Ahab. Jimmy was First Mate. Kenji was the Admiral, though the only thing commanding about Kenji was his low, booming voice and a baritone that could dive into the lowest reaches of the bass clef. On the high end of the clefs was Fred, a tenor with a falsetto that made him the Smokey Robinson of Japanese America. This foursome, in the gravity of the inner city, crooned, choreographed, and styled themselves into the PersuAsians. *Think it over.* Someone had to show that sanseis were in the groove.

"Oh Helen," Mrs. Ekubo said, "you dated in the day. Well, who didn't you date? There was Tomate, then Eiji, then Yozo, then Katsu, then . . ." She fumbled for the memory. "Now who was that? I forget his name."

"That's beside the point." Mrs. Aka shifted in her seat.

"She didn't marry any of them," suggested Mrs. Nendo.

"Who's getting married?" Mrs. Ekubo exclaimed, then she leaned over the table and said, "Katsu would've been a good catch. Missed that opportunity." She shook her head.

"How is it," asked Mrs. Nendo, "that we all ended up widowed?"

Mrs. Ekubo bristled. "I was never actually widowed. I divorced him. Then he died."

Mrs. Nendo forked the buttery crust of her potpie and sighed, "Maybe in the stars."

"Oh rubbish." Mrs. Aka pushed aside her cobb salad. "The other day, Anne suggested that Fuyuchi boy and she are a thing."

Mrs. Nendo said, "That's old news, Helen. He's at the house every other day. And so is his group."

"What are you and Walter doing about it?"

"Walter?" The Girls giggled.

"They sing a cappella for him," Mrs. Nendo offered. "So talented. So cute."

Mrs. Ekubo dabbled her lips with her napkin. "Michi, maybe Helen is right. Could be a problem, these prancing boys in the living room."

"Problem?" Mrs. Aka threw the gauntlet on the table. A folded piece of lined paper unwrapped itself into a letter.

> *Sugar Pie Honey Bunch:*
>
> *As you know, we got a contract to be the warm-up for the Wonders, and we go on the road in a few weeks. It's a commitment of at least six months going across the country and then, who knows, maybe the world, but along the way we might eventually get a better deal. My sister Sophie and the Admiral are getting married, so my folks will let her go with us. And Ahab's sister Fanny is also thinking of coming along after a while, to be with First Mate Jimmy. I know it's a lot to ask, but would you come with me? Maybe we could meet somewhere along the way. New Orleans? New York? Paris? You know you're my girl. Darling, darling, will you stand by me?*
>
> *I am forever,*
> *Your Captain*

"Curious," said Mrs. Nendo. "Who's this written to?"

"Who's Captain?" asked Mrs. Ekubo.

"Oh, that's Fred Fuyuchi," Mrs. Nendo answered.

"And who's the Admiral?" Mrs. Ekubo scrutinized the handwriting, then queried, "Ahab?"

"What does it matter? It's written to Anne!" Mrs. Aka threw up her hands.

"Anne? Are you sure?"

Well, that was the end of that. Fred must've *heard it through the grapevine and lost his mind.* And then it was eight years later.

If you were eighteen, living your entire life in a provincial community, graduating valedictorian from a suburban high school in the sticks of outer L.A., with a free ride to Sarah Lawrence, would you go off with a cover band with one single that got some airtime on KGFJ, even if Wolfman Jack growled it into recognition, even if First Mate Jimmy had poetry flowing from his fingers into original songs and the Captain was the J.A. answer to Motown, and even if it were an international tour headlined by all-stars the Wonders? O.K., a missed opportunity. Just saying. Truth is, even with the Summer of Love just around the corner, it would've been a knuckleheaded thing. Mrs. Aka and the Girls knew what they knew: *no no, you can't hurry love.*

So check this out: Anne went on to college, double majored in biochemistry and comparative literature, did a year abroad at the Sorbonne, joined the Peace Corps in Ecuador, then got an advanced degree in public health and did fieldwork in Senegal and Cameroon, translated and co-published numerous articles in international journals of public health and epidemiology, wrote a collection of short fiction set in Dakar, married and divorced an African diplomat, and by year eight, fluent in four languages, was traveling internationally for the World Health Organization for the prevention and study of tropical diseases.

Then there was Fred. With an associate's degree in musicology from the local community college, the Captain took his free spirit and the PersuAsians on the road, surprising audience after audience that oriental guys could sing and dance like blacks. *Baby, let's cruise away from here.* The open American road was a revelation, and, one by one, the group parted ways. One day, Sophie and Kenji the Admiral disappeared into the NYC subway system and emerged in Chinatown, where Yellow Power *really got a hold of* them. On the southside of Chicago, Harvey aka Ahab let the music take his mind and fell for *my girl*. But before that, some-where in the middle of nowhere Iowa, First Mate Jimmy checked into a program for poetry; by his side arrived sweet Fanny, because no cornfield was that *high*, that *low*, or that *wide*. As for Fred, he didn't just sing the stuff, he lived it in many an encounter, breaking hearts and losing them too. However, in the day, there were only two ways to avoid getting shipped out to die in Vietnam; since marriage wasn't an option, Fred took Cal Berkeley. Not that Fred spent much time in the classroom. There was free speech to attend to, freedom summer in Mississippi, the March on Washington, fasting with the United Farm Workers, breakfast with the Black Panthers, unionizing Chinatown garment workers, draft counsel-ing, Marxist-Leninist-Maoist study groups, nonviolent protests, sit-ins, and jail time. Fred finished in poli-sci and criminology, then took on Boalt Hall, passed the California bar, and joined the Asian Law Caucus. *Oh mercy, mercy me. No, no, no. My, my, my.* Time passes us by.

What's eight years? Time flies. So get ready. *Get ready.*

Predictably, the Girls were there waiting just outside LAX International. Anne could see them over her luggage as she pushed the cart around the corner and out of customs. Coming and going they were always faith-fully there, prim and proper, their hairdos and hair color always exactly the same, but this year, Anne noted, they were all wearing pantsuits. Mrs. Aka was the most stylish, her purse and shoes matching. Mrs. Nendo had probably put on some weight, and Mrs. Ekubo was holding a box of mochigashi from Fugetsu-Do. Recognizing Anne, the Girls jumped around, waving excitedly. Their excitement always transcended the diffi-culty of having three nisei moms, parsing out their positive attributes—wise, cuddly, spoiling. Hugs all around.

"Where's Dad?" Anne searched around, already chomping on mochi-gashi.

"Oh." Mrs. Nendo smiled. "Liz took him to get his hair cut."

"It's a surprise." Mrs. Ekubo waved around the remainders of Fugetsu-Do.

Mrs. Aka clarified, "Walter doesn't know you've flown in for his birthday."

"Yes," Mrs. Nendo chirped. "We've kept it a secret."

Mrs. Ekubo studied Anne, who had arrived in jeans, but said, "Dear, you've cut your hair. It's lovely, this new style."

"He might not recognize you." Mrs. Nendo looked worried.

"Oh nonsense." And Mrs. Aka led them away to her capacious Cadillac. "Let's get Anne home. She needs to rest."

"Jetlag," Mrs. Ekubo commiserated. "The last time I returned from Tokyo, it took me two entire weeks to feel normal."

Derailing an encounter after eight years is the work of fiction, but you know the details. Anne's younger sister, Mary, and her husband, Chuckie Nezuyabu, had a household of kids. Chuckie's sisters, Luisa and Henrietta, came around to babysit, chatter, and remind Mary of her happy solo days. However, remaining solo wasn't an option; Luisa and Henrietta required dates. So, when Mary found out Fred Fuyuchi was still single and his old crew was back in town, she staged a party for her dad Walter's birthday with ballroom dancing, featuring the original PersuAsians. Besides, everyone should be reminded of Mary and Chuckie's fabulous wedding.

"Surprise!" announced Mrs. Nendo, as Anne, in a stunning deep-blue gown, walked up to her dad.

As Mrs. Nendo had supposed, Walter gazed with interest and pleasure at the lovely woman approaching him without at first recognizing her until she exclaimed, "Dad, happy birthday!"

Of course, it wasn't as if he hadn't seen his daughter in eight years. She was constantly jetting in and checking in, and hadn't he met her ex-husband, that African? That was years ago. It was just that Anne was out there globe-trotting, and he had no interest in traveling to some backward place with disease and mosquitos, where she might be. He preferred *National Geographic*. He stared as if seeing his second daughter for the first time.

Mrs. Aka moved forward balancing a martini, her eyes sparkling, and pecked Anne's cheek. "Gorgeous!" She pulled out the fluffy toothpick with the olive on the end.

On cue, the band began with a waltz, and Mrs. Aka nudged Walter, who took Anne's hand with practiced overgraciousness. "May I have the honor of this first dance?"

From the stage, Fred Fuyuchi watched Mr. Kikukatana and Anne glide over the dance floor. He was suddenly distracted by Luisa Nezuyabu, who had climbed the stage to his side and grabbed his hand. "Aren't you going to ask me to dance?" she pouted, leading him down to the floor as the music ended. The music would eventually evolve into the fox-trot, the cha cha cha, and swing. Mr. Kikukatana exchanged Anne for Mrs. Aka, and yes, they did the fox-trot. He took turns with Mrs. Nendo and Mrs. Ekubo dancing to the cha cha cha, and then swing. Then, Mrs. Aka pulled Walter away dramatically for the tango. The couple stared at each other with trained hostility, strutting intensely forward and backward, their cheeks so searing they could have, between them, fried an egg.

Anne looked on in amazement, and Liz pranced over to her side. "What did I tell you? Dad and the Girls are into ballroom dancing."

"Great leg work."

"Great legs." Liz nodded toward Mrs. Aka, whose spiked heels doubled as weapons.

"Is that you, Anne?"

Anne turned to see Jimmy Mameda. "First Mate?"

"That's me!"

"Jimmy, I read your book of poetry."

"I've read your short stories." He looked at Anne meaningfully.

Harvey wasn't far behind; Anne recognized his uneven stride and nodded at both young men. "I'm sorry about Fanny."

Harvey put his arm around his buddy Jimmy, who blurted out, "I'm brokenhearted, Anne. She was my everything. I don't know how to go on living. She was a muse, my best reader. At least she got to see my published collection before—" He choked back a guttural sob.

Harvey patted Jimmy on the back saying, "My sister had a long battle with cancer," then changed the subject and waved in Sophie and Kenji. "Soph! Admiral! We got ourselves a reunion here. Hey, where's Fred?"

Fred sauntered forward with both Nezuyabu sisters in tail, Luisa and Henrietta, like backup girls. If, after eight years, he was going to make a reappearance, he did look like a confident ladies' man.

Anne looked on as if she were back in high school. *Let me tell you 'bout the birds and the bees and a thing called love.*

Trying to seem distracted, Anne looked across the room and watched a young man strut over to greet her dad. It was Bill Kikukatana, dressed expensively and with the overconfidence of a guy who was the heir-apparent slated to take over the Kikukatana import-export empire. Walter, who always thought him a snotty kid, suddenly warmed to his appearance. Bill was a cousin of a cousin by marriage, or some such long-distance but same-name relationship, but you don't have to look far to figure out that all J.A.s are, by complicated patterns of ken and camp, related. Of course no one ever said they all looked alike, because Bill was absolutely hand-some, and standing next to a radiant Liz, in haute couture, Walter thought, finally, a match made in J.A. heaven. *Don't mess with Bill.*

Mrs. Aka pulled Anne from the high school reunion, walking away with her and asking significantly, "Do you remember Bill?"

Bill pushed out his hand to shake Anne's.

Mrs. Ekubo declared, "Bill has an MBA."

Bill demurred with a touch of arrogance, "Actually, I have a PhD in business."

"Oh yes," Mrs. Nendo agreed for some reason.

Bill turned to Anne. "I noticed your article in the *Journal of Medicine.* I happened to be flipping through it and, well, I saw the name Kikukatana. What a coincidence."

"Do you read the journal?" asked Anne.

"Not really. I was checking the ads for pharmaceutical and medical equipment." He coughed. "Investment ventures, you know."

Mrs. Aka perked up. "Oh, Walter, remember I gave you Anne's article? Did you have a chance to read it?"

Mr. Kikukatana stuttered to life. "Well, I did. Very interesting."

Mrs. Nendo admitted, "I didn't understand a thing."

Mrs. Ekubo took out a Japanese fan and fanned herself. "Anne is just brilliant."

Bill, attentive to his position, added, "I agree. It's an excellently re-searched article. I learned something new about viruses, and I'm sure that Anne has made a critical contribution to the field." He tapped Mr. Kikukatana on the shoulder. "We Kikukatanas are at the forefront of our professions." He pretty much gushed himself into pride.

Liz, who'd been forgotten, looked bored. Anne managed a half smile.

Mrs. Aka and Walter Kikukatana both sighed at the very same time.

The microphone on the stage squeaked, and everyone's attention was turned to the stage, where Mary announced that she had used her special powers to persuade the PersuAsians to reunite for her dad's birthday. Relieved of being put to shame by nisei ballroom dancing, the sansei in the crowd all cheered and stepped forward onto the dance floor. The PersuAsians all pranced up to the stage, grabbed the mics, and moved into formation. "We want to wish Mr. Walter Kikukatana a happy birth-day and dedicate our first song to him!" *Father, father. Talk to me so you can see what's going on. What's going on.*

Then, *don't look back.*
Then, *reach out, reach out for me*
Then, *since I lost my baby.*
Then, *la la la la la means I love you.*
Then, *you really got a hold on me.*
Then, *I second that emotion.*
Then, *I was made to love her.*
Then, *I'm gonna wait till the midnight hour.*

And then, *the tracks of my tears.* This must have been Fred's last chance, because he searched the crowd for Anne and sang into her eyes. *If you see me with another girl, she's just a substitute. You'll see my smile looks out of place.*

For the finale, "Going to a Go-Go," Luisa climbed up to the stage again as if she'd been choreographed to dance with the guys. Admittedly Luisa could move, jumping and turning, but at some point, she lunged forward toward Fred, expecting him to catch her, but instead slid forward and off the stage. Kaboom. Unfortunately, Mary complained later, this happened before the cake and all the candles were lit and the happy birthday song. Harvey, who worked as a medic, moved into ER action, managed to jump off the stage and examine Luisa, who looked up groggily, then, eyes rolling heavenward, seemed to see her lights turn off.

You know what happened next. Fred felt guilty at not having anticipated Luisa's move, but also admitted to himself that he had no desire to catch her flying body. And if he hadn't stepped aside, she might have banged into the mic held in his tight fist. But what if she died?

The Girls gathered in the hospital waiting room.

"A coma is very serious." Mrs. Aka shook her head.

"How sweet of that young man, Jimmy," remarked Mrs. Nendo. "He's been there every day by her side. Do you know he's been writing poetry in that notebook of his?"

"Oh," said Mrs. Ekubo. "I thought he was making medical observations."

"He looks so despondent," observed Mrs. Nendo. "I hope his poetry isn't too sad."

Meanwhile, Fred paced the corridors. Sometimes Kenji joined him. Sometimes Harvey. One day, the PersuAsians converged around Luisa's bed and did their a cappella thing: *My girl is gone and said good-bye. But don't you cry. There's a right girl for every guy.* And that was all it took.

Luisa's eyes fluttered open, and there was Jimmy Mameda sitting at her side with a notebook full of poems.

Moments later, Anne appeared with a spray of yellow chrysanthemum. Fred jumped up and did a twirl over the hospital linoleum. *I'm just a love machine.*

No matter what happened after. No matter. Might as well end it here. Eight years is long enough. *I've been for real, baby.*

# Omaki-san

Mukashi, mukashi, the war came with planes that dropped bombs and destroyed everything. Not that the planes were anonymous nor were the men who piloted within, but from that distance in the sky, who could know where exactly the bombs fell? Would it have been different had the eyes of the child who pointed upward and those of the bombardier met? In this assumed indifference, many people died, but there were those who crawled away from the rubble and found a way to survive.

## Postcard from Bob Hannoki to Charley Hannoki
### APRIL 14, 1946 TOKYO

Charley Lil' Bro!

Arrived in Tokyo. Supposed to be cherry blossom time, and here's a post pic of the old days. You can use your imagination. Entire neighborhoods blasted away, but we're here pulling together reconstruction. Weird to be here in uniform with this face. Guess that's the job.

How's UCLA treating you? Hope you're keeping up your schoolwork, buddy.

Bob

## Aerogram from Bob Hannoki to Charley Hannoki
### FEBRUARY 3, 1947 TOKYO

Charley Bro,

Thot I'd write to you before I let Mom know. Been dating a gal here and planning to get married. Met her in a bar here, but it's not like how that sounds. She was doing errands for the owner and pouring tea, just trying to get by. It started that I'd pass some cigarettes on to her that she could sell to scrape up something to eat. Then I started to bring k-rations or leftovers from my lunch, and we'd eat together. Thing is she lost her entire family in the war, grandmother, mother, and little sister. Her father and brother were called up, died somewhere out there in the Pacific. She thinks Guam or Burma, but all the letters and documents were lost. She thinks maybe she has some relatives in the countryside, but she doesn't know. When she visited the village with her mother, she was too young to remember. We went over to see what's left of her home, scraped around in the char, and this was just before they bulldozed the site clean. Sad story. Now I'm all she has. I don't want this to sound like she's a charity case, but she is. Maybe she's my fate. Irony of getting out of camp and getting drafted to come back to a homeland I never knew and finding it pretty much destroyed. Believe me, I have mixed feelings, but I've never felt this kind of tenderness and love for anyone. Well, when you hear it from Mom, means it's official. Just wanted to be sure you knew the backstory. Got no one else to tell this to.

Miss you, bro. Keep up your studies and write me when you have a minute.

Bob

---

## Aerogram from Bob Hannoki to Charley Hannoki
### JUNE 1, 1947 TOKYO

Charley,

By now you've heard from Mom that Omaki and I tied the knot in a simple ceremony in May. According to custom here, we did it Shinto style, though

Mom would have preferred a church wedding. Maybe we can come to L.A. and do it again, though that doesn't seem likely for a long time.

How's college? At least you get to start as a freshman and can finish, won't have to get your studies disrupted by a war, and you can plan a future. It looks like I'll be here awhile since the pay is good and comes with housing, and now I got a family started. I used to think maybe I'd get back home and get another degree, but got to save that dream for another time. Keep me posted on your studies, not that I'm looking over your shoulder, just living the college life vicariously.

Did I say start a family? What I didn't tell you or Mom is that Omaki is pregnant. I would have married her anyway, but this sealed the deal. When we went to get registered to marry, we had to try to dig up her records, but everything is pretty much gone. But what I found out was that she had lied to me about her age. She's actually only 16, so imagine my shock. Turns out it's all legal, but to register with the government, she'd have to get parental permission. So then I had to get death certificates, and so it's been a hassle. And I admit I've been pretty angry about this, because we could have waited, and you know me, straight arrow kind of thinking. So I feel like I've been had, but then Omaki apologized and cried, and I melted. I'm fine now, just blowing off steam with no one to talk to. Anyway, you wouldn't get into a situation like this, but let my experience be a warning.

Sorry to lay this on you. Don't mean for you to get distracted by my problems. Just between you and me.

Bob

---

### Wedding invitation from Dr. and Mrs. Reginald Higuchi to Captain and Mrs. Robert Hannoki

Dr. and Mrs. Reginald Higuchi
request the honor of your presence at the wedding of their daughter

CATHERINE ICHIYO

TO

CHARLES KIYOSHI HANNOKI

Saturday, the twelfth of August
Nineteen Hundred and Fifty-Eight
at four o'clock in the evening

Centenary Methodist Church
Thirty-Fifth and Normandie Avenues
Los Angeles, California

reception to follow

---

## Note accompanying invitation from Charley Hannoki to Bob Hannoki

Bob,

Hope this finds you and Omaki well. I guess it was about time.

Yours,
Charley

---

## Card from Bob Hannoki to Charley and Cathy Hannoki
### JULY 15, 1958 TOKYO

Dear Charley and Cathy,

Sorry we can't be there. Glad I could see you last year at least, even if it was at Mom's funeral. Sorry that Mom's not alive to see you married.

Sending you a photo of our little girl Midori. She's already 10. Hard to believe.

Omaki sends her good wishes too.

Cathy, take care of my little brother. I know he's a handful, but he's a good guy.

Yours,
Bob

### Christmas card from Charley and Cathy Hannoki to Bob and Omaki Hannoki
CHRISTMAS 1959 LOS ANGELES

Dear Bob, Omaki, and Midori,

*Merry Christmas and Happy New Year!*
Here's a photo of our little Timothy, just born.

Love from Charley, Cathy, and Timmy

---

### Christmas card from Charley and Cathy Hannoki to Bob and Omaki Hannoki
CHRISTMAS 1962 LOS ANGELES

Dear Bob, Omaki, and Midori,

*Wishing you Love at Christmas and Peace in the New Year*
Sending you a photo of your namesake, little Bobby.
Photograph of Timmy (age 3) holding newborn Bobby.

With love from Charley, Cathy, Timmy, and Bobby

---

### Letter from Omaki Hannoki to Charley Hannoki
JULY 4, 1963 TOKYO

Dear Charley,

I have a hard time to write this letter to you. I should telephone you, but I can not. I got the news that Bob died. They said it was an accident. It happened in Korea. I don't understand. The war there is over many years. I know that was Bob's work, but I can not forgive. I will come to America.

I will bring Bob's ashes to bury with his mother and father. I think this is what he would want. I am sorry to write this to you.

Omaki

---

## Letter from Hannoki Omaki to Sato Otsuma

おつまちゃん (or お妻ちゃん)

お元気ですか。
　ボブが亡くなってから、遺品を整理したり家を片付けたりで大変でした。弟のチャーリーが一週間来てくれて、アメリカのほうの書類などを手伝ってくれました。これでやっとこっちを離れて、サンフランシスコで会えるわね。貴女と一緒に暮らして新しい人生を始められることに、本当にほっとしています。貴女のお店にきっとお役に立てる。前に夢見ていたように、ついにアメリカで暮らすのね。これはボブが約束してくれたこと。私がさんざん頼んだのをボブがちゃんと聞き入れて、とっくに任務を辞めていてくれたらよかったのに、あの人は死んじゃった。貴女はやり手のご主人が見つかって、運がよかったわね。
　美登利は寮のある学校に入れました。卒業まではこっちにいます。あの子の歳のころには私は完全に自立していたのよ。あの子は甘やかしちゃって苦労を知らない。アメリカで学校に入れるほど頭が良くないと思うの。いずれはアメリカに行かざるをえないけれど。だって、ボブの年金だけでは学費がいつまで持つかわからないから。
　またすぐ、東京からの旅程を知らせますね。
　こっちは寒いのよ。貴女と一緒にサンフランシスコの春を迎えられるのを楽しみにしています。

かしこ
おまき
１９６４年３月１０日、東京

*– translation –*

Otsuma-chan,

My dear friend, I hope this letter finds you well.

Since Bob died, I have had a difficult time sorting out his things and closing down this house. His brother, Charley, came for a week and helped me with the American paperwork. I am ready to finally leave and to join you in San Francisco. I am so relieved to be able to live with you and start a new life. I know I can be useful to your business. As you and I dreamed, finally I will come to live in America, something Bob promised me. He should have resigned his commission earlier, and I kept asking and insisting, and now he is gone. You were so fortunate to find a man with business prospects.

I have placed Midori in a boarding school here to finish her education. At her age, I was already completely on my own. She has been spoiled and innocent of hardship. I don't think she's smart enough to come to America and go to school. She will have to come later anyway, since I don't know how long I can spend Bob's pension on her schooling.

I will send you my travel itinerary from Tokyo very soon.

It is still very cold here. I await a springtime with you in San Francisco.

Your old chum,
Omaki
MARCH 10, 1964 TOKYO

---

## Letter from Omaki Hannoki to Charley and Cathy Hannoki
MARCH 10, 1965 TOKYO

Dear Charley and Cathy,

I will come to America in a few weeks. My friend Mrs. Otsuma Sato lives in San Francisco. She is married to Mr. Sato, who owns Daikokuya import store near Nihonmachi. She can help me with a job at the import store. I think this is the best decision for me since Bob died. Midori will stay in Tokyo to finish school. When I arrive, I will write to you again.

Yours,
Omaki

## Letter from Omaki Hannoki to Charley and Cathy Hannoki
### SEPTEMBER 9, 1965 SAN FRANCISCO

Dear Charley and Cathy,

I am in San Francisco for 6 months now. I should come to Los Angeles to see you now. I will bring Bob's ashes to bury with his parents. I can stay at your house. Thank you for this imposition. I will arrive by Greyhound bus.

Yours,
Omaki

---

## Letter from Cathy Hannoki to Dr. Reggie and Natsuko Higuchi
### SEPTEMBER 30, 1965 LOS ANGELES

Dear Mom and Dad,

How are you both? Have you settled in by now? It's difficult to imagine that you'll be in Nagasaki for an entire year. Though you've just left, I miss you already. I know the work there will consume Dad, and I know Mom will find a lot to explore. Keep us up on everything, what you see and do.

The news here is that Omaki has come to live with us. She kind of just moved in, but Charley is, of course, very nice and solicitous of her. It's his way of mourning Bob, even though he won't talk about it. I try to be supportive, but the boys keep me very busy. Omaki tries to be helpful playing with the boys. Sometimes she talks to them in Japanese, and they laugh. Maybe they'll learn the language.

Charley's been terribly busy. He's partnered with another dentist, and they are making a go of orthodontics. I think he's a bit stressed, and it's difficult to have another person to take care of. I feel sorry for Omaki, but in her needy way, she's rather pushy. I'm sorry to complain.

Timmy just started kindergarten. On the first day, he was shy, but as soon as he saw another child crying, he showed me a look of disdain, looked back at me once, and broke away. I admit I'm surprised at his independence at such an early age.

Here's a recent photo of the boys. Tim (age 5) Bobby (age 3). We're fine. Send us news about your adventures.

Love,
Cathy

---

## Letter from Hannoki Omaki to Sato Otsuma

おつまちゃん

やっと涼しくなりました。インディアン・サマーっていうのかしら、このお大気、よくわからないわね。でも東京とちがってこっちは暑いといっても湿気がなくて乾燥しているから、しのぎやすいけれど。暑かったせいで、サンフランシスコのひんやりとした霧を恋しく思っていました。慣れていたから。スチュワートと一緒に桟橋に行ったりゴールデンゲート橋を歩いたりして、夕陽が沈むころ霧が流れこんでくるのを見ていたのを思い出します。こういうとなんだかバカみたいにロマンチックに聞こえるかもしれないけれど、彼のことをとてもなつかしく思っているのよ。あんなに生き返ったような気持ちになったのは、本当にひさしぶりだったから。ボブはいつも家にいなかったし、もちろん私にもやることがいろいろあったけれど、家にいるときでもあの人は私が何を必要としているかに、スチュワートほど気を遣ってくれなかったから。スチュワートの噂を何か聞いたら教えてね。こっちではすごく退屈しているの。どこにも行くところがない郊外で、家から出歩くこともできない。時期が来るのを待って方針を決めなくちゃいけないとはわかってるんだけど。毎日、がまんしなさい、って自分に言い聞かせています。ご存知のとおり私はこうと決めたら決意は固いけれど、計画は慎重にしなくてはね。アメリカという国が、やっとわかってきた気がしています。

　ここではチャーリー一家と一緒にいます。奥さんは、まるで私のことはちゃんとわかっているとでもいうように、用心している様子。私を信用してないみたいだけど、チャーリーはとても親切です。二人とも私を哀れに思ってるんでしょう。少しでも役に立ちたいと思って、男の子二人の世話をしています。いつもうるさくかけまわって大げんかばかりしている、やんちゃな子たち。テレビを見ていいときだけ静かなの。キャシーは子供にテレビを見せないけれど、彼女が出かけてしまうと漫画番組をつけてやるでしょう、すると私はのんびりできるというわけ。そして隙を見て自分の部屋に逃げこめば、やっと落ち着けるのよ。それでいま、こうして部屋で手紙を書いている。

　貴女、あのお年寄りの旦那さんをどう操っているの。佐藤さんはいずれはお亡くなりになって、あなたにお店と財産を遺してくれるでしょう。そうなったら私たち、旅行でも何でも好きにできるわね。でもあの姪っ子、ルーシーには気をつけなくて

は。泣き言ばかりいって。本当に、あの子はスチュワートの人生をみじめにしなくちゃ気がすまないんでしょう。

　あ、やんちゃどもが私の部屋のドアのところで騒いでるわ。晩ごはんの時間。また時間を見つけて書くわね。いまは取り急ぎ。

おまきより
１９６５年１１月５日、ロスアンゼルスにて

*– translation –*

Otsuma-chan,

Finally the weather here has cooled down. I don't understand this climate they call Indian summer. But unlike Tokyo, when it is hot here, it is dry and not humid, so bearable. Because of the hot weather, I have been longing for San Francisco and the coolness and the fog there. I had become accustomed to this. I remember walking with Stuart on the pier or over the Golden Gate and watching the fog roll in with the setting sun beyond. I must sound like a silly romantic, but I do miss him very much. It had been such a long time since I had felt alive. Bob was always away, and of course I had my other interests, but when he was around, he was never as attentive to my needs as Stuart. If you've any news about Stuart, please write to me. I'm really so bored here, stuck in this house in what they call the suburbs with nowhere to go. I know I must bide my time and find my way. Every day I tell myself to be patient. As you know, I am very determined, but I must plan carefully. I think I am beginning to understand this America.

　Meanwhile, I am here with Charley and his family. His wife is rather cautious, as if she knows something about me. I don't think she trusts me, but Charley is very kind. I guess they pity me. I have tried to be useful, taking care of the two boys, both brats who are constantly running around, fighting, making a commotion. They are only quiet when they can watch television. Cathy won't let them watch television, but when she leaves, I turn it on to some cartoons, so I can have some peace. And when I can, I flee to my room to get some quiet. That is where I am now, writing to you.

　How are you managing with that old husband of yours? Old Sato should one day keel over and leave you his business and fortune. Then you and I can travel and do as we like. But you must be careful of that niece of his, Lucy. Such a whiner. Really, she must make Stuart's life miserable.

Oh, those brats are making a ruckus at my door. It must be dinnertime. I will find another moment to write to you again. In the meantime, sending my affections.

Omaki

---

## Letter from Sato Otsuma to Hannoki Omaki

おまきちゃん

ご存知のとおりサンクスギビングで、あのぞっとする七面鳥とか他にもアメリカ人の大好きな食べ物を耐え忍ばなくてはならない時期ね。でももっと困った問題は、親戚の集まりを我慢しなくてはならないこと。佐藤家はいたるところに子供たちがいて、一族郎党、集まりたくてたまらないの。もちろん私はこういうお料理はできないので、佐藤と私は毎年ウォルナット・クリークの、彼の甥のところにご招待されます。部屋がたくさんあるすてきなお家で、時々都会から逃げ出せるようにあんな家を買いましょうよと、佐藤を説得することもできるかもしれない。でもこういうことを書こうと思ったのではないのよ。

　サンクスギビングの時ね。もちろんスチュワートとルーシーも来ました。みんなディナーの食卓について、ご自慢のあの巨大な黄金色の七面鳥が切り分けられて、スイートポテトや詰め物やあのげんなりするクランベリーソースやグレイビーの器が回されたりなどなどがあったわけ。スチュワートとルーシーは互いに話をすることを避けていたけれど、ふたりのあいだのこのピリピリした感じに気がついていたのは私だけだったわ。スチュワートは相当みじめに見えたのよ、ほんとに。ふたりは一見幸せそうなふりをしていたけれど、ルーシーはいつものごとくおしゃべりで話が飛ぶし早口で、私はあの人の話はさっぱりわからないので正確なところを伝えられないんだけれど、ルーシーの話し声がどんどんどんどん大きくなって突然ヒステリーみたいな金切り声になり、テーブルの一方の端からあの人スイートポテトのマッシュしたのをスプーンでたっぷりスチュワートのお皿に投げこむのでお皿からそれた分が彼の胸にこぼれて、あげくの果てには器いっぱいのグレイビーを彼のお皿に空けちゃったの。それでグレイビーがお皿からあふれてテーブルにこぼれて彼の膝にこぼれて、彼は立ち上がって怒鳴り、彼女も大声を上げながら部屋から飛び出

していったのよ。ほんとにねえ、おまきちゃん、とんでもない場面だった！想像で
きる？

　貴女がいないと、ここはとても退屈です。またすぐお手紙頂戴ね。

かしこ
おつま
１９６５年１１月２５日、サンフランシスコ

*– translation –*

Omaki-chan,

As you must know, it's been Thanksgiving here, and we have to endure
that horrid turkey and the rest of the food that Americans are so in
love with. But the bigger problem is to endure the family gatherings.
The Satos seem to have procreated everywhere, and they are so in need
of making reunions. Of course I don't make this food, so Sato and I are
invited every year to his nephew's big house in Walnut Creek. It is a
lovely house with lots of rooms, and I have been thinking that I might
persuade Sato to buy us a place like it somewhere outside the city to get
away from time to time. But this is not what I wanted to write to you
about.

　So there we were at this Thanksgiving, and of course Stuart and Lucy
were there. We all sat down to dinner, and there is the carving of that
gigantic golden bird that they are so proud of and the sweet potatoes
and the stuffing and that awful cranberry sauce and the passing of the
gravy and so on and so on. Stuart and Lucy were not talking to each
other, but only I noticed this tension between the couple. Stuart looked
quite miserable, really. They both pretended to be happy, but Lucy has
a way of chattering about anything and very quickly, and I could not
understand anything she was saying, so I cannot tell you exactly what
was said, but Lucy's chatter became louder and louder and suddenly
screeching and hysterical, and I saw from one end of the table that she
served a scoop of those mushy sweet potatoes to Stuart in a large plop
that spit from his plate and onto his chest, and then to top it off, she
poured the entire dish of gravy onto his plate. It spilled over the plate and
the table and onto his lap, and he stood up suddenly yelling, and she ran

screaming from the room. My dear Omaki-chan, what a scene! Can you imagine?

How dull it is here without you. Please write to me soon again.

Yours always,
Otsuma
NOVEMBER 25, 1965 SAN FRANCISCO

---

## Aerogram from Cathy Hannoki to Dr. Reggie and Natsuko Higuchi
DECEMBER 1, 1965 LOS ANGELES

Dear Mom and Dad,

How are the both of you? Thanks for your last long letter with all the details about Dad's work with atomic bomb survivors. I can only imagine the intensity of your work and what you must be feeling. And I'm glad to hear that Mom is also doing some traveling outside of Nagasaki. We received your recent postcard from Kyoto. The snow-covered Kiyomizu Temple is most beautiful.

Well, we just had Thanksgiving here, and Kevin came home to join us. So it was Kevin and us and the boys and Omaki. We missed you. I made the turkey, but it was not as good as last year when Mom roasted it. But I will say that my stuffing was pretty good. I will send you some photos when I get them processed.

Kevin is looking toward his residency and wants to relocate back to L.A., which I hope is possible. So you'll be proud to know your son is seriously following your footsteps toward a medical degree. He is ready to leave the East Coast and those cold winters. He'll be here for a few weeks to look at some opportunities here, will leave again to wrap up work in Baltimore, then return for Christmas. It's so good to have him back with us. The boys adore their Uncle Kevin.

Omaki continues to live with us. She is probably bored, but she goes over to the cultural center and retrieves books and reads the Japanese newspapers to keep up on the news in Japan. And every chance she gets, she makes me take her shopping, usually to May Co or to I. Magnin. Bob must have left her a nice bank account. Occasionally she makes us a Japanese dinner, but the boys don't like fish. I have to make spaghetti on the side. I asked her about her daughter, Midori, if she's heard from her, but she doesn't seem much concerned. I asked her if she doesn't miss Midori, and she didn't say. I've asked her about her life with Bob, about those early years when they met, how Japan has changed. Maybe it's still too painful to talk about, or she is shy. I don't really know how to relate to her. I don't think it's just a matter of the language barrier, but perhaps you can enlighten me about this since you are living in Japan. The good news is that she and Kevin really seemed to get along and that suddenly she seemed to open up with him.

The boys miss you and ask when Grandpa and Grandma are coming home. Well, enjoy every moment in Japan. We'll miss you this Christmas, but I promise to take lots of pictures.

Love,
Cathy

---

## Aerogram from Cathy Hannoki to Mrs. Natsuko Higuchi
### JANUARY 8, 1966 LOS ANGELES

Dear Mom,

Happy New Year. We missed you this year, but of course you are enjoying the real thing in Japan. I did my best to make the ozoni. Omaki tried to help, and she must have thought me incompetent. She told me that we should have the spread made by outside professionals. She actually said "professionals," but all Japanese businesses close for the holidays. I pulled out the nisei church cookbook, and Omaki looked at the recipes and shook her head. Every region in Japan apparently has their style of cooking, and whatever we're doing is not what they do in Tokyo. She was especially dismissive of the recipes that are probably from Hawaii, like the guava kanten, which I love. What style of New Year food did you enjoy in Nagasaki?

Actually I am writing to ask you for advice. Kevin came home for Christmas and stayed through the New Year, and he and Omaki seem to have really hit it off. That is to say, it's more than that. I think that they are involved romantically. This has been really awkward for all of us. Omaki is older, in her 30s, but of course Kevin is not that much younger. Maybe I'm just being a prude, but Charley also feels strange about this, since Omaki was married to his brother. It's only been a year since Bob died. I don't want to worry you with this. I feel like I'm tattling, and Kevin is a grown man. But he is my brother. Maybe it's really nothing and will go away. I guess I just want your reassurance and wisdom.

Love,
Cathy

---

## Letter from Cathy Hannoki to Mrs. Natsuko Higuchi
### FEBRUARY 3, 1966 LOS ANGELES

Dear Mom,

Thanks for your letter and reassurances. Kevin returned to Baltimore as he should have, but he promises to be back here, actually in a few days. He was really angry at me for suggesting anything to him when I had the chance to talk to him, but he seems to have his head in the clouds. But before he returns, I need to tell you some gossip I heard that I figure, considering the source, is probably true.

None of us, except for Charley, who went to Japan, had ever met Bob's Japanese wife, Omaki. So I had no idea of what to expect. To be honest, she really is a striking woman, and when we go out, you can see that men turn their heads to look at her. She also came with quite a wardrobe of clothing, which seems to be growing. Bob, the one time I met him before Charley and I were married, was a pretty down-to-earth guy, but living with Omaki, now already almost 5 months, it's been interesting to imagine what sort of style of life they lived in Tokyo. I try to understand this considering Bob's work for the military occupation and his descriptions to Charley of Japan after the war. Maybe you can enlighten me about this. After all, they've just built that bullet train.

Do you remember Susan Sato? She's my old roommate from college, from San Francisco. She's related to the Sato family that owns the

Daikokuya import store where Omaki first went to work last year when she first arrived. Apparently, Omaki and Mrs. Sato (the second wife) are old friends from Japan. I met Susan for lunch in Little Tokyo, and she told me that her cousin Lucy is married to a Stuart Kusari, and Stuart has been working for their uncle George Sato at the import store. Long story short, while working at the store, Stuart got involved with Omaki.

Kevin arrives in a few days, but I'm sure he's rearranging his schedule with promises to Omaki, but this is time Kevin really can't afford, considering his studies and finances. As I said, Kevin got really angry when I suggested that maybe he was infatuated. Of course, I didn't say that exactly. But now, with this news, I can't believe Kevin is so dumb.

Anyway, glad you are far away from this nonsense.

Love,
Cathy

---

## Letter from Hannoki Omaki to Sato Otsuma

おつまちゃん

前に手紙をさしあげてから、キャシーの弟のケビンに会いました。ケビンはアメリカの反対側ボルティモアで医学を勉強しているのですが、サンクスギビングとクリスマスに家に帰ってきたのです。やっと話し相手が、お出かけしたり人生を少し楽しめる相手ができました。ディズニーランドとプラネタリウムに一緒に行ったのよ。一時もじっとしてられない甥のティミーとボビーを連れていかなくてはならなかったので、こんな子守りは時にはほんとに疲れる辛いことなんだけど、ケビンは私にとても親切にしてくれました。あの子たちがうるさかったのを埋め合わせるために、彼は私だけをディナーと映画に連れて行ってくれて、私はやっといくつか観光もできました。

わかると思うけど私のサンクスギビングは、貴女のとは大変にちがっていましたが、貴女の手紙を読んだら笑って笑って涙が出てきちゃった。佐藤家の人たちも、これでルーシーがどれだけ非常識な人かわかったでしょうね。すてきなスチュワートのことを私は忘れてはいないけれど、将来お医者さんになる人のほうが安楽な未来を保証してくれそうだという点については上よね。愛だけで結婚できるいいけれど。貴女も私も親が決めた結婚をさせられることからは逃げられたし、それを不幸といわれても報われる部分もあるけれど、とにかく私たちは自分で相手を見つけなくてはならない。この点、貴女はすでに私より一歩先を行っているわね。

　ケビンは昨日帰っていったばかりですが、その前に姉のキャシーと喧嘩しました。これがまた私の信用と計画にとっては邪魔なの。彼はできるかぎり早くまた来るよと約束してくれました。こっち、ロスアンゼルスで仕事を探すって。

　また手紙で大笑いさせてね。

かしこ
おまき
１９６６年２月２０日、ロスアンゼルス

*– translation –*

Otsuma-chan,

Since I last wrote to you, I've met Cathy's younger brother, Kevin. Kevin is studying medicine in Baltimore, on the other side of the country, but he came home for Thanksgiving and for Christmas. Finally I've had someone to speak with, to go out and enjoy life a bit with. He's taken me everywhere in Los Angeles. We went to Disneyland and the Planetarium, although we had to bring along his overactive nephews, Timmy and Bobby, but even though it was quite tiresome and trying at times, Kevin was so kind to me in every way. To make up for their commotion, he's taken me alone to dinner and to the movies, and finally I have seen some of the sights.

　As you see, my Thanksgiving was very different from yours, although in reading your letter, I laughed so hard that tears came to my eyes. Now the Satos can see how preposterous Lucy can be. I have not forgotten my handsome Stuart, but certainly a man who will be a doctor has better prospects for a comfortable future. If only one could marry for love. You and I escaped the consequences of being married off in family arrangements, but that misfortune may be its own reward, although we must find our own proper arrangements. You are already a step ahead of me.

　Kevin just left yesterday, but not without a fight with his sister, Cathy, yet again another impediment to my goodwill and plans. He promised me that he will be back again as soon as he is able, that he is looking for a position here in Los Angeles.

　Please send me another letter with more hilarious news.

Yours,
Omaki
FEBRUARY 20, 1966 LOS ANGELES

## Aerogram from Cathy Hannoki to Mrs. Natsuko Higuchi
### FEBRUARY 20, 1966 LOS ANGELES

Dear Mom,

Kevin just left yesterday, back to Baltimore. Before he left, we got into a terrible argument. Well, I told him the story I heard about Omaki in San Francisco and the probable reason she left the city. He was outraged and said I was spreading lies, that Omaki has had a very difficult life, that she is still mourning her husband, that she misses her daughter, that she feels like a stranger, is embarrassed by her English, and is very aware of her imposition on our family but doesn't know what to do. He said that she told him she had hoped to make some money by working for the Satos, but that Mr. Sato was particularly difficult and she felt she could not make her friend Otsuma's life more difficult by staying. What Omaki told Kevin, confidentially, was that Mr. Sato was hitting on her, and she really didn't want Otsuma to know her husband's infidelity. This was all amazing to me, and I didn't know what to say. Then he said he would come back for Omaki and hoped I would be more understanding of her situation.

I don't want to bother Charley with all this. He is so busy building the business, and it is finally taking off. I go in every day for a few hours to help in the office with accounting and scheduling, and to be fair, Omaki takes care of the boys when I leave the house. But I can't keep my mind off this. Be honest, and tell me if I'm overreacting.

Charley and the boys send you their love. Love to Dad too.

Love,
Cathy

---

## Letter from Natsuko Higuchi to Cathy Hannoki
### MARCH 2, 1966 NAGASAKI

Dear Cathy,

So grateful to get the photos of you and the boys. But I admit I'm feeling uneasy about your letters about Kevin and Omaki. I shared your letter with Dad, and you know him, always philosophical about these things. And he's really very busy working with patients who are so in need of his help and expertise. But I know you are there in the thick of it, having to interact every day with Omaki and then with your brother, who can be very stubborn. And Omaki seems frankly to have invaded your household. I know you and Charley want to be charitable, but there are limits. If Kevin has become so close to Omaki, perhaps he can guide her to another future (job?) in the U.S. Not marry her, though. I wish I could come and take care of the boys and give you some time off.

While Dad has had to remain in Nagasaki, I've been able to travel with friends to other parts of Japan. Kyoto was so lovely, entirely preserved from the devastation of the war, but then most of Japan has been or is being rebuilt, and the physical evidence of the war is all but disappearing. I have been taking Japanese lessons and flower arranging and tea ceremony and any other activity that's suggested. I have also been asked to teach English to a small group of women who come once a week to the house. They are all so polite and kind to me, bringing gifts all the time. I feel very fortunate, but the conversation, even when I try to complicate it, is always very limited. There is a great reticence to speak, or perhaps there are signals that I cannot comprehend. I feel very isolated here. Perhaps this is what Omaki too is experiencing. Not to excuse her actions, but perhaps to give you some perspective.

Missing you and the boys in particular. Hugs all around.

Love,
Mom

---

## Letter from Sato Otsuma to Hannoki Omaki

おまきちゃん

お知らせがあります。お宅の美登利ちゃんがサンフランシスコの私の家に来ています。昨日着いたばかりよ。ひとりで飛行機に乗ってアメリカにやってきました。そんなことありえないと思われそうだけれど、あの子はきっとあなたとおなじくらい反抗心と勇気があって、あなたはあの子を見くびっていたのかもしれないわね。東京の学校の寮から逃げ出してきたんだって。ロスアンゼルスに行かせましょうか？とてもいい子にしてるわよ。さしあたっては、私が面倒を見られます。

別のお知らせもあるの。あの何度かお店に来て、古い漆塗りの簞笥や十八世紀の屏風をいくつか買ってくれたお金持ちの白人、ジム・マーティンを覚えてる？ 彼はすごいお金を遣ってくれて、品物はぜんぶロスアンゼルスの自宅に送ったでしょう。そう、あの人はサンフランシスコに一軒、そしてベバリーヒルズにも大きな家を持っているのよ。テレビのプロデューサーらしいわ。その彼がこのあいだ、貴女のことを知りたくて、訪ねてきました。貴女がどこにいるのか、どうやったら連絡が取れるのかを知りたいんですって。しつこいくらいで、自分が手紙を書いたら貴女に転送してくれるか、といっています。それでその手紙を同封します。

美登利ちゃんをどうすればいいか、忘れずに知らせて頂戴。

かしこ
おつま
１９６６年３月１７日、サンフランシスコ

*– translation –*

Omaki-chan,

I have some news for you. Your daughter, Midori, is here at my house in San Francisco. She just arrived yesterday, having taken a plane by herself and come to America. I know this sounds impossible, but she is perhaps as rebellious and courageous as you, and you have not given her enough credit. She has run away from that boarding school in Tokyo. Shall I send her to Los Angeles? She is quite well, and I will take good care of her in the meanwhile.

There is some other news. Do you remember that rich white guy, Jim Martin, who came into the store several times to buy some old lacquer chests and several eighteenth-century screens? He spent a great deal of money, and we shipped everything to his house in Los Angeles. That's right, he has a house in San Francisco and a large house in Beverly Hills. I think he's a television producer. He has been here lately asking about you. He wants to know where you are and how to be in contact with you. He's been very persistent and asked if he wrote you a letter if I would forward it to you. Well, here is the letter.

Don't forget to let me know what I should do about your Midori-chan.

Yours,
Otsu
MARCH 17, 1966 SAN FRANCISCO

## Note from Jim Martin to Omaki Hannoki
MARCH 15, 1966 SAN FRANCISCO

Dear Omaki-san,

I was so disappointed to come into Daikokuya and find that you were no longer there. There is no pleasure shopping there without you. I have given this note to your friend Otsuma-san in hopes that you will read it and find some time and heart to correspond with me. When I met you, I knew I had found the perfect woman, the very Japanese woman I have been looking for all these years. I have been thinking of you constantly since we first met, and I cannot get you out of my mind. Wherever you are, I will come to find you. I promise that my intentions are the most respectable. I will move and shake the world for you. I beg you to answer me with some sign but more importantly your current address.

With great sincerity and true love,
Jim

---

## Aerogram from Cathy Hannoki to Mrs. Natsuko Higuchi
APRIL 1, 1966 LOS ANGELES

Dear Mom,

How are you and Dad? Thanks for hearing me out, and for your thoughts about Japan and Japanese. Speaking of which, my house just got more Japanese in it. Omaki's daughter, Midori, arrived a few days ago. Apparently she ran away from the boarding school in Tokyo, found a way to get on a plane, and came on her own to San Francisco. She was staying with the Satos, then they sent her to Los Angeles. Midori just turned 17, but this must have been a very brave thing to do. Omaki is pretty upset about it, and I have heard her fuming and yelling at Midori. Midori, for her part, is very quiet and shy. Her English, however, is quite good. She went to American schools on the military base in Tokyo. I think she was in a Japanese boarding school that must have been very strict and even abusive from the little I've learned. I've suggested that she can go to the local high school and meet other students like herself. We went together today to meet a school counselor and get her classes arranged. Well, we'll see how this works out.

I haven't heard from Kevin, who usually writes us a few lines every week, if just a postcard to the boys. He does seem to be writing to Omaki, however. When I hand Omaki his letters, she stuffs them away in her pocket or purse without comment.

Timmy is very happy in school. He's already reading. *Dick and Jane* and Dr. Seuss. Bobby loves to ride around on his tricycle. While Timmy is in school, we go to the park. Your Japanese picture books just arrived. Thanks!

Sending love to you and Dad,
Cathy, Timmy, Bobby, and Charley too

---

## Letter from Sato Otsuma to Hannoki Omaki

おまきちゃん

美登利はぶじロスアンゼルスに着いたことと思います。美登利はとても引っ込み思案に見えるけれど、じつはあの子を見ていると貴女を思い出すのよ。何を考えているのか絶対に分からないけれど、あの子はいつもよく見ていろいろ学んでいるにちがいありません。

　　新しいお知らせよ。スチュワートとルーシーが離婚する、そして別れる以上、スチュワートは大黒屋を離れなくてはならないということを、ついさっき聞きました。佐藤のお父さんはこの件についてはとてもきっぱり決めていて、ルーシーの側の言い分しか聞こうとしません。スチュワートは、ロスアンゼルスに移って新しい仕事を探すといっています。彼は日本の骨董品を売るのはそもそもあまり上手じゃなくて、いつも誰の作かとか何世紀のものかとかをまちがえていました。私は教育がないけれど、その私だって日本の歴史は勉強してきたわ。こうした骨董品は、それにまつわるいい話をしてあげられるのでなければ、けっして売れないもの。あの人は嘘ひとつつけないから。でもとてもチャーミングでハンサムだから、きっと何か見つかるわよ。もちろん彼が引っ越しについて私に話してくれたのは、私がそれを貴女に話すと思ってのことでしょう。だから予め警告しておくわね。

　　この件がこれからどうなるか、そして貴女が最近どうしているのか、教えてね。

かしこ
おつま
１９６６年４月１４日、サンフランシスコ

*– translation –*

Omaki-chan,

I trust Midori arrived safely in Los Angeles. Even though Midori seems very shy, she actually reminds me of you. You cannot know what she is thinking, but I believe she is always watching and learning.

I have new news for you. I have just heard that Stuart and Lucy will get a divorce, and with that separation, Stuart will have to leave Daikokuya. Old Sato-san is adamant about this, only willing to hear Lucy's side of everything. Stuart told me that he will be moving to Los Angeles to look for a new job. He was never very good at selling Japanese antiques anyway, always confusing the artisans and the centuries. I am not educated, but even I have been studying Japanese history. If you cannot tell a good story about these old objects, you can never make a good sale. He could not even lie. But he is very charming and handsome, so something should come his way. Of course he told me about his plans to move so that I would tell you. So you are forewarned.

Let me know what happens and how you are faring these days.

Your friend,
Otsuma
APRIL 14, 1966 SAN FRANCISCO

---

## Letter from Cathy Hannoki to Mrs. Natsuko Higuchi
### MAY 5, 1966 LOS ANGELES

Dear Mom,

It's Boys' Day today, but you know this. We are flying two large koi in the backyard for Timmy and Bobby. It's also Cinco de Mayo. There was a dance program at school, and Timmy danced the hat dance with his classmates in the schoolyard.

Midori is going to school and seems to be doing just fine. She's a very sweet young girl and very helpful and kind to the boys. Bobby can't wait for her to come home to play with him. I think she genuinely loves to play with the boys, even when they are rough and uncontrollable. I have seen her roll around on the lawn with the boys. It was Midori's idea to fly the koi. We went together to Little Tokyo to buy them. In a short time, we've all become very attached to Midori. Despite her crazy mother, Midori seems to be her father's daughter, like Bob, down to earth, open, and very earnest.

The new development here is that lately there is a hakujin guy who comes around and takes Omaki out on dates. Apparently Omaki met him in San Francisco. He has at least two cars, a big black Cadillac and a sporty red Mustang. Depending on the date, he'll arrive in one or the other and escort Omaki away. Midori has joined them a few times. They've taken day trips to Santa Barbara or Palm Springs. Omaki's also mentioned going to concerts and the opera, and she said he's promised to take her to the Emmys. I guess he works in TV. Omaki calls him Jimbo.

Last weekend, Kevin arrived suddenly, I guess hoping to surprise Omaki. But Omaki wasn't here but in San Diego or maybe Tijuana. Kevin moped around the house all Friday and Saturday and just before his flight out of LAX on Sunday, Omaki arrived in that red Mustang with Jimbo, the convertible top down, laughing gaily. I was pulling the car out of the garage to take Kevin to the airport, and he was lugging his bag across the front porch. Somehow everyone got introduced, fakely cordial. Then Kevin got in the car, and we drove in silence to the airport.

Well, enough said. Love to you and Dad. I miss you so.

Love,
Cathy

---

## Letter from Hannoki Omaki to Sato Otsuma

おつまちゃん

ベバリーヒルズでの私の新しい住所をお知らせするために書いています。ジム・マーティンと私が結婚したと知ったら、貴女は驚くでしょうね。簡単な急ぎの式でしたが、いずれパーティーを開くし、そのときは誰よりも貴女に来てほしいわ。ジム坊はパームスプリングスにも家を一軒もっているので、パーティーをどっちでするか、決めなくてはなりません。でもいうまでもなく、サンフランシスコにジム坊がもっている東洋趣味のビクトリア式の大きな邸宅にも、貴女をご招待できます。

美登利はハイスクールを卒業して、それからもチャーリーとキャシーと一緒に暮らしたいといっていますが、これは本当に助かるわ。二、三年のうちには美登利がきっと大学に入れると、キャシーは考えているみたい。

もうひとつのお知らせです。あなたが教えてくれたとおり、スチュワートはロスアンゼルスに引っ越してきました。彼はいい仕事が見つからなくてお金が尽きてしまい、気まずくてそれが私にいえなかったのね。ある晩、ジム坊と私がハリウッドで夕食をとっていたら、テーブルにウェイターとしてやってきたのが、なんと私の最愛の、最高にハンサムなスチュワートだったのよ。私は顔を上げると息を呑んでしまい千回もとろとろに溶けてしまったけれど、なんとか間をおかずにジム坊に紹介できるまでには回復したの。「大黒屋時代のお友達でね、私にとっては兄みたいな人」って。それからはトントン拍子に、ジム坊がスチュワートを助手として雇うことに。助手といって、スチュワートがどんな仕事をするのか全然わからないけれど、それよりもいいのは彼はトレーラーハウスとかいう物を借りてうちの土地に住んでいるのね、だからいつも手が届くところにいるというわけ。

やがてはこんなふうになるのよって、貴女か私に予言できたかしらね。

いつも貴女のお友達である
おまき
1966年6月18日、ベバリーヒルズ

*– translation –*

Otsuma-chan,

I am writing to you to let you know of my new address in Beverly Hills. I guess you'll be surprised to know that Jim Martin and I got married. It was a simple and quick ceremony, but we will have a party, and you will be the first invited. Jimbo has another house in Palm Springs, so we must decide where to have the party. But soon, as you realize, I can also invite you to Jimbo's oriental Victorian house in San Francisco.

Midori wants to finish high school and to continue to live with Charley and Cathy, and that is a big relief. Cathy is sure Midori can get into college in a few years.

Another piece of news is that Stuart arrived, as you let me know, in Los Angeles. Unable to find a good job, he ran out of money and was too embarrassed to tell me. One evening, Jimbo and I were having dinner in Hollywood, and who should come to wait on the table but my dearest, handsomest Stuart. I looked up and gasped and melted a thousand times but recuperated my senses in time to introduce to Jimbo "my friend from Daikokuya, practically a brother to me." Well, one thing led to another, and Jimbo has hired Stuart as an assistant. What Stuart must do as an assistant I have no idea, but the better thing is that Stuart is renting what they call the carriage house on our property, so he is never very far away.

Could you or I have predicted how things would turn out?

Your friend always,
Omaki
JUNE 18, 1966 BEVERLY HILLS

# J.A. Cheat Sheet

In case you wondered, and with apologies to Jane Austen (rest her soul), members of the Jane Austen Society, my sister in particular, and fans everywhere.

Shikataganai & Mottainai *(Sense & Sensibility)*

Giri & Gaman *(Pride & Prejudice)*

Monterey Park *(Mansfield Park)*

Emi *(Emma)*

Japanese American Gothic *(Northanger Abbey)*

The PersuAsians *(Persuasion)*

Omaki-san *(Lady Susan)*

# Afterword: Sansei Janeite

*The Empire Dress, or To Marry: It Does Not Signify*

One day you wake up, and your sister is a Janeite. You think it might be a coincidence about her name, Jane, but as Emma says, this does not signify. Friends and family hover between amused and clueless since maybe, like you, they've seen the movies but probably never actually read Jane Austen. And now that Austen's become a pop phenomenon, folks figure it finally got easy to get your sister a gift; you name it—Jane Austen doll, mug, puzzle, Post-its, apron, newest rip-off zombie bodice ripper. Just to be clear, your sister sneers at this consumerist appropriation; she's moved on to a higher level of Janeitism. This is a serious field of inquiry. She's a gentlewoman and a scholar. She's also become an haute couture Regency seamstress, fashioning with meticulous attention to outward authenticity (the Velcro and metal hooks are hidden), the most extravagant gowns with matching headgear and purses. And you thought it was all about the empire dress fashioned after some Greek goddess. Someone asked about your sister's interest in cosplay, but you think if Austen became a Disney princess, it also wouldn't signify.

You love your sister; she has her thing, and you have yours. But isn't it time you read Jane Austen, at least one book? You've read Edward Said's essay "Jane Austen and Empire," but not *Mansfield Park*. You agree with Said, but then aren't you a fraud? So you buy the complete novels of Jane Austen with an introduction by Karen Joy Fowler. Hey, KJ is a fan; couldn't hurt to crack it open. To be honest, you don't *read* any of them, but you do listen on audio. You cook and clean, pay bills, answer emails, write syllabi, often fall asleep, and listen to one novel after another. Does this count? The English accents are authentic. It's true that imperialism and colonialism are alive and fueling the second-tier aristocracy and the nouveau landowners; guys disappear to the New World, the Middle

Passage, and Indian assignments, and return eligibly wealthy. Someone
has got to fund all those balls, concerts, carriages, and month after month
living on the considerable resources in the many rooms and extensive
gardens of those grand estates. Austen isn't telling; she's just showing.
When home gets reproduced in other worlds, you figure that this is the
memory that builds those plantations. If there are six main characters,
there has to be sixty servants who pretty much never appear or speak, but
this is not their story. And this is not the point.

It's the turn of the seventeenth to the eighteenth century. Was that a
sexual innuendo? You're making a vat of Meyer lemon marmalade. Turns
out it's 7.5 pounds of lemons to 9 pounds of plantation sugar, but that's
confidential information. You check the temperature on the Meyer lemon
marmalade, then press a sticky finger to the Thirty Seconds Back icon on
the iPad. You press the icon a couple of times, because what's a sexual
innuendo in Regency? The protagonist has been sitting the entire dance.
Totally snubbed. Bummer. Your sister has said they probably didn't wear
panties; too much trouble under all those layers of Indian silk and indigo
muslin. It's all about the clothing, the pushed-up bosoms, and the perfect curls. Beautifully powdered Anglo-Saxon people. It's got to take
hours of fine preparation. You think you could wear one of your sister's
Regency gowns without panties too. The candy thermometer creeps up
to 220. The thing is, it wasn't sexual innuendo per se, just innuendo. Like
the blue mercury creeping surreptitiously to the jam point, you might
miss it entirely. You realize that this is a romance without romanticism;
it's antiromantic, all about calculating your chances to make the right
choice, which for most of the characters, except the heroine, is the wrong
choice. Marriage is like marmalade—you could miss 220 and reject Mr.
Knightley or Mr. Darcy or Captain Wentworth, and, well, c'est la vie. You
had a boss who was an old Reaganite, and though you both agreed to dis-
agree about most things, your boss once said a true Janeite thing: *Nobody
knows why they do that.* By "that" he meant get married. Society moves
around the question, and despite what Janeites know, everyone makes the
same mistakes.

You grasp for some kind of relationship, and it occurs to you that
maybe you can compare this Janeite society to growing up sansei. Not
the carriages and grand plantation estates; face it, you grew up in city
ghettos and plotted suburbs. Still, growing up sansei was very confusing.
Fortunately no one has to do this again. Your parent's generation, the nisei,

were generally closed-mouthed, diffident people who had been burned big-time. Everything that should have been obvious about American society and its promises of freedom and the future was on a standby basis, depending on you. And everything the nisei passed on to sansei was unspoken innuendo about what kind of people you were supposed to grow up to be. Apparently the Chinese are fortunate enough to have loud-mouthed tiger moms, but in the day, the sansei were supposed to get it by just being born.

There was some sociological statistic about sansei outmarriage, something like 50 percent back in the day. You can speculate about the conditions of attraction and subtraction, but maybe your sister and the Janeites can make marmalade of something a South Asian friend of yours once said: *All marriages are arranged.*

# Stories/Essays Previously Published

"The Bath," first published in *Amerasia Journal.* Los Angeles: University of California, summer 1975.

"The Dentist and the Dental Hygienist," first published in *Asiam.* Los Angeles, 1987.

"A Gentlemen's Agreement," first published in *Review 72: Literature & Arts of the Americas: Latin American and Asian Writing and Arts,* vol. 39, no. 1. New York: The Americas Society, Routledge, Taylor & Francis Group, May 2006.

"Borges & I," first published in *International Journal of Okinawan Studies: Special Issue on Women & Globalization,* Kazuko Takemura, guest editor, vol. 2, no. 2. Okinawa: Kenkyusha, University of the Ryukyus, December 2011; and in the *Massachusetts Review,* Jim Hicks, editor; Amherst: University of Massachusetts, summer 2012.

"Kiss of Kitty," first published in *Asian American Literary Review,* vol. 7, no. 1, spring 2016.

Indian Summer," first published in *Boom California,* Jason Sexton, editor. University of California Press, May 2, 2017.

"Colono:Scopy," first published in *DSM: Asian American Edition; Open in Emergency: A Special Issue on Asian American Mental Health,* vol. 7, no. 2. Asian American Literary Review, Inc., fall/winter 2016.

""KonMarimasu," first published in the *Margins,* Asian American Writers Workshop, September 2017.

"Shikataganai & Mottainai," first published in *Red Wheelbarrow Literary Magazine,* Ken Weisner, editor. Cupertino, California: De Anza College, 2018.

"Omaki-san," first published in *Freeman's,* John Freeman, editor, 2019.

# Acknowledgments

Many years ago, while in Brazil researching the history of Japanese Brazilians, I sent a short story to Dick Osumi, then editor of *Amerasia Journal* at the UCLA Asian American Studies Center. I believe I even sent it with a long letter that explained the story. Unknown to me, Dick entered it in the first short story contest sponsored by *Amerasia*. One day in São Paulo, I received a letter saying that I had won their contest. Surprise. That was "The Bath," the first story I had ever written. That award was a small blessing. With the prize money, I was able to travel to the north of Brazil, but the award itself was a confirmation that maybe I could write. Looking at that story and its newbie writer flaws today, I wonder. After that, I wrote short fiction only sporadically, thinking that it's really not my forte. I enjoy the long distance of the novel. After a while, short pieces accumulated, and so here they are, these selected about growing up and living in Japanese America.

The first person I thank is the late Dick Osumi, whose support initiated me into a writer's life. And I thank the many editors of anthologies and small journals who over the years have published my stories, in particular to this collection: Lawrence-Minh Davis, John Freeman, Jim Hicks, Ryuta Imafuku, Rie Makino, Kat Sayarath, Jason Sexton, Kazuko Takemura, and Ken Weisner.

For the "Sansei" side of the book, thanks to those who, long ago, shared ideas, stories, and histories that contributed to the writing of this collection: Lucy Mae San Pablo Burns, Marsha Furutani, Ryuta Imafuku, Earl Jackson, and Lucio Kubo. Thanks to Lucy Asako Boltz for research support and for coming along on that incarceration road trip. Thanks also to Frank Gravier at the University of California, Santa Cruz, McHenry Library Special Collections; and Paul Shea of the Yellowstone Gateway Museum in Livingston, Montana. Thank you Naomi Hirahara for helping me to create the J.A. timeline for these narratives. And thank you with apologies, friends and family, for my appropriation of your sansei recipes.

On the "Sensibility" side, thank you to Keijiro Suga for the Japanese translation of letters in the story "Omaki-san" and to Ikue Kina with whom I conferred in the editing of various Japanese phrases in the texts.

To early readers of the Jane Austen–inspired stories: Ruth Hsu, Micah Perks, and Elisabeth Sheffield, a big thank you for your kind support.

As always, I am indebted to Chris Fischbach and the dedicated staff at Coffee House Press with special thanks to: Anitra Budd, Nica Carrillo, and Carla Valadez.

Finally, as must be obvious by now, this book is because of my only sister, Jane Tomi, to whom I apologize for my nonsense and thank for her always-generous support and astute sensibility.

LITERATURE
is not the same thing as
PUBLISHING

Coffee House Press began as a small letterpress operation in 1972 and has grown into an internationally renowned nonprofit publisher of literary fiction, essay, poetry, and other work that doesn't fit neatly into genre categories.

Coffee House is both a publisher and an arts organization. Through our *Books in Action* program and publications, we've become interdisciplinary collaborators and incubators for new work and audience experiences. Our vision for the future is one where a publisher is a catalyst and connector.

# Funder Acknowledgments

Coffee House Press is an internationally renowned independent book publisher and arts nonprofit based in Minneapolis, MN; through its literary publications and *Books in Action* program, Coffee House acts as a catalyst and connector—between authors and readers, ideas and resources, creativity and community, inspiration and action.

Coffee House Press books are made possible through the generous support of grants and donations from corporations, state and federal grant programs, family foundations, and the many individuals who believe in the transformational power of literature. This activity is made possible by the voters of Minnesota through a Minnesota State Arts Board Operating Support grant, thanks to the legislative appropriation from the Arts and Cultural Heritage Fund. Coffee House also receives major operating support from the Amazon Literary Partnership, Jerome Foundation, McKnight Foundation, Target Foundation, and the National Endowment for the Arts (NEA). To find out more about how NEA grants impact individuals and communities, visit www.arts.gov.

Coffee House Press receives additional support from the Elmer L. & Eleanor J. Andersen Foundation; the David & Mary Anderson Family Foundation; Bookmobile; Dorsey & Whitney LLP; Foundation Technologies; Fredrikson & Byron, P.A.; the Fringe Foundation; Kenneth Koch Literary Estate; the Matching Grant Program Fund of the Minneapolis Foundation; Mr. Pancks' Fund in memory of Graham Kimpton; the Schwab Charitable Fund; Schwegman, Lundberg & Woessner, P.A.; the Silicon Valley Community Foundation; and the U.S. Bank Foundation.

## The Publisher's Circle of Coffee House Press

Publisher's Circle members make significant contributions to Coffee House Press's annual giving campaign. Understanding that a strong financial base is necessary for the press to meet the challenges and opportunities that arise each year, this group plays a crucial part in the success of Coffee House's mission.

Recent Publisher's Circle members include many anonymous donors, Patricia A. Beithon, the E. Thomas Binger & Rebecca Rand Fund of the Minneapolis Foundation, Andrew Brantingham, Dave & Kelli Cloutier, Louise Copeland, Jane Dalrymple-Hollo & Stephen Parlato, Mary Ebert & Paul Stembler, Kaywin Feldman & Jim Lutz, Chris Fischbach & Katie Dublinski, Sally French, Jocelyn Hale & Glenn Miller, the Rehael Fund-Roger Hale/Nor Hall of the Minneapolis Foundation, Randy Hartten & Ron Lotz, Dylan Hicks & Nina Hale, William Hardacker, Randall Heath, Jeffrey Hom, Carl & Heidi Horsch, the Amy L. Hubbard & Geoffrey J. Kehoe Fund, Kenneth & Susan Kahn, Stephen & Isabel Keating, Julia Klein, the Kenneth Koch Literary Estate, Cinda Kornblum, Jennifer Kwon Dobbs & Stefan Liess, the Lambert Family Foundation, the Lenfestey Family Foundation, Joy Linsday Crow, Sarah Lutman & Rob Rudolph, the Carol & Aaron Mack Charitable Fund of the Minneapolis Foundation, George & Olga Mack, Joshua Mack & Ron Warren, Gillian McCain, Malcolm S. McDermid & Katie Windle, Mary & Malcolm McDermid, Sjur Midness & Briar Andresen, Daniel N. Smith III & Maureen Millea Smith, Peter Nelson & Jennifer Swenson, Enrique & Jennifer Olivarez, Alan Polsky, Robin Preble, Alexis Scott, Ruth Stricker Dayton, Jeffrey Sugerman & Sarah Schultz, Nan G. Swid, Kenneth Thorp in memory of Allan Kornblum & Rochelle Ratner, Patricia Tilton, Stu Wilson & Melissa Barker, Warren D. Woessner & Iris C. Freeman, and Margaret Wurtele.

For more information about the Publisher's Circle and other ways to support Coffee House Press books, authors, and activities, please visit www.coffeehousepress.org/pages/support or contact us at info@coffeehousepress.org.

**Karen Tei Yamashita** is the author of eight books, including *I Hotel*—finalist for the National Book Award—and most recently, *Letters to Memory,* all published by Coffee House Press. She is a recipient of the John Dos Passos Prize for Literature and a U.S. Artists' Ford Foundation Fellowship, and she is professor emerita of literature and creative writing at the University of California, Santa Cruz.

*Sansei and Sensibility* was designed by
Bookmobile Design & Digital Publisher Services.
Text is set in Arno Pro.